Also by Anna Porter

Fiction

Deceptions

The Appraisal

The Bookfair Murders

Mortal Sins

Hidden Agenda

Nonfiction

In Other Words: How I Fell in Love with Canada One Book at a Time

Buying a Better World: George Soros and Billionaire Philanthropy

*The Ghosts of Europe: Journeys through Central Europe's
Troubled Past and Uncertain Future*

*Kasztner's Train: The True Story of Rezso Kasztner,
Unknown Hero of the Holocaust*

The Storyteller: Memory, Secrets, Magic and Lies

GULL ISLAND

A Novel

ANNA PORTER

PUBLISHED BY SIMON & SCHUSTER

New York · London · Toronto · Sydney · New Delhi

SIMON &
SCHUSTER
CANADA

Simon & Schuster Canada
A Division of Simon & Schuster, Inc.
166 King Street East, Suite 300
Toronto, Ontario M5A 1J3

This Simon & Schuster Canada edition September 2023

SIMON & SCHUSTER CANADA and colophon are trademarks of Simon & Schuster, Inc.

For information about special discounts for bulk purchases, please contact Simon & Schuster Special Sales at 1-800-268-3216 or CustomerService@simonandschuster.ca.

Interior design by Wendy Blum

Manufactured in the United States of America

10   9   8   7   6   5   4   3   2

Library and Archives Canada Cataloguing in Publication

Title: Gull Island / Anna Porter.
Names: Porter, Anna, author.
Description: Simon & Schuster Canada edition.
Identifiers: Canadiana (print) 20220465363 | Canadiana (ebook) 20220465371 | ISBN 9781668017708 (softcover) | ISBN 9781668017715 (EPUB)
Classification: LCC PS8581.O7553 G85 2023 | DDC C813/.54—dc23

ISBN 978-1-6680-1770-8
ISBN 978-1-6680-1771-5 (ebook)

Julian, who introduced me to Georgian Bay

GULL
ISLAND

1

I HAD DRIVEN UP FAST. WHEN I SET OUT FROM THE city, it was still dark. There were not many cars on the highway. Dawn breaking as I turned off the 400. No one had removed the dead animals from the side road to Honey Harbour yet. There was a young raccoon, bloody teeth bared, its chest squashed, arms pawing the air, and a large snapper, its house smashed, its guts strewn across the road. Too much night traffic. But not even one car now.

It was quiet at the marina. I couldn't see the *Limestone,* though that was usually the boat they took out of winter storage first. The *Hunt,* a much smaller boat, had been left for me at the main loading dock. There was no one else at the docks, at the pump, or on the veranda of Jim's cottage. Perhaps the guys who ran the place for him had been told to take the rest of the week off. They were usually cheerful and friendly, offering to haul the bags to the boat, making rude comments about my city garb, offering to come and keep me company in the evening while I waited for the rest of our family to arrive. I was not used to silence at the marina.

When I headed out, it seemed to me that the *Hunt* was the only boat on the lake. Perhaps April was too early for other people to be this far north. There was a chill in the air. The ice had barely gone out, and the birds that wintered in the South had not yet arrived. When my hand touched the water as I tied the boat up to our dock, it felt painfully cold.

The cottage, too, was strangely quiet. In the old days it had always been noisy. Kids running and shouting, Gina doing her ridiculous exercises on the dock, country music or opera wailing away inside, the men chopping wood or repairing the roof, or moving rocks to make an easier path into the water. Sammy had been quite useful, then, and James, to my surprise, had fitted in with the rest of the family. Years ago, there used to be a lot of bellowing and even some laughter. My mother would try to relax, read, or give strident orders to complete some task we had been putting off. The last time I was here, though, there had already been too much silence. Since I hadn't come to the cottage often then, when I did, I was aware of the overall gloom, the sadness that had settled on the place. Mother spent most of the time in her room, gazing at the birdfeeders, her book lying unread on the bed. She left all the cooking to Gina and me. I knew I couldn't face the ghosts of summers past.

I carried my bags up to the deck—I had brought up only two bottles of wine, because I hadn't expected to stay long—and placed them carefully at the glass doors while I hunted for the key.

It wasn't under the small rock where we usually hid it after we locked up at the end of the season. Hardly surprising, given the winter snowdrifts, the strong winds that had blown down some of our roof tiles and broken branches off our one remaining ash tree. While I scrabbled around among the musty, dead leaves, I thought I heard something scuttling toward the cabins. Maybe a squirrel or a chipmunk, but I saw nothing when I stood up. Still no key. I searched under the steps, no key, and nothing on the big nail where Gina preferred to hang it.

We had fought about that.

We did not have the warmest relationship, my sister and I, but we rarely engaged in open combat. It was more of a standoff. We knew each other too well for prolonged battles, but toward the end of that gloomy summer two years ago, we had allowed ourselves to express the anger we both felt—at least, I know I felt—but had kept under control. I found it oddly liberating. We argued about a whole lot of subjects we had avoided before. Mother's choice of a condo and how long she would be able to stay there, Scoop's ashes, Father's mansion, Gladys, Eva, and why she kept showing up (Gina was sure that she still hankered after our father, and I was equally sure that she was secretly gay and in love with our mother). Gina suggested once that Eva had something on our parents, a secret they didn't want her to reveal. (I thought that was ridiculous; if she had some sort of hold over them, she would cash it in, not take it in time spent at the cottage.) We argued even about little things like cleaning the place and who left dishes out the last time. Everything except William. I stayed quiet when she talked about him.

The fight over the placement of the cottage key was one of our nastiest, and it ended by not ending. It started with each of us explaining our different positions—me saying the key had to be in a place where no one could easily find it, Gina saying that everyone put keys under rocks and that our mother preferred the nail option. I viewed bringing our mother into the discussion an unfair thrust and parried with a variety of instances of my sister's ignoring our mother's wishes. From there, the fight escalated.

Given that we had grown up together, we both had a veritable smorgasbord of each other's failings to choose from when we decided to be nasty. These days, our fights veered off into mutual accusations of indifference to Mother's needs, then on to the familiar grounds of sibling rivalry over holiday plans (whose plans had most inconvenienced the others) and selfish or inconsiderate choices of long ago. I brought up her failing to show up at our mother's bedside when she had been ill a few years ago. Unusual for Mother, she had asked for some help with her shopping. But, as was usual with our mother, the shopping wasn't what she had meant. For reasons that hadn't yet been obvious, she had become afraid of being alone at night.

She had been proud of her independence. She not only didn't ask for help, but she also rejected all offers of assistance—and that attitude was still there that winter, three years ago. She insisted on doing her own Christmas shopping with only Nellie's help and ignored our, I thought unanimous, decision to reduce the volume of gifts and the attendant headaches. We would each buy a present for just one person, drawing a name out of a hat. She wanted to buy gifts for everybody.

Gina said that it was a ruse. One of our mother's completely unnecessary ways to show affection and demand, by implication, the same in return. I thought it was her basic insecurity, her feeling that unless she continued to earn respect and admiration, she would cease to matter. As she once described it to me, if you are no longer who you have persuaded yourself you are, then you are no one, a nonperson. That remark had been in response to my suggestion, long before her diagnosis, that she needed a break from her endless schedules, that she could allow herself time to relax.

Back then, she had been a respected academic, a sought-after public speaker. A couple of years later, she was still able to deliver her Current Affairs Lecture at Trinity College, yet she persisted in repeatedly proving her own relevance. She worried that she had been supplanted by other, more effective, or worse, younger speakers.

Perhaps it was her form of blackmailing everyone into appreciating what she did. An extreme case of impostor syndrome. Or a reasonable dread that her failing memory was no longer a secret.

Naturally, no one would ask Mother whether Gina's contention about her preference for key placement had been correct. Gina had mentioned several times during that winter her amazement that I had managed to be invited to give readings throughout the month and that all my readings were far from home, so Gina must have had her way with the key, the reason I couldn't find it.

After about twenty minutes rootling around under nearby rocks and feeling along the edges and undersides of all the steps and everywhere a key could have fallen from a nail, I stomped upstairs and tried the glass door. It was unlocked. Strange, I thought. We always lock up when we leave. But as I slid the door open, I had the weird sensation that I had already done this, that the damp leaves on the mat had been left there by my own boots.

The living room looked as if we had just left for a quick trip up the lake. There wasn't that familiar musty smell we used to comment on when we opened the cottage. Seat cushions pressed down where we had sat, chairs facing one another, the Scrabble board still on the coffee table, a couple of cups nearby, the unfinished puzzle on its table, Mel's baseball glove and ball near the couch, fishing rods with their dangling lines in a bucket, ready to deploy. There was still ash in the fireplace and logs in the iron log-box. Perhaps the photographs were a bit more faded, but they were still standing up in their plastic frames. But I was sure at least one photo was missing. At first I couldn't tell which one, because there was such a plethora of family pictures, so many from the time Gina and I were gawky children, and so many more of her children as they went from babies to almost teens. Well, that's not exactly right. There were a lot of photographs of Gina's daughter, Mel, but only a couple of photos that included William seeming almost relaxed. He had been carefully posed, I am sure. Otherwise, he wouldn't have been looking up. He usually stared fixedly to the right.

My mother had put the pictures out herself and added to them as the years went by. She used to fuss about their placement, making sure no one was in the back row more often than anyone else. I used to count the number of pictures of me and compare them to the ones of Gina. I always came up short.

The missing picture had left a thin line in the accumulated dust, suggesting that it had been there as recently as last summer. There was now a small gap in the area where Gina and I were teens and our mother was young and still pretty. She had remained attractive, in a small, fragile way, well into her sixties. The lines in her face were so muted that, ignoring the obvious fact that I was much bigger-boned than Mother and Gina, people would say the three of us must be sisters. Lines had started to appear on my face, I think, already in my very early thirties—a series of thin, knife-edge lines on my forehead and a couple of softer downward ones from the corners of my mouth. "It's because you frown too much," Mother had said when she noticed me looking at my face in her round magnifying mirror. "You could try being less worried about things."

When I didn't reply, she said, "Or you could try standing on your head for a half hour every day. Let the blood circulate to your face." She told me she had found standing on her head restful.

I turned on the electricity and went to check the toilets. I had watched the men starting and closing down the water often enough, it should, I thought, be easy to restart the system.

It wasn't.

I turned the taps full on, nothing happened.

Oh yes, of course, the pump.

I hated going into the basement. Despite the tiny gaps that remained between the concrete slabs of its outside wall, it was murky and stank of decay and, I thought, peanut butter. Early in the season, Father used to drown mice in a bucket he kept there with peanut butter smeared around the rim. They would fall into the water after they scaled the outside of the bucket. "They're really stupid," he told Gina and me as we watched the desperate creatures trying to get out. You could see their little claw marks on the inside of the bucket after Father threw their tiny bodies into the woods behind the house. "Lots of animals like a good meal of mice," he told us. "They'll be gone by tomorrow." And they were. I know; I looked.

I tried to ignore that memory and instead remember how to turn on whatever it was that our father and, later, Sammy used to turn on when we first came up.

The outdoor furniture and summer things occupied the space at the front of the basement. The water tank was way in back where there was impenetrable blackness.

There was no point in turning the water on in the cottage if there was no water coming into the tank.

I thought it was getting darker.

I went upstairs to look for a flashlight. Amazing how warm it was inside the cottage. The afternoon sun had been bright and the wide windows captured the heat just as they held in the cool air in July.

I should start a fire in case the evening was cold. April was a deceptive month here. Some days it would be warm enough to walk around in shorts, then it would snow and we were back into winter. There was a pile of wood by the fireplace, a bundle of kindling and old newspapers.

The flashlight didn't work. Whoever had used it last—and I put my money on Gina—hadn't taken out the batteries when she left, but why would she remember to do that when she hadn't even thought of locking the doors or putting away the Scrabble or puffing up the cushions on the sofas? I tried and failed to feel sympathy for her.

Best to leave the water till morning.

I put my groceries into the fridge and closed its door. It had begun to hum contentedly.

I made the bed in my room. The sheets felt frigid as I spread them out and patted them down on the mattress. We always left the sheets and duvets in big plastic bins for the winter. They had a damp, musty odor, with a hint of rosemary. We used dried rosemary instead of mothballs. I plumped up the pillows in their too cool covers. Would I have to get a sleeping bag? I couldn't remember where we had stashed the sleeping bags. I hadn't used one since that disastrous camping trip some years ago.

James and I on the French River. What could I have been thinking?

It rained the first day and drizzled the rest of the week. I was not an experienced paddler, and James was impatient with my "lily-dipping." I hated sleeping in the cramped, damp tent reeking of fetid socks, and James had forgotten to pack the padded ground-sheet. He had also left the whiskey behind. I had shivered all night in my dank sleeping bag, while James snored happily in his. Luckily, I had brought along a bottle of Chablis, imagining it would be good for celebrating our first night in a tent. As it was, I drank it all on our second night while James slept. About halfway through the bottle I had proposed a toast to James's solid back.

2

THE SKY HAD TURNED SMOKY DRAB. THE TREES, EVEN the birches, their long, thin, skeletal branches backlit by the setting sun, were black now, as if they had been sketched in charcoal. There were a few rows of green buds, but the leaves hadn't appeared yet. Only the lone willow that Mother had planted twenty years ago near the lake showed long light-green shoots. There were minuscule buds on the oak and, of course, the red pine seemed to be thriving in the cold early spring air. The peaked roof of Father's cabin caught the last of the bleak light; the building itself was blacker than the trees.

It was very still.

I hadn't known that I had been waiting for the prevailing west wind to rustle the dead leaves until I went out on the deck with my glass of lukewarm white wine and noticed myself watching for the ripple of waves or the sound of the boat rubbing against the dock. There had been only the scrunch of acorns under my feet. Nothing else.

The lake was beautiful in its mirrored stillness. In past years I would look at scenes and linger over objects, pondering the right angle, or the right light, approaching closer, backing up, holding my hands up to form a frame around an image. I used to carry a sketch pad for the occasions when I couldn't resist the desire to make something appear on paper. Had I left one here last time? Or my paints? I hadn't seen them at the apartment, but I hadn't really looked for them either. I hadn't wanted to paint.

Mother said I had shown some talent when I was younger, that had I stayed with it, I might have become a passably good artist. Eva, she had said, could have taught me so much, had I been willing to listen. A small gallery in the city had even sold a few of my smaller paintings, and I remembered a suggestion from the owner—was his name Yves?—that he have a modest exhibition of my work. I would have to help with the promotion, of course, and make sure all my friends and acquaintances came.

Mother said my friends would buy some of the paintings because, hey, what are friends for if they're not willing to shell out a bit of money for a painting? They didn't have to hang them to prove their fondness for me, all they had to do was buy them. For a while I had made lists of people to invite. It didn't last. I didn't have enough friends to make the effort worthwhile. Sure, I knew quite a few people, but the only real friend I'd ever had was Annabel, and she had decamped to Paris.

Mother had been even less encouraging about my writing than she had been about my attempt to be an artist. "You're not going to make a living at it, that's for sure," she had said. "You have to be famous to make money writing, and you're not famous."

Too dark to look for my paints now. Leave it till the morning. I would still be alone then; the one thing I hated about painting was that anyone could watch you.

I went inside again and lit the scrunched-up newspapers in the fireplace. The matches, I thought, were sure to be damp, yet one of them caught after only a few tries. The kindling was slow to get going and I had used up most of the paper by the time the maple log caught. My father had been an advocate of burning maple—it lasted longer, the logs were tidier. James had favored birch; it was easier to get going. "The man lacks patience," Father said, returning to one of his old jokes. "He must be a lousy lover." He wasn't, but I had no desire to discuss sex with my father.

When I opened the packages of food I had stashed in the fridge, I couldn't find anything I wanted. The closely packed lettuce and sliced chicken breasts reminded me of the times Gina did the shopping and filled the kitchen with her health foods, big cabbages and cauliflower, broccoli, legumes (I hated the way she pronounced legumes—the *u* elongated, the *g* swallowed), brown rice, flatbread, vegenaise. Never a single thing I was interested in eating. Naturally, when it was my turn to shop, I indulged my inner carnivore with spicy salamis, Italian prosciutto, pork sausages, rib eye steaks, and, when it was my turn to cook, I took delight in watching Gina's discomfort. She would thank me for the effort, then prepare something for herself from her own food supply. Chickpeas and beans that smelled and looked like mush heaped onto her plate. Except when it came to dessert. She liked my desserts a lot more than the fascinating things she made with honey and imitation chocolate. Her children always preferred my cooking to hers, but they rarely got a choice. Mel used to watch me preparing my beef Madras recipe and told me she needed to learn so she could prepare her own meals when I wasn't around.

I took my glass of wine to bed and huddled into the cold sheets. Curled up with my knees against my chest, the pillow scrunched under my head, I could see the sliver of moon and the motionless trees. My father had replaced most of the windows of the original prefab design with wide sliding doors. When he was younger, he had loved the early mornings while everyone else was still asleep and he could open the door and slip out, unnoticed, for his dawn swim in the lake. By the time the rest of us woke up, he would be sitting on the deck, reading his papers and sipping his coffee. The only signs of his swim were the wet footprints that crossed the kitchen floor and the sound of the grinding beans for the percolator. Preground coffee, he had told us, lost its flavor.

There used to be a photo of him sitting on the porch in one of those old, paint-peeling red Muskoka chairs, his feet up on the wooden railing, coffee mug in hand, squinting into the morning sun. I realized that was one of the photos my mother had taken from the collection in the living room. I couldn't remember when it had disappeared from her carefully curated family shots.

I wondered where that picture was now.

I hadn't been aware of it earlier but I did, now, surprisingly, miss him. Not so much his actual being, but the assumption that he would be here in the morning, sitting on the deck, drinking coffee, the momentary peacefulness of it, before the day unfolded. Nostalgia for something that never existed in real time, only in the way I had chosen to see the world when I was about five or six, when I still believed in innocence.

3

UNTIL NOW, ALONE ON GULL ISLAND, I THOUGHT I hadn't believed in ghosts. I didn't hold an aggressive or fanatical position; after all, I had played once with Gina's Ouija board, and she had almost convinced me that the island had a ghost.

The board, Gina's birthday gift from our mother, was black with two rows of silver letters—all capitals—in a slight curve across the middle, a large YES and large NO above on either side of what looked like a moth or a june bug with spread wings. There was a stylized sun-face on the left and a moon-face on the right. A separate silk pouch contained what my sister called, rather portentously, the "planchette," a smallish, roughly heart-shaped piece of wood on casters. The idea was that we would ask the spirit questions and it would answer with the planchette, using our energy to point at letters or one of the two words. The problem was that our energy, Gina had explained, had to be transmitted through our fingers "lightly" laid on the piece of wood.

She had insisted we wait until it was dark. "Much better for ghosts," she said authoritatively, as if she had the faintest idea about what ghosts preferred. She also said that ghosts liked teenagers because they were young enough to believe what they saw and old enough to know what was real. I told her that was typical Gina bullshit but I let her persuade me to play. I think I felt sorry for her because she had put on so much weight—I was taller and thinner—and had taken to wearing loose tops to hide her very large breasts.

It was late September, windy, rough out on the lake. We had brought a low table over to the fireplace because Gina swore that the room had grown unnaturally cold when we first unwrapped the board. The only light was from the flames, because Gina had turned the lights off to create a "bit of atmosphere."

The wind must have blown down the chimney because the flames flickered and almost died out. "Rain," I said, though there was no rain against the windows.

"Shush," Gina whispered. She had just asked a question about what she would do after school. The planchette moved quickly to *e* then *s* finishing with *ape*. "Escape," Gina said, loud enough to wake the parents. "It's talking to me," she added, her voice rising.

"You were pushing it," I said.

"I wasn't," she almost yelled. "Were you?"

"No," I said. I was pretty sure I hadn't been pushing the thing, but it was hard to keep your hand steady over the top of it as it flew from letter to letter. "My turn." I asked it whether I was going to be a great artist.

This time, it rolled right away to the big NO and waited there, like a well-trained dog ready for the next command.

I took my hand off it and rubbed my fingers. They felt frozen, though the fire should have kept the room warm. Some ash had dropped on the board from the fireplace, and as I watched, there was another gust of wind down the chimney. More fine dust and Gina shouting that it was her turn again. She asked a question about a boy she had met in her French class and the Ouija board didn't think he would call her. Not tomorrow. Not next week. When she didn't believe either of those answers, she asked if he would ever call. The answer, as far as I remembered, was *Never.*

I liked that because that boy had asked me to go to prom, and I had every intention of accepting his offer. He was my age, a year older than Gina, but he had been kept back in the class because he was seriously bored by French. I thought he had shown some independence of spirit by asking me, not only because I was older but also because I went to private school. I had met him only once, on a holiday weekend when he had walked Gina home from some teen pool party and they stayed talking at the front door until I told them it was almost midnight. I still remembered Gina's fury when I told her about my prom plans. Though she had already lost interest, she still regarded him as private property.

If asked, I would have said I prefer to keep an open mind about ghosts. I have never been religious either but keep an open mind about God. Possible, but highly unlikely. Perhaps, as James pointed out years later, a characteristic unwillingness or inability to commit. Either way. It could be remnants of a childhood of being pulled in both directions, never knowing which way to jump and almost always regretting whichever decision I had made. My father was a determined, vocal, forceful, always-ready-to-state-his-case atheist. My mother was Roman Catholic. She had studied catechism, both the Old and the New Testament, according to Ignatius. When Father wasn't around she could quote chunks of the Bible. She believed in saints and angels, devils and sinners, heaven and hell, and the afterlife. She always wore a silver cross on a chain around her neck and kept both a Bible and a rosary in the nightstand next to the bed. She didn't engage in debates about religion. She ignored my father's categorical statements because she was certain she knew better. For his longer, more vociferous pronouncements, she had perfected a look of complete detachment, blank eyes staring into the distance. She went to church on Sundays for as long as she could.

She had asked Gina to be sure to call the priest for last rites when the time came. She hadn't asked me.

"She hadn't even told me that she was still Catholic," I told Gina after one of my infrequent visits to mother's new condo.

"Nobody," Gina said, "no one at all, ever quite stops being Catholic."

She had, however, stopped going to confession and communion sometime after she married Father, because the Church didn't recognize marriage to non-Catholics and she could hardly keep confessing to living in sin every time. She had told us this when we were little. Back when we lived in Forest Hill, she would sometimes take us to an Anglican church, which is why, for a while, I assumed we were Anglican. She didn't like Anglicans, she said, but Grace Church's service was close to a Catholic mass, and it was only five minutes' walk from where we then lived.

Getting to the nearest Catholic church would have required a car, and the family's cars were, definitely, our father's. Asking for one of them would have meant an extended argument about religion and no car to drive. So, we went to Grace.

She had insisted that we needed to learn a bit of religion. "Something for you to reject later, if you turned out to be like your father," she said. Besides, Grace was "high Anglican." It had a sort of confession and a sort of communion and a recitation of the Apostolic Creed, which announced, among other bits and pieces, that "I believe in the Holy Spirit, the holy Catholic Church . . ."

"See? It's a leftover," Mother said, "from before the time Henry the Eighth, still married to his queen, ignored the pope's objections and took a new wife." She added, "The reason for this silly religion was the English king's desire to keep marrying."

Gina told me that Mother had chosen Our Lady of Perpetual something as her church once Father was out of the house and no one would criticize her for being Catholic, or for taking a taxi to church every

Sunday. She had given up driving a long time ago. Later, when she was in the condo, she would walk there with Nellie. And the home, Fairview, had Sunday services for most Christian religions, even Catholics, Nellie told me.

Spirits, both shining well-lit ones and dark, evil ones, were accepted presences in her religion and we read about them in church and in her Bible. There was the Holy Ghost having his way with Mary and Satan lurking among the apples, so why not a few ghosts on Gull Island?

4

WE HAVE HAD A FAMILY COTTAGE HERE FOR AS LONG as I can remember. We were told that Father had purchased five lots from a business acquaintance—"not a friend," he had said, emphatically—days before the bank foreclosed on all his not-friend's properties. "I slipped in as the vultures were circling," he added with a smile. He was already ostentatiously proud of his business acumen.

He bought four more lots later, for "protection," in case another curious "vulture" bought them and built a cottage near ours. He didn't want anyone near us. "This is my escape hatch," he said. "Besides, those four were irresistibly cheap. I've always found it hard to resist a bargain." In the end, the whole island became his. He had the best protection: open water and hidden rocks close to the surface. Not even seasoned boaters came this way if they had other places to fish.

In the city, he was social. "Perforce," he had said. He often used big words to show that he was smarter than Mother, though she was the one with the academic career. "But I'm tired of all that bowing and scraping, greeting and smiling that's part of the job." The firm of architects where he worked when he was young used him to welcome potential customers and sign them up for big expensive jobs. On the island he didn't have to see strangers. I thought that was the reason he learned to do the maintenance jobs himself. Back then, he would spend hours studying books on how to fix wiring, plumbing, roof tiles, props on boats, broken engines, docks, and even that infernal generator he had bought—secondhand—for when the lights went out.

We assumed, then, that what he wanted to escape was his work environment, but now I am sure there was more to it than that.

He always allowed some phone calls to invade his peace. After he left architecture and took up real estate investing, he installed a special Wi-Fi router, and a printer for long, complex documents. He kept all this in the cabin farthest from the main cottage. He said he didn't want us to interrupt his work.

Still later, one of his secretaries would phone to ask which pieces of his mail he wanted to read. When he chose to be on the island for a few days, his driver would deliver large packages of mail to Jim's marina, and either Gina or I would take the boat in to bring them back. He never wanted to miss his city mail (every city where he had an office).

He used to boast about building the cottage. It is a simple wooden structure, most of it a prefab he had bought from another defunct company—he had an unerring instinct for bargains—that promised to make cottage-building easy and inexpensive. He hired a local company to dig down and lay the foundations. Our parents were young, so the prospect of raising a prefab, he had told us, hadn't seemed daunting. The frame is pine, treated with dark preservative that still smells like motor oil some thirty years after the cottage was assembled. The walls between the rooms are plywood. Because there is no insulation, walls and doors are almost irrelevant. Except for my father's own room, whose walls were stuffed with foam, they provide a mere illusion of privacy. We could easily hear one another through the walls.

When my sister invited her first real boyfriend for the weekend—

I think she was about nineteen—we all knew they were making out on one of the bunk beds. Mother went to her room, turned up the radio, and pretended to read. I went down to the dock. Our father sat in the living room, softly playing one of his old country and western records. In the morning he remarked on the boyfriend's inability to hold back. "Does not bode well for the long term," he said with a wink, "but what can you expect of the Irish."

He then told a relentless joke about how different nationalities approached foreplay. The Irish, as you can imagine, hadn't a clue. The boyfriend had the disadvantage of an Irish name. My sister and her boyfriend left the room minutes before Father arrived at the Irish bit. She knew what the punch line would be. We didn't see her again until after she had ferried the boyfriend back to the mainland. She had gone straight to our room—the one with the bunk beds—and listened to loud rock through her earphones.

It's weird, I think now, that neither of our parents seemed to be concerned that Gina, at nineteen, was having sex with her boyfriend. Father seemed to think it was funny, and Mother, though the Church certainly frowned on sex before marriage, made no objections. Didn't they care?

When James came to the cottage, he used the small cabin, and I joined him after my parents went to their separate rooms. I hadn't expected them to object, I just didn't want to hear Father's comments.

The cottage floors are also plywood with a thin pine overlay. Father and a couple of his friends—he used to have friends back then—had laid them and raised the plywood walls over one summer about thirty years ago. It was exacting work, but he said he had enjoyed it, fitting the pieces together, making sure each one was true to its function. All that happened before I was born and long before he made what he called his "serious money."

The foundations are concrete slabs with unintended gaps where the local workmen forgot to insert caulking. At first, Father had been furious. He had demanded they take them apart and remake them exactly as planned, but later he agreed to a reduced bill and caulked the gaps himself. The basement is big, dark, and damp. It's used for the pump, the heater, the hot water tank, the generator, and for winter storage. It's where we stash everything in late October, the barbecue, the lounge chairs and tables, the children's outdoor toys, the swing set, buckets, plungers, rakes, shovels, the power saw, and assorted gardening and fix-it tools.

It's also where he locked me up when I couldn't stop crying about the dead mice. Another time, when I was around five or six and had snuck into the basement to save one that was still swimming around, he left me there overnight. I couldn't be sure whether that was the first time he hit me. Not hard but it was across the face and my nose hurt all night.

The main cottage has five bedrooms, three in back, one at each side, a large living room that stretches across the front, and a kitchen with old appliances that still work most of the time. Father's study had been the largest of the back rooms. It has a skylight and wall-to-wall windows with a view of our pine forest. Gina and I used to share another back room with the two sets of bunk beds, so we wouldn't fight over who got to sleep on top. Later, it was the room Gina's kids shared, William always in one of the bottom bunks because he flailed around so much at night, Gina said he would fall out of bed and hurt himself. Gina and Sammy had the room in the middle, next to their kids, and I moved to the end room, closest to the steps that led down to the path. It was smaller than the others, but it had a lot of sun in the mornings, and in late summer I could see the red clouds through the trees as the sun set.

There are two prefab sleeping cabins, with only wash basins and a path between them that leads to the outhouse. The doors are low, the roofs red and peaked, the windows have multicolored frames, like meticulously assembled LEGO constructions. They were meant to serve my sister's growing family, but she hated them and she hated the outhouse with such passion that she never used it.

Almost four years ago Father, with all his equipment, moved to the bigger cabin. It was as though he had decided to leave us gradually. Eva, who used to stay in the small cabin, took over his bedroom. I don't remember any discussion of this move; it just happened.

Eva was my mother's best friend and a frequent visitor everywhere she lived.

The front of the cottage is all windows looking out at the lake. There are a bunch of thin birch trees, a few big oaks, some white pine, red pine, spruce, an ash that had somehow survived the weevils, a couple of maples, a lot of low sumac, young sapling oaks, and raspberry bushes that hadn't had a chance to grow.

In the spring, Father used to take the scythe to everything he thought might block his view of the water or was superfluous or useless. He hated fast-growing asters, long ferns, young oaks, lilies, goldenrods, even black-eyed Susans because they grew too tall. He would stand with his legs apart, one arm out straight, the other bent at the elbow and whip the scythe from side to side. I remember the whoosh as he swung it. He used a pair of huge shears for what was left by the scythe. He could have paid someone to do the work, but he chose to do it himself because he said he didn't want anyone spying on us. Besides, it would be done right this way.

I couldn't imagine anyone wanting to spy on us, but I did understand his absolute belief in being the only one who could do everything the right way.

We rarely used the place in the winter. When my sister and I were little, the pipes had heating ducts and insulation, but he didn't repair them when they frayed. Back then, he still enjoyed driving his old Jaguar and the Alfa Romeo. They were sporty, low-slung cars, deep two-seaters with a sort of rumble seat in the back that Gina and I shared by squeezing into each other's laps. Usually my lap, because she was younger and smaller. On the long trips from the city to the marina, she would beg our father to stop. When he refused, and he always refused, she peed on my legs.

Later, he went to the Bahamas or London (where he had offices long after both Gina and I had left home), or to Barbados, sometimes to the Caymans or someplace in Spain. He didn't have offices in all those places, but he had what he referred to as "a man" and some sort of winter deal that gave him a big house, a housekeeper, a gardener, and a car with a chauffeur when he wanted one. Even when they were still living together, Mother would not go with him.

After he was no longer living in our house, he informed us that he didn't like to drive. He sold the little cars and got a Mercedes with push-button windows and a glass partition between the front and the back seats. Now, only his chauffeur drove, and no one else was allowed to sit next to Father. On the few occasions when he came to take us out to dinner, we sat with our backs to the chauffeur, and our father sat facing forward. When we argued, which was often, he pushed the glass partition up so the chauffeur—the only one he had for longer than a year was Gerry, and Gerry was hired only a couple of years ago—couldn't hear us.

On sunny days, the cottage was cooled by the prevailing wind—northwest and coming straight at the dock—off the lake. We seldom needed to turn on the ceiling fans.

Some of my early memories of the cottage are cheerful. Though I am not a great swimmer, I loved swimming here; though I am not confident landing boats, I do love being out on the open water in a boat; I love kayaking, being far enough away from others that I can think; and though I am not much of a cook, I loved cooking in that kitchen because it is open to the dining area and people—not my father—would come and talk with you and sometimes offer to help chop vegetables or peel potatoes, or clean the pots and pans. Later, someone, usually Sammy, would pour the wine and bring glasses, someone else would set the table, the kids would help put out the cutlery, and all the time there would be music under the chatter of voices. Even William helped out, and though he often placed the cutlery on the wrong side of the plate, I was glad to see that he tried.

Only Father liked country and western. My mother liked classical. Opera: Mozart, Puccini, Tchaikovsky, and long symphonies—more Mozart, some Beethoven. "It's the ultimate music," she said, "perfection. It can't be improved upon. No reason for creating music if you can't make it perfect." Some evenings she would listen to her Mozart and he to Garth Brooks, both pretending that they couldn't hear each other's music.

5

THE KITCHEN WAS THE PLACE WHERE I USED TO CATCH
up with my mother's news. It's where I learned that she had been diagnosed with dementia.

She was very forthright about it. As if she were adding to our list of
groceries. It was a Sunday evening, and since I had an event at a writers'
festival, I had to head into the city the next morning. My mother, never
an early riser, dictated the list while we were both in the kitchen. I was
making dinner. She was slicing a lemon for drinks. Gina was listening to
Mother's *Così fan tutte* (my father hated that one with a particular passion). Gina's kids were rehearsing a play they intended to show after dinner. Mel had dressed up as a witch, and William was planning to be a tree.

"I decided to go for the test," my mother said, casually, as if she were
talking about something simple, like an eye exam or a boating test. She
had never bothered to get her boating license. She was sure the marine
cops would not bother her. They all knew her and knew she had been
boating long before they donned their first marine cop outfits. In rough
weather they sometimes docked at our place to get out of the wind.

"I've been forgetting things," she said, "so far, nothing crucial, but last week I left a pot on the stove and it almost caught fire. All the alarms went off, of course." She laughed. "Your father had installed a very effective system. Before he left." She very rarely mentioned my father's leaving.

"Oh my God, Mom, you could have been killed." I drank more of my wine.

"Not a great loss, all around," she said. Her voice was calm but crackly, coming from the back of her throat. "In the Arctic, they used to put the old folk out on the ice. Here, we keep them alive for years after their best-before date, so long as they stay out of sight and they can afford to pay their own bills at the nursing home."

"Aw, Mom . . ."

"The fire department arrived, attractive young guys, a bit stern with their instructions on how I had to make sure to turn the burners off when I left the kitchen. As if I didn't know. There was this one guy—cute, blue-eyed, with a fringe of dark hair—but I didn't like the way he looked at me, as if I were a small child who didn't know any better and shouldn't be playing with things in the kitchen anyway."

"When did you start . . . ?"

"Noticing? Oh, months ago. At first I lost only words and familiar phrases. I knew they were hiding somewhere in my brain but I couldn't grasp them and pull them out when I needed them. Sometimes in the middle of a lecture. Awkward pause and a quick replacement with another word or a phrase that wasn't quite right but would have to do. Then I started to forget appointments, repeated what I had already said, sometimes in the same conversation. I am becoming a bore."

"I hadn't . . ."

"Of course, you hadn't. You tune me out. But friends have become impatient with me." She stressed the word *friends* to make the difference between them and me clearer. Guilt had always been one of my mother's weapons of choice in combat, but now, while my pen hovered over the blank piece of paper still waiting for her shopping list of body lotions, shampoos, face creams, I hadn't thought we were at war.

"What did they say when you took the test?" I asked, ignoring her invitation to fight.

"Not much. There wasn't much they could say. It's a creeping disease. Slow. Relentless. Incurable. Goes in one direction only. Forward. I think the word is *inexorable*. Can you fill my glass?"

She took the roast out of the oven and carried it to the table. There was an ugly red burn mark on her wrist. I wanted to ask her how that had happened but decided to raise it later, maybe after dinner.

I filled her glass and sloshed some more wine into mine.

I had wanted to tell Gina right away but she was in one of her moods. She had been complaining about some perceived slight from one of her now former friends. She discarded friends the way some people discarded old clothes: seasonally and without regrets. She was only a year younger than me but seemed a dozen years younger. I had been baffled by her decision to marry when she was twenty-one, much too young even for someone who was mature for her age, which Gina wasn't.

She had moved on from *Così fan tutte* to one of our mother's Wagners, something she knew our father hated even more than *Così*. "Incontinent squealing of angry women," Father had said of the Valkyrie. "All to get that son of a bitch to pay attention," he said of Wotan, the super-god of *Walhalla*.

Gina had turned the Wagner on especially loud so she would not have to hear William's halting, slow reading for his father. The kid was doing his best, but it was irritating. I think both Gina and our father had detested him pretty much since he was first diagnosed. They were both perfectionists, and he'd had greater hopes for William than he'd had for Gina and me. Or for Mel, because she was just another girl.

Afterward, the evening had unfolded as a typical cottage evening. Mother led the political discussion at the table. She was opinionated, sure of the rightness of her views on world affairs, dismissive of opposition as irrelevant for even questioning her certainties.

I would have argued with her about new troubles in Mali—I had heard about Mali from James, who had actually been there—but I was busy looking for signs of her forgetfulness. When she did repeat something she had said earlier, I thought it could have been for emphasis, except that I now suspected it wasn't. Father hadn't been at the table. He rarely came to the cottage now, and when he did come, he took his dinners to his cabin. He hadn't bothered to make excuses.

After dinner Gina put her children to bed and didn't return. She was too young to be a mother, and Sammy, jovial, friendly, bearish but only marginally more mature, as usual, had had too much to drink. I was hardly the one to be critical of someone else's drinking habits, since I rarely went to bed sober, but Sammy had two kids and more responsibilities.

He fell asleep over a book that slid down his knees to his ankles. As the years loped by, there was only one reason for his presence: William. I had often wondered why he and Gina were still together, and I always came up with the same answer: William with maybe a dash of Mel. Sammy didn't have to worry about Mel so much because she had been such an easy child. He chose to come to the cottage although he knew he annoyed both Gina and our father, but he seemed to think a stable home—one with two parents—was important for a child. Especially a child such as William. Sammy had some very traditional ideas of what a family should be and his being around us hadn't yet changed them. Otherwise, I assumed, he would have stayed in town with William.

Gina had inherited Father's fastidiousness, his love of order and his desire to see everything in its place. Sammy was disorganized. He left his wet bathing suits on the floor and rarely cleaned his clothes ("they're cottage clothes, who cares?").

Perhaps he hadn't expected our father to be here. Frankly, neither had

I. Those days, he rarely came to the cottage, and when he did, he kept pretty much to himself. I wondered whether it was the hunting and fishing that brought him, or his pride in having built most of it himself and that not much, not even the old appliances, had changed here since then. He rarely talked with us anymore and never spoke with Mother.

I washed the dishes and watched our mother take her glass into her room and shut the door firmly. Obviously, she had no desire to continue our discussion.

Early the next day, I tried to wake her to say that I was leaving. Mornings were not her best time, so I hadn't expected she would choose to talk, and least of all about the dementia, but we had, I felt, an unfinished conversation, and I wasn't sure when I would see her again.

She lay on her side, very still, one arm over her face, the other under the pillow. Her shoulder was bare. It was just one small round ball of bone with a covering of paper-thin blue-white skin. The loose skin of her arm folded under her armpit. Her breasts had almost vanished. When she was younger, she used to wear push-up bras to accentuate her figure. Now, she no longer wore a bra.

Her left hand lay lifeless on the duvet, the nails were all painted pearly beige, the cuticles carefully trimmed. She had the prettiest hands. Long, slender fingers, tapered at the ends. They made my own square hands feel clumsy.

I hadn't noticed how frail she had become.

As I pulled up the blanket to cover her shoulder I lied that I would try to be back in a week. Though I was pretty sure she had heard me, she didn't stir.

Father stood at the end of the dock, still wet from his early morning swim, his back to our mother's empty chair. He wore his linen cottage robe, too short but tailored to fit, even now that his belly had become rounder. He was approaching seventy years of age. Perhaps I hadn't really looked at him for a while. I noticed, however, that his legs had become thinner, his knees bulkier, his chest narrower. His shorts hung down his hips, barely covering his bony ass. Even his casting arm was thinner, the tendons taut over the softening muscles. He was casting for bass the way he had taught me. "It's all in the wrist," he used to say. His wrists had been thicker then, and his voice deeper. "Bend it just so, snap it and gentle it as far as you can into the water, let it rest for a moment or two, then reel it back so the fish can see the lure dancing on the surface."

That morning, he didn't speak to me.

It was a soft, late summer morning when I left. The sun was barely over the horizon, ducks gathered in loud, busy flocks; long lines of cormorants ready for migration, hummingbirds anxiously feeding at the four red birdfeeders we should have removed already to encourage them to leave, raucous gulls circling near the small fishing boats I passed, only the oblivious geese carelessly foraging near the marina, where I'd tied up the *Limestone*. I usually got the *Hunt*. The *Limestone* was Father's, though Gina felt entitled to use it when he wasn't here. It was the bigger boat, more stable than the *Hunt* in the waves, and she had kids. But that morning, I felt I had the choice of boats. Father said nothing. I assumed that he was too busy with his fishing rod to notice, but now I think he no longer cared.

I didn't know then that I wouldn't be back at the cottage for more than a year.

6

THE SHOPPING LIST STAYED IN MY WALLET LONG AFTER
it had become obvious that I wouldn't use it. It had become a sort of talis-
man, a lucky charm that could bring us all back to a place where Mother
gave me shopping lists, the kids set the table, and we could still pretend
we were a family. I had been busier than usual. I missed Thanksgiving at
the cottage that year. It was not my first time, but I knew I needed to give
an excuse. I was going to schools in the north, speaking about my young
heroine, Kitty. Kids liked to hear about her adventures, especially the ones
that hadn't happened yet. I got to try out my future story ideas on live
audiences and frequently changed them in response to their responses—if
they found them too outlandish, or too impossible for Kitty to survive, or
if they looked weary or bored. I thought of it as market research. When
I had mentioned this to my mother, she said that it showed I had never
taken my writing seriously, and no wonder, since I had chosen to write
wholly unlikely fantasies for children with little imagination of their own.
She said I should have stuck with painting. But I enjoyed writing, and it
earned me money.

Afterward I went to give some talks at a convention of librarians in

Atlanta, Georgia, and left for Newark the end of the week for a series of interviews about writing for teens. It was a feeble excuse for postponing my return, but it would have to do. I had not been ready to deal with my mother's illness.

By the time I came home, it was almost winter, and the first thing Gina said was that we should move our mother. Sell the house and use the money to buy her a condo. The house was too big for her alone, and Nellie, her housekeeper, was barely managing the cleaning and upkeep. She said it was time I went for a visit to see for myself.

I think I had been afraid to see Mother. I didn't want to talk about her dementia with her. Perhaps talking about it would make it seem more real.

"Caregivers," the Alzheimer Society's website said, "often live in denial. They hope the condition will pass. It doesn't."

Obviously, I wasn't a caregiver, but I feared I could be sucked into the role. Gina would use her own kids as her reason for pushing me into it. I had no obvious excuse, other than my sense of never having been close to my mother, never having the kind of relationship that fostered easy intimacies, and caregiving implied intimacy. I did not think we would be comfortable in that role. Neither of us. She would no more want me to see her struggling to make it to the bathroom than I wanted to witness her humiliation. I don't know whether other families can manage those roles, but ours, for certain, couldn't. I knew Gina felt much the same way I did, or she would not have taken the first opportunity to move out of the house, but I think she felt easier around Mother than I did. Or vice versa.

When I finally visited her, it was late November, and both of us pretended nothing was wrong, that nothing had been said about the dementia. We also pretended that I was sober.

She chatted about plans for Christmas, the price of turkeys, a speech she had canceled because she did not want to fly to Victoria (not because of her declining mind) and, though I knew she wasn't interested, I told her about my new book. Anything to avoid the subject of dementia. Or our father's new living arrangements. It was difficult not to connect the two subjects, since the year of her diagnosis was also the year Father had finally moved out.

7

I WASN'T SURE WHAT WOKE ME. IT WAS VERY DARK. I think I had forgotten how much darker it was here than in the city. No streetlamps, no moving cars, no neon signs, no office high-rises with all-night lights, and now even that sliver of moon had vanished. I lay still and listened for the sound that must have woken me. Nothing. I reached for the flashlight I always kept next to the bed, then I remembered that I hadn't been here for a couple of years and no one else would have put in new batteries.

Scratching somewhere under the window. Softly, then more vigorously, more quickly. I thought of paws trying to dig out something left underground. Raccoon? They eat bugs, don't they? We used to have a couple of raccoon families on the island. One lived in a hollow high up the tree near the steps that led up from the path. In the spring the kits would crawl down and balance along the railing, glancing down from time to time, looking for a soft place to land. They were not afraid of us. Scoop, my mother's dog, didn't like them, but he did find them fascinating. He growled but never attacked them. He indulged in prolonged staring contests with the mother when she followed her kits down the tree.

I sat up. Throughout the summers I usually didn't draw the curtains on the big screen doors, enjoying the night sky, and like my mother, I loved to wake up to the birds and the early morning sun. But I had never been alone up here, and now, in the impenetrable dark, I thought coming here had been a dreadful mistake. Had Mother not insisted, I wouldn't be in this room, clutching my blanket, pulling it to my chin. My fingers were frozen claws.

I decided not to turn on the light. It would make my presence obvious to whatever was digging out there. Just as well the flashlight didn't work. Its light would pinpoint me, and whatever that sound had been, I didn't want it to know I was here.

I got up very slowly and, feeling my way around the bed, padded over to the side window nearest to the sound, and waited for my eyes to adjust. I could hear my heart beat inside my ears.

Something was moving in the darkness, blacker than the all-around black, bulkier, close to the side of the cottage, close to the steps that led up to the deck. My door was the first after the steps and it wasn't locked. We didn't lock our doors at night. We locked them only when we left for the winter.

I hadn't known I was holding my breath until I had to let it out, and now I worried it might have been heard. Who knew that breathing made so much noise?

For a minute or so the scratching and digging stopped. The bulky thing moved sideways. I could have sworn it looked at me, but how I could think that, I don't know, since it was pitch-dark. When it started to dig again it was louder and, I thought, more determined than before, but by then, I was sure my imagination had taken over. I told myself to stop being scared. It was only a raccoon. And if not a raccoon, maybe a large squirrel or a porcupine.

Squirrels are not nocturnal. Okay, so porcupine. There must still be porcupines on the island, though we hadn't seen one for some years now.

Perhaps they had been scared away by Scoop's sharp-edged barking. He didn't bark at raccoons but became agitated about porcupines. Or maybe my father had shot them. Sometimes he would head out with one of his shotguns and be gone all day. We would hear the gun pop at the back of the island and he would come back, pleased with himself. But perhaps he had missed, or he hadn't planned to kill a porcupine and there was still one left on the island somewhere. Or it could have come over from the mainland.

Do porcupines swim?

My feet were icy. The rest of me was also cold, but I was more aware of my feet on the wooden floorboards than of the rest of me shivering in my thin flannel nightshirt. Abruptly the scratching and digging stopped and the bulky thing stood up. Yes. I thought it stood but it was almost impossible to see anything in the dark. Then it disappeared. Bear?

There had not been bears on the island since the raspberries disappeared.

Rustling of last year's fallen branches and leaves as it walked away. Or was that the prevailing wind getting up at last? Softly. I hadn't seen any movement, so how could I imagine it had walked away?

As if on cue, the thin slice of moon illuminated the lake and the birches in a scintilla of patchy pale light. I peered down through the window. There was nothing at the foot of the stairs and nothing near the birches, though I was sure that was where it had gone.

I stood waiting for a sound to tell me where it was, for a sense of something real, an animal searching for food—but why at the wall? Or walking into the lake for a drink, or because it lived in the lake. An otter? Why would an otter come this far out of the water? Not an otter. A beaver. Yes. There had been beavers on the west end of the island. We saw a few trees they had felled, and some years ago, as Gina and I paddled around the island, we could see their dam. But that was many years ago. Father said he wanted to discourage them before they wrecked our island.

He had probably shot them. He didn't tell us, but when he announced that the beaver problem had been solved, we just knew it.

Still, there were more beavers in Georgian Bay. One of them could have swum to the island last year, after the others were killed.

I slid the screen doors shut and locked them, drew the curtains, peed into the empty toilet bowl (definitely not going to the old outhouse), tossed more wood into the fireplace in the living room, poured myself a glass of wine, and curled up next to the still smoldering fire, where it was warmest. I was determined to start the pump in the morning.

I couldn't remember what I had been reading, so I picked a book at random from the bookcase and dove into *Sapiens,* a history of our species in some five hundred pages, from the earliest unrecorded times to nearly today. I had abandoned it years ago because I didn't want to feel as insignificant as the author had made me feel. But tonight, being alone in the cottage, with something digging under the bedroom window, feeling insignificant would be useful.

8

ONE OF THE ADVANTAGES OF WRITING MYSTERIES IS being able to almost effortlessly enter imaginary worlds. My books are in a category called YA (young adult, teenager really), and they are supposed to be riveting page-turners. On the long drive up the boring highway, I had been trying to picture Kitty, the wisecracking high school dropout-turned-juvenile-detective heroine of all my books, skillfully evading a paid killer. She had recently discovered that a mining company was dumping waste into a river and was determined to "out" them. Hence their hired killer.

Once I was off the main highway, I made myself super aware of large trees, perfect for hiding behind, and impenetrable bushes lining the side road. In the parking lot I gave wide berth to everything a killer could slip behind, only to determine that this would not work if the killer had a gun. And why wouldn't he have a gun? He could hardly be expected to set out on his assignment armed with only a knife. I had debated the matter of guns with my editor, who thought YAs would be too scared to keep reading about an armed killer chasing a sixteen-year-old (always pick someone a bit older than your audience; they don't identify with kids their own age) through the woods. It could even be "triggering," she had said. How in hell could someone with a gun trigger a traumatic experience in a kid, unless the kid had a bad experience of his or her own with a gun? I thought.

"Trigger warning?" I said. "You're joking. Right? Gun, trigger, etc. . . ."

"No. We would have to put a trigger warning on the cover," she had said, pursing her lips with the disapproving forbearance editors display when you disagree with them.

"Bullshit," I told her. Nevertheless, I changed the killer's weapon to a knife, thus reducing his chances of causing Kitty—she had taken a course in martial arts—any serious damage.

"It must be comforting to all your readers," my mother had said, "that no matter how dangerous the situation, Kitty will come through it all right; we all know she will be featured in the next book in your series. Unlike in life, there are no real risks." She was not a fan.

My writing didn't make much money, but I didn't need much, and so long as I could churn out one book a year, rarely ate in restaurants, and didn't frequent the clubs near my apartment, I got by. The royalties covered the cost of my one-bedroom in what was billed the Entertainment District—an area of clubs, theaters, bars, restaurants—safe during the day, at night not so much. I lived there because the rent was low, not because I liked it. Sometimes I went to the theater, but I avoided the bars and the clubs. They didn't exactly charge admission fees but you had to buy a drink if you wanted to stay and the drinks were very expensive. The fact that I could never resist a second drink, a third, or more as the evening wore on, and sometimes didn't quite remember where I lived, made these outings not only exorbitant but also dangerous. I could usually foresee how the night would unfold even before I entered a club, and the picture of myself staggering home with someone I had just met or someone following me was scary enough to keep me home.

After James moved in, the attraction of the bars had grown stronger.

His disapproval of my reaching for another glass of wine made me want martinis with olives, or manhattans with cocktail cherries, or some other fancy concoction a barman would make. James was a securities lawyer but he often worked at home, and I had nowhere else to go to write. He suggested that we rent a bigger apartment with two studies, a large bedroom, a larger living room, and more space for books. He would have paid more than his share, but I didn't want to feel like our arrangement was permanent. So long as he was staying at my place while still keeping his own vacant apartment, I'd felt I could end the relationship when I wanted to end it.

Knowing how our father lived and how much he spent on entertaining himself, I had also assumed that one day there could be enough for me to stop renting and buy my own place. But it didn't matter whether I was even in his will. I could live like this for the rest of my life—no matter what the therapist suggested. She certainly hadn't known me long enough to know how I saw my own future or what price I might not have been willing to pay for a home I could own.

Father had begun to accumulate money when I was still at university, and while he never talked about it, the signs were there soon after he gave up architecture for real estate.

We didn't know how much money there was, but Gina had been confident enough for her and Sammy to take out a gargantuan mortgage on a three-story house near a hip area of the city. It was for the children, she told us; the location had excellent schools. Instead of splurging on a new house, our father had suggested enrolling Mel in a private school, but she told him that a good area to live in was more important. She didn't have his money, she said pointedly, so they would make do with public schools. The schools nearby were, she insisted, a cut above the downtown schools where genuinely poor people lived.

What worried her more, she said, was that William took up too much of her time, rather than his not catching up to his peers. Sammy made enough to pay the bank its monthly mortgage rates, but not enough to hire help in the house, let alone what Gina called "special needs" help for William. Father thought her notion about William catching up was inane. The best she could hope for was that he pass through life without causing lasting damage to himself or anyone else. Not that she ever talked directly about William's imperfections.

He may have been a bit slower than others, but he was not even ten years old.

Now, of course, all that discussion was unnecessary.

9

I NEVER DID GET BACK TO SLEEP. I LISTENED TO NOISES from the woods behind the cottage, the buzzing of mosquitoes or black-flies against the screens (too early for mosquitoes?), a loon, and once a rac-coon calling its mates, but no more sounds from near the steps. Nor did I see anything near the lake. For a fleeting moment, I recalled the Ouija board, the ashes, and the wind, but I still didn't think I believed in ghosts. I was trying to convince myself that I had dreamed the figure outside, that it was one of my odd reflective dreams—and I have had many during the past few years—where I was both present and absent at the same time, observing myself from a distance and not liking what I saw.

Those dreams, the therapist had thought, might represent how others saw me and how I had begun to see myself. When she asked whether I had felt close to my parents, I laughed. Close? We had never been closer than din-ner guests at the same event, but at different tables. Father's indifference and Mother's disapproval might have made me feel worthless or, at least, insecure, even as an adult, she said. Had I been avoiding them? I had been concerned about Mother, but not concerned enough to go and see her, I realized.

Now, I could not persuade myself that the bulky form under the window had been a figment of my overactive imagination. I couldn't even distract myself by thinking about the difficulties facing Kitty. Under a harsh blanket of guilt, I was churning over what Mother had told me about her memory loss. Though she had named it right away, I didn't want to name it, not yet. I settled on "cognitive impairment." Mild, early form, perhaps.

Already more than four years ago, there had been no doubt we had to move her out of the house and then, last winter, out of the condo we had bought with her money. We decided to put a deposit on the space at Fairview. We could not be sure of a room without a deposit, because Fairview was one of the most coveted retirement and assisted-living places in the city. It was also one of the most expensive, big airy rooms, a good kitchen with an extensive menu, choice of wine by the glass, and a classy dining room with white tablecloths that would appeal to Mother's genteel snobbery. We had to ignore the fact that she didn't want to go there. "These places," she had told us when we first broached the subject, "are not for the old, most of them would rather stay where they are. Their sole purpose is to comfort their families, make them feel they no longer have to care." She had looked at me when she said that. "Not that you need to care wherever I am," she added.

She was right. Fairview prided itself on its "care-staff."

At dawn another loon called, not far from the dock, enthusiastically answered from farther away, and I was trying, I have no idea why, to remember all the items on that last shopping list of Mother's, from the evening five years ago when she told me she couldn't remember words and phrases and that she had left the burner on.

After "Part One, The Cognitive Revolution" in *Sapiens,* it was almost a relief to read the appropriate bits of our manual for the pump: First, you turn on all the taps, make sure the water intake is connected to the tank, and the electricity was connected to the pump. The instructions warned in red not to start the pump without "priming," and that meant a complicated set of directives on "flushing water into the system."

I finally ventured outside at eight o'clock. For a couple of hours, I had been watching the deck for signs that would confirm that the night visitor had been a raccoon.

No signs, no turds, no sounds. Not even the screaming of seagulls or honking of our neighborly Canada geese. They nested on one of the outer islands and foraged along our shoreline every summer. No screeching jays, no wrens. Nothing. It was so quiet, I could still hear myself breathe.

I replaced the batteries in the flashlight—they were last year's but had astonishingly survived the winter—and descended the stairs near where the scratching had been during the night. No evidence of an animal now, but there were some scratches all over the cottage's weathered pine boards, not only where I thought I had heard something last night. My father used to put preservative on the wood, but no one had done it for some time now and there were rotten bits, turned dark and soft where claw marks should have been, too, but weren't easy to see. Could it have been searching for something in the wood itself? I was fairly sure raccoons didn't usually do that, but maybe I knew less about raccoons than I needed to know if I was to spend time up here alone.

Somewhere close to this set of steps, Gina used to bury her "precious things," stuff she wouldn't risk leaving in our bunk room because she thought I would take them from her. Her colored, transparent beads, her woven bracelet, a note from a boy she had kept in a small square box, and that planchette I had saved from the fire. But that was long ago, when we were twelve or thirteen years old. I only knew about the spot because once, when I thought Gina had taken my sketchbook and I had complained to Eva. She told me not to worry, she would take care of it. Later that day, Eva said she had found it dug into the ground near the steps. She asked me not to tell Gina, to say only that I had another sketchbook, that it was best Gina think her secret hidey-hole was still safe. Had Gina ever discovered the ruse? I didn't know, but I was sure she hadn't talked about it.

It was a murky, cloudy day, delicate gray-blue waves on the lake, the kind of day I used to welcome in the middle of summer, when there had been too much sun and heat, but now it was merely cold and bleak. In the basement, it was light enough that I was able to fight my way through the remnants of past summers that barred the way to the back, where the pump and the water tanks sat in impenetrable darkness. The light switch crackled when I tried it, but the lone bulb hanging from the low ceiling didn't come to life. The flashlight produced the faintest of yellow beams, but enough for me to make sure the intake pipe was connected, find what I assumed was the relief valve, and set about trying to open it. Twisting the metal lever needed a whole lot more strength than I could muster in such a confined space. James used to say I had butterfingers. My mother said I had the beginnings of arthritis. "Most of us get arthritis, so you can expect to have it soon," she had said, cheerfully. "Maybe sooner than you think."

"Thank you for that," I told her.

She, of course, didn't have arthritis. Her fingers may not have been as supple as in her youth, but they remained as long and tapered as ever.

I found a piece of wood outside and wedged it in next to the lever, trying to make it easier to turn, but it still wouldn't budge. I vaguely remembered my father taking a screwdriver down after he turned the water on, so I got a screwdriver and a hammer from his big red toolbox in its usual place near the entrance to the basement. I hammered at the wood to push the lever. I am not sure how long I kept trying before the flashlight faded, flickered, and went out. Again I had to wait for my eyes to adjust to the darkness, so I could feel my way out of the pump room, over the old hammocks and Muskoka chairs and children's plastic wading pools we had been keeping long after the kids no longer used them. They had learned to swim, and I think Gina had been surprised that even William, spluttering happily and flailing away with both arms, managed to stay afloat. He had really loved being in the water.

I grabbed one of the rakes leaning up against the concrete. Its prongs were rusted and bent from our strenuous efforts over the years, but it would do to gather the dead leaves—a job I usually shared with my sister and, back when she was younger, our mother. I needed distraction, and it would be good to have some exercise.

I ducked under the low doorframe and stood blinking in the dreary morning sun. Though it was far from warm, it felt good on my skin after the sleepless night. I was desperate for a cup of coffee but had not been able to make coffee because there was no running water. I took a kid's red plastic bucket and filled it with water at the lake to take upstairs for my coffee.

There were a few tentative tulips poking their heads through the dry leaves. Amazing that they had survived the squirrels' winter hoarding preparations. Gina had said she had scattered cayenne pepper over the bulbs to save them, but I had seen a squirrel digging down for a bulb and holding it in its mouth as it scaled one of the oak trees. I could have sworn it liked the taste of cayenne.

Maybe a squirrel had been digging for bulbs by the wall?

It was too early for my father's blue periwinkles to flower but I could already see the leaves showing on the far side of the path. It was the only plant he had ever brought up here, and he'd planted it himself. "An invasive species," my mother had said.

"Exactly. That's why I brought it up," he replied.

It was May, a number of years ago, and he had been pulling out and discarding other plants, mostly lilies, digging hard to make room for the periwinkles. We found out later that they had been a gift from Gladys. A most unusual gift, but one he seemed to have relished. It was early days for their relationship, but she apparently had wanted to give him something that required effort. His, not hers.

Mother stood behind him, hands held just behind her back. "They have no business being on the island," she said. She kept her voice low but I knew she was angry, and so did he. But while both Gina and I were usually attuned to her disapprovals, he had the ability to slide over her moods, as if they were quite irrelevant. He finished planting his periwinkles, stood up with a broad grin on his face, wiped his hands on his jeans, swept the dirt off his knees, and strolled down to the hammock where, within easy reach, he had left his chunky scotch glass and his book.

Our mother continued to stand, looking at the tiny periwinkle plants, scowling and shaking her head. Then she mounted the stairs to the deck, saying over her shoulder, "I do not understand you." She spoke artificially slowly.

He kept sipping his scotch and reading. The only sign that he had heard her was his sideways smile. I had seen that smile before. It confirmed my suspicion that he enjoyed annoying her. There may have been a time when he had loved her, but I doubted he had liked her very much even then. Sometimes he played the part of the agreeable husband, but never convincingly. I thought—and that's what I thought even when I was a child—that he put on the performance for our benefit and over-acted the part to make sure we knew he was acting. We were his designated audience. And Mother, of course, would also have known.

I ran upstairs, hoping for the sound of running water. I had left all the taps open and I had half hoped that the water would have started while I was fiddling with the lever in the basement, but there was still no water from the faucets.

I looked down at the periwinkle patch. The little plants were thriving despite the cold. They had spread through the woods and into the meadow close to the water. When I had found out who had given him the plants, years later, it had made sense that our mother had hated them and that she called them "invasive." They were intended to invade our place and remind him of this other presence in his life.

10

THE COTTAGE HAD ALWAYS BEEN THE ONE PLACE where our family would be together. Even if we stayed apart during the winter, here we would talk with one another. Father, as far as my memories stretched, had always traveled a lot, but he made a point of coming to the cottage during the summer. He would even try to teach us to fish and, less successfully, to hunt. Hunting had been his passion.

I don't know why I was determined to find a photograph of my father somewhere in the cottage. Perhaps I was trying to understand when he had changed or if it was only my perception of him that had shifted and whether there was a precise time when I began to see him differently. Was it gradual, or was it a singular moment?

There had been that photo taken at their wedding, and another that used to be on the chest with the other family photos, but it had disappeared long ago.

Father had been very handsome and Mother delicately pretty in those days. She had said he was the best-looking young man she had ever met, and she always suspected that his whole life was affected by his looks.

Everything came more easily to him than it should have. Certainly, his partnership in the firm was due, she said, to the impression he had made on the partners and on prospective customers. It wasn't, she said, his talent as an architect.

"If that's so," I asked her, "why did you try to stop him from leaving his firm?" I still remember them fighting about it, and Father shouting that none of it had ever made him happy.

"Because it was something to keep him busy. I didn't want him to have too much time on his hands."

The houses Father designed were, at best, Mother said, ordinary, a result of his nostalgia for a past era, solid red brick, tall windows, central hall, rooms on either side, kitchen in back, straight-up stairways to the second floor, imitation Georgian, lacking in imagination. But then, he was never expected to design anything that required more than basic skills.

Instead, he attended meetings with prospective clients, listened attentively and respectfully to their wishes, took notes with a serious expression, smiled at the women if there were women involved in making decisions, and left the details to others. One of his senior partners had once told me, jocularly, that had our father designed Thomson Hall, it would have been square. That was long after our father had left the firm. He had made that joke again when I had called him to ask whether he had spoken to Father in the last few weeks.

"Why?" he asked.

"Because he's vanished."

"What do you mean 'vanished'?"

"He hasn't been seen for at least three or four weeks, and no one knows where he is. I wondered whether he called you."

"Me? Why would he call me?" He chuckled, as if the very idea of our father calling him were preposterous. "He hasn't been in contact with anyone here for years. No reason why he should be. He wasn't cut out to be an architect."

"But you hired him."

"Yeah. He was a good salesman. God forbid we should have allowed him to design a building." Then he repeated the joke about Thomson Hall.

I thought perhaps Father had assumed no one would mind if he took off for a while. He might have gone on a hunting trip somewhere and failed to mention it to anyone. Not even his daughters. Or especially not his daughters.

Gladys, who had moved into his big house with him at least four years ago, wasn't sure when he had been at home last when I asked her, and she didn't seem to care.

"We had a bit of a fight," she told me. "It's not like we fight a lot, so maybe, just maybe, he decided to take a bit of time away. Sometimes that's the thing to do," she added, seemingly for emphasis.

"What is?"

"You know. Be on your own for a while."

"Could he have gone on a hunting trip?"

"No idea."

"What was it about?" I asked.

"What?"

"The fight."

"Nothing," she said. I assumed she meant nothing that she wanted to tell me because who was I even to ask.

Gerry thought he might have gone on a trip to visit a client. Sometimes they sent their own cars and planes for him.

"But wouldn't he have told you where he was going?"

"No. He has a lot of clients and he never even mentions their names to me. Not my business. I just drive the cars."

That was why none of us knew for certain how long he had been gone.

In the cottage kitchen, I found the jar of instant coffee and began to boil the water. On second thought, though I was concerned about running out of wine, I poured myself another glass.

The basement would have to wait.

11

MOTHER HAD KEPT BOXES FULL OF PHOTOGRAPHS
and a few neatly organized albums in her room. The loose photos, she
said, were waiting for her to have the time to put them into albums.
Suddenly—perhaps not suddenly, because I realized that I had my own
reasons for coming here—I wanted to see those pictures. And any other
secrets she may have buried here. Mother asking me to find a copy of
Father's original, and perhaps only, will had given me permission to
rummage. Not that I felt I needed her permission to look through old
photographs—perhaps there would be a cute baby photo of me somewhere.

I crossed the cottage to her room. I hadn't been here since August
the year before last and even then, I had ventured in only to pick up a
few items of clothing I thought she might have wanted for the winter.
She hadn't asked for them. She hadn't asked me for anything, but I knew
that she liked her blue woolly socks, the fuzzy brown slippers, the heavy
knitted cardigan that made her look like her inner old lady, someone she
had so long defied as she continued to give her talks about Europe and the
European Union, its relationship with the United States, and the future of

the euro. She wore that cardigan only at the cottage and never when we had visitors. The past five years there had been no visitors, other than Eva, and she no longer counted as a visitor.

There were still a lot of clothes left on her hangers. A fluffy blue dressing gown, a couple of striped summery blouses, the long slit-sides gowns she liked to wear in the evenings, something comfortable to slip into before dinner. I remembered that she had worn the dark green gown the last time we were all here. I thought she had been making an effort to make the place seem normal, as though we were all still a family. Father was here that weekend, sitting on the porch in the evening, sipping his wine, listening to his music. She had never yet mentioned that our father had moved out and left her. Not the cottage, only her. Occasionally, he still came to the island, expecting one of us to pick him up at the marina. I wasn't sure whether she hadn't remembered, or knew but chose not to talk about these things. Perhaps the fact that Father still considered the cottage shared territory kept up the illusion of his presence in her life. The cottage, I thought, remained essential for him, no matter what he had decided to do with his life.

Her sandals were in plastic bags, as were those long scarves she had taken to winding around her neck when the skin under her chin had loosened. "Turkey neck," she had said, examining her image in the mirror.

Her walking shoes were arranged in neat pairs, toes out, a few of the better ones with inserted shoe trees to keep their shape. There was a pair of suede slip-ons with wedge heels I hadn't seen her wear for years. At least not since Father had stopped having dinner with us at the cottage. For that matter, he no longer had dinner with us anywhere. "He has his own life to live," Mother had said, almost convincing me that she didn't care. The rest of the shoes were made for comfort—thick-soled black lace-ups, and a pair of brown slip-into Clarks and the soft slippers she had taken to wearing even outdoors during the past couple of years.

Funny, I had forgotten how small her feet were.

Her room, even in the sunshine, felt gloomy, abandoned, though that might have been only my imagination. Her sheets and her duvet had been folded into their winter plastic containers. The mattress was covered in a silky, bluish fabric, worn threadbare on the window side, the side where she used to sleep. I pulled her duvet out and put it on the bed. It was a soft pink and blue and made her room feel less abandoned. She liked to look out at the trees and watch for hummingbirds at her red birdfeeders. Her headboard was sturdy, dark oak, with a circular pattern in the center and sides. She explained that she hadn't chosen it, not really, it had chosen her. It was something she had bought at an antique dealer's and she picked it because the circles reminded her of the Green Man and his penchant for living life to the fullest, while you could. Perhaps to compensate for the pagan symbol, once Father moved to the cabin, she had placed a black wooden cross above the headboard, and there was a painting of a crucifixion next to the prints of Georgian Bay rocks and windblown pines on the wall across from her bed.

Her bookcase was almost empty. She had taken her treasured books down to the city, but there were a few leftovers, all history and philosophy—Thomas Aquinas, Chesterton, Kierkegaard, Kershaw, Hofstadter, Fukuyama, Judt, Keegan, Tuchman, and many more—with a couple of Ruth Rendell mysteries she had read and didn't want to reread. "It's entertainment," she had told me, "like your own books. They have no staying power."

I was surprised that she had taken her framed photographs with her.

The chest of drawers, another dark brown castoff, faced her bed. Even now, I hesitated before I reached for the wide handle on her top drawer. An assortment of clothes, a few soft silk scarves, carefully folded, a plastic bag with what looked like folded underwear, a silver woven bracelet I didn't remember ever seeing before, white ankle socks also folded and regimented along one side, blue shorts near the bottom of the drawer. She had stopped wearing shorts some time ago because, she said, her legs had become too "bumpy," adding, "I hate even looking at them." Under the socks, there was a brown set of shiny wooden rosary beads. They felt well used. I had the sensation of her hands rubbing them as she counted down the Hail Marys. I had seen her here, sitting on her bed, near the window, the rosary beads flowing through her clasped hands as she recited her prayers.

The drawer smelled of her. I had never noticed that she had her own personal odor half hidden by her perfume. Lily of the Valley. Slightly sweet, pungent when freshly sprayed, it settled as a light scent, cool but amiable. The plant itself is poisonous. The flowers produce something defined by the plant dictionary as "toxic, can lead to death." Mother's little white, bell-shaped lilies of the valley bloomed along the path and under the trees near the cottage early every spring. She herself had planted the tiny bulbs back when the cottage was still new.

The scent seemed to linger near the window, where she had often sat, looking out at the birds. Not just the hummingbirds, but also a pair of wrens that came back every year to build nests under the eaves.

The middle drawer also smelled of perfume and of her. A little tinge of baby powder—she didn't use deodorant—and sweat laced with wine and spray freshener she used in her bathroom every time after anyone else had been there. I closed the drawer so fast I caught my finger in the opening. The pain dulled that other pain I hadn't been willing to acknowledge. I held on to the window frame for a while, choking down the hurt. It was the familiar pain of my childhood, one of rejection, of knowing that no matter how much I cried, no one would come to comfort me.

The sun was glistening on the deck.

Unlike the big open space of the living room, the air felt thick here in my mother's room, redolent of winter dampness over the lilies of the valley and something else, dank, moldy, slightly saccharine, maybe something decomposing. I thought I should look for dead mice. I opened one of her windows. It had always been the first thing she did when she arrived: let the breeze in.

This morning there was no breeze, though. I thought the deck vibrated in the sun, heating up slowly. I stared at it through the now open window as it seemed to shift ever so slowly sideways, thin undulating lines vibrating toward the cottage. A snake? It lifted its flat snout and flicked out its tongue, smelling something (snakes don't have noses; do they sniff the air?), swiveled toward the window, and froze. It was looking at me. I jumped back against the chest of drawers, knocking over my mother's perfume bottle, her red opaque glass with her toothbrushes, the small blue vase with withered flowers.

I yelled, and the snake lowered its head. Perhaps it had heard me. Or not. Snakes have no ears, I told myself, they respond to vibrations. Something rolled off the chest, bumped into one of the drawers, and landed on the floor. I leaned forward and snapped the window shut.

Rolling toward the door was an amber-color plastic bottle full of small blue pills. I took my eyes off the snake to pick it up. The label identified the medication as "diazepam, anti-anxiety and containing Valium." Was this another version of Ativan?

How long had Mother been taking these? Since she hadn't been here since last summer, she must have started long before Fairview. I had read that it was normal for people with encroaching dementia to feel anxious. I had looked it up. The website I found also informed me that as symptoms became more pronounced, anxiety would build, and anxiety made the symptoms worse. Early signs of dementia include repeating what you had just said, or asked, forgetting midway what you had started to say, and getting lost in familiar surroundings. Long before Mother had told me about her dementia, I had noticed some of these symptoms, but I had ignored them. I assumed she wasn't listening to what I said because she didn't find it interesting, or she wasn't paying attention because she had moved on to another subject in her mind. She often lost interest in a particular line of thought or discussion. She had always seemed so much smarter than anyone else that she would get bored easily.

She must have made a prodigious effort not to show the signs.

The snake slithered along to the railing, stopped to explore the gaps, thought better of it, and curled into itself. Greenish brown, about four feet long. Just a fox snake. Harmless. Unless you're a rodent or a small bird.

A couple of years ago a similar snake had crawled up the side of the cottage, along the roofline, hung its head down to the phoebe nest above our mother's window, and eaten the baby birds. The two adult birds flapped about desperately while it carried on with its silent meal.

Our father used to pick up fox snakes, let them curl over his arm rattling their pathetic imitation rattler tails in panic, and thrust their smooth flat faces, their forked tongues, toward us. We would scream and run. He would laugh. "Nature red in tooth and claw," he would say. Though, as I told Gina, snakes had neither teeth, nor claws.

Father didn't kill snakes unless they got in his way or threatened him. That's why he sometimes shot rattlers, though, but he considered them relatively useful because they ate rodents. He hated mice.

12

I WANTED TO LEAVE MOTHER'S BEDROOM, BUT I hadn't found the photographs yet. And one of the reasons—my main reason, if I was going to be honest with myself—for agreeing to this solo expedition to the cottage had been to discover what she had stored in her room. I had always sensed that she kept secrets here—secrets from me, ones shared only with Eva. Perhaps some were about me. I had noticed the two of them sometimes stopped talking abruptly when I entered a room.

All photographs—other than those she chose to display in the living room—were kept in this room in shoeboxes on a shelf in her closet. On special occasions—our birthdays, for example—she would bring out a box and show us how we used to be. The boxes were labeled with years and sometimes occasions, such as when Gina was brought home from the hospital wrapped in a pink baby blanket and placed in her new bassinet.

There were no baby pictures of me. Not a single one. Had I been too ugly to photograph? Gina's first birthday, not my first birthday. Her second birthday with a cake and a candle in the shape of a number two. My second birthday. No chance of confusing them, we didn't look remotely alike. Gina had fine white-blond hair, brushed back on the sides and plastered down her forehead, and she grinned as if she had known that's what you were expected to do when you were confronted with a cake on your birthday. Our parents were on either side of her. They were both smiling.

I had dark hair in tight curls and I looked angry. I usually looked angry, Mother had said. My cake was close but not too close to me, and its candles were in disarray. Mother told me that I had punched the cake with both my fists and wouldn't eat it. "You were upset," she said, "because it didn't have a soft chocolate topping." How would I have known about soft chocolate toppings when I was only two years old? Unlike my sister, flanked by both our parents, I was alone.

Mother had also kept a photo of me ready to leave for boarding school. I looked suitably sullen in that dreadful uniform. Short blue-green tartan skirt, striped tie, dark green knee socks, white button-up shirt, a green jacket she called a blazer, horrible black patent leather shoes she called "Baby Janes" with a strap across the instep. Later, I discovered they weren't even compulsory—you could wear any style of low-heeled black shoes—but, since they were the only shoes I took with me that day, they were the only ones I could wear the first semester.

At the end of November, Eva dropped off a pair of sturdy black brogues for me—nasty-looking but not as embarrassing as the Baby Janes. She blathered on about how awful she had found her own uniform when she first wore it. She said the nuns had been sticklers for perfection when it came to skirt lengths and loose ties and even rolled-up sleeves. My school, she said, would be a lot less regulation-conscious. I was lucky I had not been enrolled in a Catholic school, she told me. At least I wouldn't be growing calluses on my knees from all that kneeling.

"Luck has nothing to do with it," I told her. "Father would never agree to pay the tuition at a 'Dogan' school."

"My parents," Eva said, "were what you call 'Dogans,' or Irish

Catholics, and they would never have sent me to a secular school. You do know that your mother's parents were also Catholics?"

I did, of course, though whatever religious overlays Mother had hoped would stay with me for life had already rubbed off.

There were also a lot of pictures of Gina's wedding. Mother had hired a professional photographer, and he had obviously doted on Gina. Pretty much everybody doted on Gina. She used to be pretty in a doll-like way and so very young. In a few of the photos she still looked like a child. There were close-ups of her dreamy face, her eyes gazing into the distance, her left hand with the rings—one of which had belonged to Sammy's grandmother and he said the setting was real pink diamonds—resting on Sammy's arm. A couple of years later I took the ring to a jeweler when Gina was in the hospital with her first baby and he said they were pink glass.

I really don't remember why I had wanted to know whether the diamonds were real. It wasn't because I didn't like Sammy and wanted to catch him in a lie. He was a sincere, immature, loveable bear of a guy with no pretensions. My problem was with Gina. Always had been.

There was a photo of James and me preparing for that disastrous camping trip. We were standing next to the packed canoe, both of us grinning, leaning on our paddles. James was at least a foot taller than me, broad-shouldered, muscular, a little awkward in the way tall men are sometimes awkward when they are next to someone much smaller. I must have taken all the photos on the trip itself because that is the only picture of me from that time. The others are all of James alone. I remember the long hours of paddling, James in the stern, both of us sweating, James singing old camping songs and criticizing my paddling.

There was a much later photo of James and Father standing at the end of the dock, both of them with their hands in their pockets, looking at the lake but seeming preoccupied with something other than the view. About ten years ago? Father was dabbling in real estate. "A tricky business," he had told us. "There are too many useless lawyers involved." I had been watching them, wondering what they were talking about and why they needed to discuss it at the end of the dock and not at the cottage. I remember that close to shore an osprey dove down, splashed claws-first into the lake, grabbed a sizable fish, and wings battling to take off again, it rose low over the waves, then higher as it aimed for its nest at the west end of the island. Neither of the men looked in its direction. I didn't think they even noticed the drama of the moment.

James had arrived earlier, in Father's boat. He was still wearing his business suit, navy with thin darker stripes, white shirt, black loafers, blue tie that he had tucked in between two buttons of his shirt about midway down his chest. He used to do that when he came home. After he popped the top button, he would loosen his collar with two fingers, stretch, and swivel his neck. Our father, who had been here for some time, was barefoot and in his beige cottage shorts, the ones with the many pockets that sagged from too much wear and too many times in the laundry. I had gone down to help James with his bags, but Father waved me away. He had started talking as he tied up the boat, and then the two of them continued to talk quietly, looking incongruous.

Father was at least two inches shorter than James, wider in the hips and shoulders. James was what I would have called "lanky," had he appeared in one of my Kitty books, long slim body, long muscles on his arms, slender ankles and wrists. He wore his hair longer than was usual in his line of work, and by the end of the day he always developed a five-o'clock shadow on his jaw. I liked it, even when he left a beard-rash on my face and my belly. I often pulled him down to the floor in the entrance of my apartment, or pulled him into the kitchen, his back against the counter, his jacket still on, his pants around his ankles. And I always tried to persuade him not to shave before he came to bed.

Then there were all the photos of our parents' famous twentieth-anniversary dinner.

Everyone remembered that dinner. Mother had rented the entire basement of a downtown restaurant, in a chic area of the city, and she had preordered the dinners. Smoked salmon on round crackers. Chicken in some kind of sauce. A green salad. Rice with mushrooms. A large cake with icing and candles. There was that photo of the cake with the twenty miniature white candles and of two larger ones of the soon-to-be knocked-over couple in the center. Both figures had candlewicks protruding from their heads.

I had been twenty (born twelve months after the wedding), Gina was a year younger ("thoughtfully spaced," according to Mother), but that evening was so fresh in my mind that I could still smell the smoke from the blown-out candles. One for every year they had been married. When Father blew out the smaller candles, the two figures remained, stubbornly, with their flames intact. Our mother licked her thumb and forefinger and pinched the male figure so hard that it came out of the cake and toppled over, making a small ditch in the icing. Then she knocked over the woman candle as well and squished her into the icing facedown, next to the male figure.

At the time, everybody had laughed, but I had wondered whether it was an omen. Our parents' marriage had already started to fall apart. When I came home from boarding school, I noticed the cracks had begun to show. I had wondered at the time why it had taken so long. Both Gina and I knew that something was off, like the air in Mother's bedroom, a whiff of something rotten even though you couldn't quite determine the source.

Some of the boxes of pictures were no longer there.

I pulled at the handle of the bottom drawer of the dresser. It wouldn't budge. I jiggled it up and down, then side to side. Still no movement. I held the handle with both hands, one over the other, sat on the edge of the bed and planted my feet below the drawer as I pulled. Part of the handle came away in my hand, and I hit myself on the chest with it as I fell onto the bed.

"Shit! Shit! Shit!" I yelled, holding my sore fingers with my other hand. Mother had been right about the arthritis. My joints were painful and swollen. Shutting the middle drawer on my finger and now struggling with the recalcitrant lower drawer had made the pain worse.

Maybe she hadn't wanted me to open that particular drawer.

Undaunted, I got a large knife from the kitchen and attacked the sides and top of the drawer. It took patience and determination but I did, finally, shift it loose and, wedging the knife into the opening, pulled the damned thing out, not all the way but as far as it would go.

At some point she must have shoved most of the photos from the boxes into this drawer.

They had been thrown in carelessly, and a couple in the corner got caught as the drawer had closed and were now folded over, their shiny sides cracked. I pulled those out first. One was of Gina and me sitting on Santa's knee, she cute and blond in a lacy dress, me screaming, my arms flailing, wanting to be free of the man in the red outfit. I still remembered his smell. Sweat and oil. Perhaps he put pomade on his hair to hold it down. It was yellowing and patchy, and there was hair and wax in his ears.

Mother had told me in her deep steady voice that I shouldn't be frightened, but she didn't hug me when I ran to her. Santa doesn't hurt little kids, she'd said. I should tell him what I wanted for Christmas. But I hadn't been scared. I had been revolted.

The other photo was the wedding picture that had once been in the living room. The rest of them used to be in a white album with squishy covers, the photos positioned in order from the church to the entrance to the restaurant, our parents side by side under the marquee, she in her white gown with embroidered sleeves, a white cardigan over her shoulder (it was a cold evening), he in a suit with the Harvard tie, his face impassive, his eyes looking into the distance past the photographer.

They were not touching.

She had a small, oval face, tiny chin, big blue-green eyes ("My best feature," she used to say), though you couldn't see the color of her eyes in that picture. It was black and white. She was slender, wore her blond hair up, her shoulder fit into Father's armpit.

The flowers in her hair were angel's breath, a token of hope, trust, innocence, sincerity, and everlasting love. "That's how stupid I was then," she said one day when we—Gina, our mother, and I—were looking at the photographs. They were all posed, everyone aware of the young man with the camera—the same professional photographer who later shot Gina's birthday party. He was the one who told them when to look up, or hug each other, or raise their glasses and smile. I wondered why no one minded being posed or told to lower their forks, though our father did manage to have a mouthful of cake for at least one shot.

When I was fifteen and had begun to think like a teenager, I had insisted on telling our mother what I thought. I mentioned that her smile was forced, and her face drawn, skin close to the bone, while Father's was soft and slack.

"How observant of you," she had said with more than a hint of disapproval. "We're the ideal couple; I am pinched and he is spent." They were still together at that point.

Our father was beautiful then. But he also managed to look tired and uncomfortable in all the wedding photos. He had worn a dark suit, maroon tie, shirt a little bit open at the neck. It was a hot day, he told us, and he could hardly wait to take his jacket off. Gina said he seemed out of place. As if he had happened upon the scene while on his way somewhere else. I thought he looked anxious. Or wishing he were somewhere else.

He had loosened his collar, as James used to loosen his, but he never took the tie off. It was, our mother said, his Harvard tie. He always wore it. She said he would want to die wearing it.

It didn't, of course, turn out that way.

13

THE ALBUM HAD CONTAINED THIRTY-TWO BLACK
pages with plastic overlays proceeding chronologically, ensuring that
all the guests were shown at least once, and that the celebrating couple
appeared either in the foreground or the background of most shots. Now
the pictures were scattered, but I could easily put them in the order they
had once been. There were our grandparents, whom no one ever mentioned, and the Johnsons (it was Bob Johnson I had called to find out
whether he had spoken with Father when he hadn't been in touch for
four weeks or so), the Donavans, Kovacses (I still called them all by their
surnames), a couple from our father's office (she was a secretary, I have no
idea what he did), the two principals of the firm with their wives (both
wives got religion late in life, one became a minister, the other a warden
in her Anglican church), a few others I barely remembered, people I don't
think stayed long in our parents' lives. In all, fifteen couples including
Eva and an odd-looking man who may have been her husband or a friend
she had brought for the occasion. Mother had told us that Eva once had a
husband but no one knew what happened to him. She wore a long, loose
dress, not very flattering.

I remembered her being very drunk later, at the anniversary party, and that she had kept drinking until she passed out sometime before the speeches. Her head had dropped onto the table in front of her, and she'd slid sideways into one of the Johnsons, I think the man because he didn't seem to mind.

It was at the anniversary party, too, that Frank Donavan had told me that Eva had once been a girlfriend of Father's, "not a steady one, but close enough," he added with a wink. Mother said, when I asked her, that she couldn't recall who had put her on the invitations list, but of course she would have been asked. They had gone to the convent school together, so I assumed that, since Mother had planned the whole dreadful event, she must have asked Eva to come. They seemed to have become good friends. So good, that Eva came frequently to the cottage, always bringing food and expensive wine, always on her own. She never paid special attention to Father, ignored him most of the time, acting as if he were not even there. He dealt with Eva in the same way, though there was one sign that he was aware of her presence: he never joined us for dinner when Eva was there.

She even took over his room in the family cottage, eventually.

As far as I know our parents never discussed her.

She was a quiet presence, tall, erect, dressed in soft linens, her hair drawn back and up into a careful topknot, a look of concern and a pious smile as she hovered around Mother. Nellie told me she visited Mother once a week in the new condo. "She is Catholic," Mother told us, as if that would have explained everything.

Mother must have removed all the pictures from the album, tossed them into this drawer, and thrown the album away. I was pondering what, if anything, that meant. Perhaps she had decided that the album had conferred too great an importance to the images. Perhaps she had meant to throw them all away but changed her mind and kept some of the photos after all. Or she had done it after one of her forgetfulness episodes.

I still couldn't pull the drawer all the way out. I sat next to it on the carpet and tried to peer into its depths to see what held it in place. There were some folded papers or pictures in the back, but hard as I tried, I couldn't budge them. I shuffled through the top, took out bunches of photos, and laid them on the bed. A lot of the cottage, Gina's children when they were little, our mother reading in her usual chair on the dock, the boat tied up and another boat departing the island, a lot of us waving. I almost remembered that one.

It was the summer William turned eight and we flew some kites with happy birthday wishes from the end of the dock. By that time, he had perfected his characteristic far-away-and-to-the-side look that either failed to focus altogether, or was looking at something other than the person trying to engage him. "Not his fault," Sammy had said, "and he does hear you," he added with a defensive chuckle. Though naturally untidy himself, Sammy usually picked up William's messes. He enjoyed being with his son. Even here, with all the tension in the air, the musical battlegrounds, the fierce arguments, he had managed to relax, and keep an eye on him.

He had told me once that Gina couldn't be trusted to watch William. She had too much on her mind. Though I couldn't fathom what Gina's preoccupations might be, I didn't argue with Sammy. She had nothing to do but take care of her children, and she was the one who had chosen to be a mother. Sammy would have waited till they had more money and could afford the bigger house. Given her natural bent to utter selfishness, I assumed she had expected a ton of cash from Father once she produced a son. She hadn't anticipated William's imperfections.

Already when he was six or seven, Gina had started telling our father how difficult her life had become and how William needed to be in a place where kids with problems like his problems could be taught to live independent lives. How hard it was for her to care for him on her own. How expensive special schools were and how she couldn't afford them.

Because she thought Father wasn't paying attention, she usually raised her voice. He had ignored her lobbying for money, even when she said, rather pointedly, that she wanted to get William admitted to a special school, if only they could find the money for it. She said she was sure he would love boarding, surrounded by other special needs kids and she would, finally, have a chance to return to her own career. Whatever that was. She had already begun to blame her own education for her not having more options in life.

Gina, of course, hadn't been to boarding school and always assumed it was something special that only I had been privileged to enjoy. I had assumed that my being sent away was some kind of punishment, and I hated Gina for being able to stay at home.

Father, not wishing to miss an opportunity to fuel Gina's animosity toward me, had explained that I needed a more comprehensive education because I was more ambitious. I had always been aware of his desire to see us compete and, unlike Mother who resented our noisy battles, he enjoyed them. A good school would set me up for life, he had explained. I would make connections that would, later, when I was an adult, turn out to be useful. He said his own example should serve as a lesson. He wouldn't have been able to join such a prestigious firm had he not been a friend of the senior partner at school. His first clients had all been to the same school. That was the reason why they had trusted him.

Mother's explanation was simpler: Gina was more manageable. I argued about everything, refused to keep my room tidy, was always late coming home from junior school, or I was sent home early for fighting. Besides, she said, when she saw that Gina envied me those unpleasant years away from home, what was the big deal about going to boarding school? An Anglican school with no discipline? She, herself, had been sent to a Catholic school for girls. Run by the Sisters of St. Joseph, it was more like a convent than a school, chapel every morning, prayers four times a day. "Discipline. And I was all the better for it," she said. "I would have achieved so much less in life, had I gone to a school with no discipline."

Our father said he saw no point in educating William. He would never be "useful."

He said that he didn't even know how to talk with William. Not that anyone else did either, but the rest of us tried.

14

IT WAS GOING TO TAKE HOURS TO LOOK AT ALL THE
pictures, really look at them, not in the way I used to when I was younger,
but in a way I would see them and understand what I saw. Not that I
knew exactly what I was seeking to find in them, but I was sure there
would be some explanations, something hidden in these old photos that
would help me deal with my life. I needed to make sense of my relationships with my father and with my mother. I needed to know why they
cared so little for me when I was a child. Why there were so few pictures
of me in this drawer and so many of Gina. Had I genuinely been so much
more difficult as a child? Simone de Beauvoir had noted that mother-
daughter relationships are usually catastrophic, but that wasn't true in
our case. I think I just hadn't been able to adjust to Mother's lack of love.
"Catastrophic" was how I would have defined my relationship with my
father.

There was still no running water, and no matter how much I resisted
the prospect, I had to abandon the pictures and go back to the basement
to resume my struggle with the pump.

I peered out at the deck in front of my mother's window. Well, at least the snake was gone. I put another battery into the flashlight, squeezed through the half-opened door, walked slowly along the deck to the steps, checking for the snake all the way. I went down the steps cautiously, avoiding snakelike sticks. When I glanced at Father's cabin I was overcome with such a sense of foreboding that I had to take a few breaths to steady myself. I wedged the basement door open with a large maple log, wondering, Do snakes like cool dark places? I remembered the night—cold—when I was locked in here, the noises, the scratching, the skittering feet, the raccoons clawing into the compost behind the cottage, but no snakes. There used to be snakes sunning themselves on the dock in the summer, though, and once we found two curled over the exhaust pipe of the boat. They must like warmth.

I marched in as my young heroine would have done, going into battle with some evil mastermind who had underestimated her. Many of my stories turned on this failing that villains shared. They could not conceive of someone so young being so smart and so enviably brave.

I pushed hard with both hands at the piece of wood I had used earlier, and finally the lever moved and I could hear the water starting to bubble in the pipe from the lake, gurgle upward, swish around and sigh, and then it stopped as breathily as it had begun. I ran, too quickly—I was still a little dizzy from standing up too fast, and it was too dark in the pump room—but I had to see if there was water coming out of the taps upstairs. I ran so fast I didn't notice that I had thumped my head into the low beam under the deck and skinned my ankle on the log I'd used to keep the door open, and though it didn't hurt, I was trailing drops of blood on the pine floors. A trickle of water from the kitchen tap. Then nothing.

I wiped off my blood with a mothball-smelling towel I pulled from the laundry basket. It was the one place where we used the mothballs to discourage mice during winter. I took a bandage from Gina's first aid kit and taped it over the wound on my ankle.

I decided to postpone my next battle with the pump till after lunch.

My watch said eleven o'clock but it felt like noon. The sun was high and almost warm for this time of year. Time for a glass of wine. I thanked whatever gods there were for the steady humming of the fridge, wiped a glass from my mother's not-too-carefully-arranged glasses cabinet, took the second bottle of Chablis to the porch, and poured the wine from a few inches higher than necessary. It was a deft move from my waitressing days, when I could pour the wine in such a way that the punters could snuffle it as it hit the glass. Then, with a practiced lift, I twisted the bottleneck upward to avoid a drip and cradled the bottle on my right arm. Still perfect. The glass had clouded over beautifully. Hot air meets cold glass.

"Waitressing," my mother had said, "is the perfect preparation for life. Serve. Smile. Repeat. Sometimes there would be a tip. Sometimes not. Get your reward in heaven. A bit like marriage. For a woman." If she intended that little speech for my father, it was a waste of effort. He hadn't been listening.

She did very little cooking herself and certainly no serving at home, but she insisted on the right to complain about being in charge of her home and her children. Even if our father had been capable of taking care of us, which he wasn't, she was always the one who made the decisions. From when we had to stop sucking our thumbs to what we were going to wear the first and last days of school and for the grad ceremony and which university we would choose. She was certainly the one who decided to send me to that boarding school, some distance from home.

Much as we disliked each other, Gina and I tended to keep our battles private. We rarely told on each other because there was no point in tattling. Neither of our parents was interested, though Mother had often observed that I had a nasty way of drawing attention to myself. Once, when Gina was about seven, I told our father that she was still sucking her thumb, and he said, "Good" and grinned, as if he was proud that she had failed to follow our mother's orders. That might have been the only time he had expressed pride in one of his daughters. Or had I forgotten some key moments of our childhood?

I drank the wine so quickly the last swallow still felt icy when it went down my throat. I placed the glass next to the bottle on the wide flat board at the top of the railing close to where our father used to sit and where the snake had been. Shouldn't it be hibernating still? I was sure I had read that snakes don't emerge until May, but it was such a sunny day, it could have decided that the time was right to take a look at the world. I peered over the edge of the deck, in case it was down there waiting for something to happen. Much as I had been waiting these past many months—years?—to see whether I would make some big decisions about my life or continue to write forgettable books for preteens, drink too much, and pretend everything was fine, even though nothing had been fine for many years and I expected it would never be fine.

There was a long procession of large brown ants crawling up to the deck. They marched toward the dining room's open screen door, and then one of them turned and I could see it raise its nasty little ant head toward me and come at me, decisively; its followers stopped, too, and the whole column marched in my direction. I watched, fascinated, curious to see what had made them change direction. When the first one reached my foot, I could have sworn it sniffed the air before it mounted the side of my running shoe and climbed up to where the blood had seeped down through the bandage and pooled on the collar of the upper part of my shoe. I wiped the ant off with my hand and stepped on his followers, grinding them into the wood.

I poured some more wine—not so cold now and no ceremony—took an old blue-and-white-striped shirt off a hanger in my bedroom closet and went down to the lake to wash the blood off my leg and my shoe.

I hadn't noticed that the shirt was one of James's until after I had dropped it into the lake and began to wring it out. The water was so cold

I had to keep rubbing my hands together after clutching the shirt, closing one fist, then the other, then rubbing each hand, in turn, on my jeans to try to warm them. My fingers had turned white.

Thinking of James made me even sadder than I had felt before driving up to the cottage. It's not that I would have changed anything about how things had ended. We had continued to live together long after I thought our relationship was over. He obviously disagreed.

Our relationship might have been dead already when I decided we needed the break from each other. He thought I had meant a few days and moved his stuff into the so-called guest room. I waited a year before telling him that I thought some months apart might be better for me. He nodded and continued to come home, as if we still had a real home rather than just an apartment we shared, offered to make me a martini (never more than one), watched the news in the living room, and went to sleep in the guest room. A couple of perplexing years.

In the end, I packed his clothes into his own handsome Bric's Bellagio suitcases and left them outside my front door. "Our front door," he protested when he saw them. "How could you?"

I said it was, in point of fact, my door, since this had been my apartment long before he had moved in, and I was still the official resident. "We both pay the rent," he had said in a voice designed to annoy me—his little boy whine that may have been effective with his mother but had never worked for me.

I dunked his shirt in the water again, washed the wound on my leg, then held the shirt against it. I remembered wearing this shirt early one morning when I went down to the lake for a swim. It had been a warm midday then, too, mid-August, slight breeze wrinkling the waves, at the water's edge a small fox had looked at me, wearily, then, deciding I posed no threat, it strolled into the woods. James was still sleeping in the first cabin and, though I wanted to call out to him, I didn't want to wake him. He had a habit of sleeping on his stomach, face deep in the pillow (he preferred feather pillows), the back of his neck looking surprisingly vulnerable, and on that hot summer morning, soft sweat-soaked bits of his brown hair strayed over his neck. I must have loved him then. Perhaps if it hadn't been for his wanting to control me, I wouldn't have wanted it to end, wouldn't have wanted the relationship to be over.

Now, as I sat shivering on the dock, I was trying to remember why that had been so important. Had I linked James with my father in my mind? Was it his assumption that he would take charge of our lives? Mine with his? Perhaps had James not shown signs of wanting to start a family, had he not shown me a new, much larger apartment and told me we would both give up our places and move in there together, had he not insisted that he knew we would need more space, perhaps then I wouldn't have felt threatened. I couldn't think of having children. Not when I was still sorting through the detritus of my own childhood.

My leg was still bleeding. Pink water ran down my foot and dripped into the lake, leaving a trail on the dock, pooling in the deep indentation where my mother's chair used to stand, out of the sun but not so far that she wouldn't feel its heat on her ankles. It's where she had sat the last time I was here, gazing at the lake, her book lying facedown on her knees.

I trailed my hand in the water to rinse the shirt. Still very cold, but a few strands of sticky reed attached to my fingers as I lifted them out, thinking how they felt so much like hair. Strands of fine hair. A flash of white shimmering under the reeds. I looked closer, my face near the surface now, where something was moving gently, shifting left then right near the rocky bottom, shunted by tiny waves, though I could see no waves. I came even closer to the edge, my shoulders angled downward, my hand trying to touch the white thing.

A loud shriek behind me and I was in the water, flailing about at the thing that seemed solid and yet soft, almost mushy on the surface. I panicked, my head under, the water frigid, desperately gulping for air, more water in my nose, reeds on my face, that sound of water buzzing in my ears. I surfaced coughing, trying to breathe. It was deeper than I had thought, my feet not quite touching the bottom. The water streamed down my body, thick, icy, my pulse was racing. Got to move. I grabbed the dock and kicked at the thing, whatever it was, so it drifted away from me. Drew myself up, arms so cold I barely noticed I had cut myself on a nail sticking up near where our mother's chair would sit.

I threw myself onto the dock, faceup, arms stretched out, shivering. I focused on breathing. There was a big yellow-billed gull stomping its feet, at the far end of the dock. It shrieked again, lifted up and hovered, its head turned sideways, cold yellow eyes fixed on me or something near me, then it flew off, its wing tips skimming the waves, toward the far islands.

I lay there in the sun, trying to feel my hands and my feet before rolling off my wet T-shirt. I tried to remove my jeans but they were too stiff and the zipper wouldn't cooperate. I sat up slowly, carefully. Shoved my hair out of my face and tried to peel off my running shoes. Felt dizzy bending over. Hands shaking too much. Blood oozing from my knee where I had scratched it earlier and more blood on the board where my right hand rested after its losing battle with the shoelaces. There was blood pooling between my fingers.

The path to my father's cabin seemed to move, the small stones refracting the sun, then hiding in the shadow. The edge of the blue tarp he used to cover his canoe each winter rose and fell back with the ebbing of the wind.

"What is happening?" I asked and didn't realize that I had spoken out loud until a ragged-tailed red squirrel stopped at the end of the dock and glowered at me. Its tail looked as if it had been chewed by another animal. Judging by its angry chattering, it held me responsible for its troubles.

Squirrels on the island had become used to us since Scoop had stopped harassing them. He used to rush at them with great enthusiasm and wild barking that would alert them to his approach long before he was close. He would stand on his short hind legs and continue barking up the tree that the squirrel had scaled. The squirrel, it always seemed to me, would view him with casual indifference. There was never a chance that Scoop would get to it before it climbed a tree.

For a long time, all that was left of Scoop had sat in a blue and white ceramic pot on one of my mother's bookshelves. Was it still there? I caught myself trying to remember when he had died. It would have been great to have him here today. His warm, fuzzy presence, his general good cheer would have made this trip to the island less lonely. He had been shoved into a big crevasse between two flat-surfaced boulders. I remembered that spot. I had always thought that that's where the entrance to the old stone quarry had been, the quarry they used in the eighteenth century for railway bridge piers and for facings for houses.

Late one summer he had been dug up by something, maybe a coyote or a fox.

No one wanted to show the body to Mother. James—it was only his first time on the island—offered to take it to an animal hospital in Barrie and ask them to cremate it. Later, when he returned with the ashes, he told me that the vet had said the dog had been shot. The bullet was still lodged inside the skin and bones of his rib cage. We never found out who had shot him or why, and it was only by accident that we had found his body. My father blamed the locals, "they mistook him for a rabbit," he said; Mother glowered at him but said nothing.

I thought Father had shot him, perhaps by accident. He had been spending more and more time duck hunting, coming back late, when it was already dark. Besides, he didn't like the dog.

He liked to think that everything was supposed to be a certain way, that everything had a function and without such, the world would collapse. Unlike Gina, he wasn't only a perfectionist, he was also a functionalist.

If something had no function, it either had to be fixed, or eliminated. Flowers, for example, were a waste of space until I convinced him that they were like lintels, their purpose was to be decorative. "Like women," he had said, with a lopsided grin.

It would have been difficult to argue that Scoop was either useful or decorative.

15

I SHOULD GET MYSELF A DOG. A WEIRD THOUGHT AS I lay back on the dock in my wet tightening jeans, trying to remember what had propelled me into the lake.

But all I could think of was Scoop, his small, inquisitive snout, his many foibles, his sharp voice, his soft body lying next to me on the sofa. Perhaps time at the cottage had divided itself into the Scoop years, when we were sometimes happy, and the unhappy Scoopless years that followed, the memory of his poor broken body that haunted us every day for more than a year.

The therapist had said I was "obsessing" and insisted that if I were determined enough I could switch it off. At least try to understand what a dead little dog had to do with my inability to connect with my life. I had to force myself to be fully aware when those unwanted thoughts were sneaking in, make a conscious decision to think about something else, stay with that other thought long enough, and presto! The misery would be gone. Not immediately, but over a few weeks if I persisted and tried the mindfulness exercises in tandem with the switch . . .

I had to change into dry clothes.

But first, I needed to get up. I tried more deep breaths. I was dizzy.

The idea of wanting time away from the city, time alone to think and to sort through some memories, now seemed as fraught as the memories themselves. Why that urgent need to know what my parents had thought and done with their lives? Why had that seemed so important when I'd set out for the island yesterday? Why was I so eager to find photographs of myself as a child? And why was I obsessing about my mother's small dog? And my relationship with James? There had been other short-lived relationships before him and a few one-night stands fueled by Entertainment District cocktails after, but they hadn't seemed relevant to my decision to stop living with James.

I felt the back of my head, gently, where it ached the most, then looked at my hand, now streaked with blood. Had I hit my head on the dock when I fell in? Or on that weird rock when I went under?

Had there really been a squirrel looking at me at the end of the dock or did I imagine a squirrel because I was wet and woozy and confused? I turned on my stomach and placed my good hand down on the board and tried to push my chest up, but one hand couldn't hold me. I felt like a fish flopping about out of the water. Was there a fish flopping about near the dock where I had fallen?

Was that hard white thing in the water a dead fish?

We had about a dozen fishing rods in the cottage, a lure box, extra plastic line in case the line broke hauling out a particularly heavy fish, but the only one of us who had ever fished was Father. He said he used to get swordfish off the coast of North Africa. "Real, tough fighting fish," he said, "forty, fifty pounds of sheer muscle. Angry." The biggest fish he had ever caught in the Bay was a mean-looking carp. "Lazy bottom-feeders," he said, dismissively, but he still had trouble landing it.

Our mother snorted not only about his catching swordfish in Africa but also about everything he ever said about Africa. She particularly hated his fishing and hunting stories.

About ten years ago, when he made his first million on the Wilson development, he told us, he celebrated by hiring a hunting guide in Kenya. He flew to Nairobi to meet the team—the guide, a tracker, and two guards who would guarantee a fun week in the savannah and at least some antelopes, a kudu, and maybe a zebra. I remember he showed me the pictures of the animals he had been promised. He said the outfit he'd chosen provided the guns, real beauties, high-powered repeat rifles with telescopes. He said he had bought one for his own collection and planned to go bear hunting in the fall.

He showed us a photo of a dead elephant. It was smaller than elephants I had seen in the zoo. It lay on its side, and there was blood all over its face where its tusks would have been. He said he had been lucky. He got a chance to hunt elephants. Though killing elephants was already illegal in Kenya, the "right man" could find you one you could shoot and no one need know about it. Our father always knew the right men. He never explored a new business opportunity without first contacting the right man. And there was always the right man wherever he traveled.

If he ever went bear hunting, he didn't mention it.

Mother had escaped to her room when he was gutting the fish and refused to come to the table for dinner that night. She held a handkerchief over her nose and mouth, and she said through the cloth that the smell made her gag. I remembered the fine texture of her handkerchiefs, the minuscule flowers embroidered in the corners, and that she used to keep them in a sandalwood-scented box on her dresser next to her perfume bottle. She must have taken the little box with her the last time she left the cottage.

After gutting the fish, Father dunked it in flour, salted it, wrapped it in tinfoil, and started the barbecue. The pike was rubbery and the bones were hard to remove. He threw a few chunks of fish at Scoop and encouraged him to try them.

I was relieved that Scoop hadn't wanted to. Generally, he didn't like fish. Smart dog. If he didn't choke on the oily taste, the bones would certainly have killed him.

Dad had never liked that dog. A noisy, busybody with a long inquisitive snout that used to sniff at our plates and burrow under our blankets during the night when we were too sleepy to object, he was a black and tan dachshund or mostly a dachshund. He was happiest at the cottage, where he could chase chipmunks and squirrels and sometimes try to square up against raccoons too surprised to argue.

I don't know why thinking about Scoop made me tear up again, but the sight of his small broken body wedged into that crevasse seemed more pathetic now, years later. Made me want to howl.

I was still lying on the dock, dizzy and now blubbering. I rolled over and pulled myself up onto my elbows. Looking at it from this angle, the boards seemed darker than I remembered them. They had more cracks and fissures for the blood to seep into.

So much blood . . .

16

SCOOP KEPT INVADING MY THOUGHTS. I ALMOST expected him to trot out to where I was trying to get all the way up on my hands and knees. Maybe he'd lick my face. I had begun to run through my memories of James bringing his ashes home from the vet's, debating whether to sprinkle them at the water's edge, where he had loved to run and bark at the waves, or bury them under the woodpile with Mother's other dog—was it a spaniel? It had died when I was about five. I must look for it in the photos. Scoop's ashes stayed in that blue and white ceramic pot in her closet because we couldn't make up our minds. Had I seen that pot in her room? I couldn't remember.

I edged over to the side of the dock and looked down again at the water. It was a sharp angle from where I had raised my head and where the water rippled toward the shore, but I caught sight of something that seemed to be bobbing near the surface, something with wisps of dark green that moved on their own over the smoothness of the gray. Or was that an illusion? If it wasn't a big dead fish, it could be a smooth, dappled rock. There were large rocks that had been worn smooth and slimy by the water near the shore. I would slip on them when I tried to get into the lake too quickly. During the summer there was a metal ladder attached to the end of the dock, but that was only after we officially opened the cottage, not now, not in April when I was the only person here and the water was much too cold for swimming.

One summer, when she was about six, Gina fell in backward with the ladder on top of her. The top step cut her forehead, and one of the middle steps hit her in the chest so hard she couldn't even scream. Our mother, who was a terrible swimmer, jumped into the lake, pushed the ladder off Gina, and towed her to shore. She fell twice on the slimy rocks but didn't seem to notice the blood oozing from her knees. I stood there, looking at them, not moving, not even when Gina started screaming or when Mother yelled that I should help. It seemed as if I were watching a movie, a particularly affecting scene of two people in some sort of trouble or pain, but distanced from me, as movies usually are.

I wondered whether Mother would have waded in to save me, had I fallen in from the ladder. Would she have let me drown?

Eva said later that I must have been in shock, that's why I hadn't moved, but neither Mother nor Gina spoke to me for a while.

I've had more of those distanced feelings since then, even more these past four or five years, a greater sense of dislocation. When I told James about it, he blamed my excessive drinking, but as I pointed out, I hadn't yet started drinking at age seven when I watched Gina fall and our mother rush in to help her.

Slowly, carefully, I maneuvered my aching body onto its knees, pushed back on my haunches, then into a crouch, and stood, still dizzy, blood pooling in my shoes, more blood on my face and running into my right eye, or was that water? Strange how sharply every rock stood out on the path to Father's cabin and even the tree trunks, each strip of bark so distinct from the other, dead leaves redder than I had ever seen them before. A carpet of them like blood near his cabin. Last year's dead leaves.

Again the shriek of that gull. This time, I managed to ignore it.

I would have to start the pump right now. My jeans were stiff and still stuck to my legs. I went up the stairs with them tight over my knees and cutting into the backs of my legs every step I took. Thank God the fire hadn't quite died. Bending over while trying to keep my legs straight, I threw on two more logs. Birch this time, so it would catch quickly.

I squelched my way over to the counter, poured myself a large glass of wine, and tried to dry a little by the fire.

The sun was cooler now. At last a little breeze. Tiny waves sparkling magenta and yellow.

I must have been on the dock longer than I realized.

My summer wardrobe offered only shorts, flimsy shirts, sun hats, sandals, and out-of-date sagging bathing suits. There was a pair of soft gray joggers, some socks, and a warm sweater in my bag, but I hadn't brought another pair of shoes. Still shivering, I managed to yank off the shoes. Blood had seeped through the laces, painting my feet pink. As I peeled off the jeans, blood spread down one leg and colored the gray pants when I tugged them on. My fingers were swollen, taut, and clammy. Still shaking. I ignored both the wound on my ankle and the deep scratch on my arm. I used my wet T-shirt to dab at the cut on the back of my head. Yes, it must have happened when I fell on that rock. I had turned and now remembered the roundness of it, touching it with my face as I went down and that it had felt like skin. Hard skin, slimy but not like a rock. The denseness was also different from our yellowish rocks or the white stones that drifted onto the shore. Those soft drifting strands of weed or grass were so much more like hair. Long brownish white hair combed forward, now drifting back with the waves. But it couldn't be. Weeds. Smooth limestone rock.

I sat on the porch in what remained of the sun's rays and finished the bottle of wine.

I hadn't expected to start on the liquor till tomorrow but I had planned on an easier day. Not altogether easy because I wanted to take my time thinking about the past year and looking at the photographs in our mother's room. Not necessarily in that order. What I hadn't planned on was falling into the lake, bashing my head, cutting my hand and my leg. Worse, there was the problem with the pump—before I arrived, I hadn't even thought of the pump. In my mind, the cottage would be more or less as I had last seen it almost two years ago, water coming out of the taps.

There was always a bottle of scotch in the liquor box we had left here. And, for sure, a bottle of rum (Sammy drank rum and Coke) and some sort of sweet liqueur I used to slosh on my cut-up fruit. We would always leave the liquor bottles at the cottage, not only because they would survive the winter but also because our father contended they would serve a purpose: if some of the locals drove up on snowmobiles to look for something to take, the bottles would be easy prey. No need for them to take his music or the carpet, or anything else of value. It had been his idea to leave the bottles in a big pine box near the entrance. Back then, we would also leave the door unlocked to spare anyone the trouble of breaking the windows. "Don't blame them," our father had said. "They need a little pick-me-up after a day of hunting." He would grin and nod to make sure we understood he shared that hunting instinct with the locals. I remembered this conversation from a number of years ago, when he was still living in our old house and usually came to the cottage in the summer.

"There is no hunting on this island," I said.

"No hunting on any of these islands," Mother said.

"Oh sure." Father nodded some more. "Too many goddamn rules. Too many prohibitions. It's a country of don'ts, always looking for reasons to rein in man's natural instincts. Next they'll ban fishing."

There was no point telling him it was catch and release in this part of the lake. He said he always killed what he had caught and insisted we eat it with him. "It's only fair," he said.

"Did you eat the elephant?" Mother asked.

He laughed that loud, toneless laugh he used to disparage something he had heard from one of us that he thought was outstandingly stupid. It's the same laugh he used when Mother talked about going to church or one of the men at the marina reminded him that he had no fishing rights, referring to how the locals could fish anytime because they were Ojibwa. The Ojibwa, I told my dad, had inherited their rights to fish and hunt here. It used to be their land.

"Sure they did," he snorted.

After Thanksgiving, when duck hunting opened on the lake, he used a blind he had made at the back of the island to shoot ducks as they gathered to migrate. He would shoot into the middle of a flock of mallards, scaring them up and when they were about sixty feet from the water, he would pick them off, one at a time. He had tried to interest Scoop in retrieving the still struggling bodies. When the dog resisted, he picked him up by the scruff of the neck and carried him to the blind. He held Scoop captive on his knees while he slaughtered the ducks, then dragged him along to where the thrashing birds still tried to get up into the air. The dog was terrified. He scrabbled back from the dying ducks and ran to the cottage the first chance he had. "Useless mutt," our father yelled at his retreating tail.

"He is not a hunting dog," I told him when he came back with what he called "a brace of birds." "He is a dachshund."

Scoop wouldn't leave our mother's bed for days after the attempt to transform him into a useful dog, and he avoided our father altogether from then on.

The "brace" lay on the porch, bleeding, for a few hours, and once it was obvious no one would get them ready for dinner, Father boiled the water himself, plucked their feathers, cut up their bellies to remove the intestines, stuck some of the bodies into the freezer, and put three or four others into the oven. "You bake them at three hundred," he said. "Don't rush it, even if it takes a long time. They're tougher than you think, all that exercise during the long summer."

I never tasted the ducks. Mother stayed in her room with her dog.

17

"I LOVE HOW DOGS FEEL," SHE SAID WHEN I VISITED her in her eighth-floor condo. "Love the softness of their fur." She was on the balcony overlooking a small park and some large buildings. It was the winter, about three years ago, and we had been relieved we would no longer have to hire guys to shovel the steps to the front door of our old house.

We had helped her move here because the place had no stairs outside and none inside for her to climb up or fall down. Plus the move gave us permission to turf most of the detritus of her marriage (and our childhood) so that her eventual shift to an old-age home or a nursing home would be easier. We had expected her to protest, since her antique furniture, her paintings, her favorite Persian carpets, a ton of her books would all be gone, but she had been relatively compliant. I think there were too many memories in the house. The furniture had absorbed them, and even the Persian carpets she had loved so much managed to retain her memories. Perhaps some happy times with our father, though those—perhaps those, in particular—were good to leave behind. She said she didn't want to save anything, except for a few of her own books and some photos, for the new condo.

She was sitting in a lounge chair, listening to barking and enjoying the last of the sun. It was one of those crisp cold days that we sometimes get in the winter here. She wore her long mink coat—"faux," she said, but I was pretty sure it wasn't—woolen mittens, a knitted peaked toque with earflaps, thick white socks, and fur-lined slippers. Nellie, who had endured Mother's criticisms longer than any of her previous attendants, poured us tea. She had gone shopping earlier and bought a package of lemony biscuits of the kind she thought I liked. Mother was gloomy that she hadn't gone to the shop with Nellie, there were so many more things she had on the shopping list. She complained that Nellie often ignored her wishes—she hadn't even taken the list with her. Nellie told me that there was nothing on the list, that she had taken the piece of paper with her for the sake of peace but it had been blank.

"She is forgetting so much, these days," Nellie said. "Not so much the past—that she remembers too well, but recent things. Yesterday she insisted I call her dentist to make an appointment she had already made, and she got up in the middle of the night, got dressed, woke me up, and asked why I hadn't made her breakfast. I am not sure I want to be here much longer," she added later when I followed her to the kitchen.

I had already looked on the Comfortcare website for live-in care-givers offering help for dementia patients. There was a waiting list.

I broached again the idea of Fairview, how, as the name implied, the view from its windows was even prettier than here, that they had people to drive her to shop, if she wanted to go herself, or would deliver anything she needed.

"But they don't allow dogs in that place," she said.

"You don't have a dog," I told her.

She smiled indulgently and looked past me into the park. I remembered that look from all the times when I had said things to her that she considered silly, uninformed, or ill-suited to the conversation, the time, for example, when I said I would report our father to the authorities in Kenya, or the World Wildlife Fund, that he had to be stopped from killing elephants. She had let me go on about how unfair it was to slaughter animals that could not fight back against guns, that I thought it was stupid of him to call it a sport, that he had no possible reason for slaughtering them. As I became more and more agitated she had watched me and listened with that same indulgent smile. I may have been crying already when she said, "He hasn't shot any elephants. He tried, but he failed. The guide shot the elephant. He had a permit."

"Why?"

"So your father could take the picture."

"But he said . . ." I protested.

"He says a lot of things." She had nodded then, as she did now, when I stated the obvious fact that she didn't have a dog. Hadn't had one for more than fifteen years. She never replaced Scoop.

I remembered thinking that making someone else shoot an elephant so you could have a photo posing with its corpse may be even worse than shooting the animal yourself, but by the time I decided to contact the World Wildlife Fund, that photograph had disappeared. I had also discovered that if you pay enough for the privilege, you can kill anything legally.

"I will miss walking on that path near the Brickworks, you remember, where the koi are in that pond . . ." she said. "That pond . . ." She paused. "I think it was yesterday. You said you don't think it has a name. It's near the dog park . . ."

"You were walking with Nellie?" I asked.

"Nellie?"

"Yes, your housekeeper."

"Of course. And there were all these dogs. Love to watch them play. Not a care in the world. Dogs are such a comfort, don't you think?"

"You could still have a dog," I said.

She shook her head. "Can't. But I like looking at them in the dog park."

"Nellie could still go walking with you after."

"After?"

"Yes, after you check into Fairview. She will be there." Gina and I had agreed that we would pay Nellie to visit Mother every day in the home, to make sure she was comfortable, brush her hair (she hated to be touched, but Fairview's information page told me touch was essential to "well-being"), tidy her room, bring her flowers.

"Some of these places don't provide constant care," Gina told me, "and at least we would know she is with someone we can trust. Peace of mind, you know, it's worth the money."

I did know. I also knew that Gina was not going to offer the extra money. She assumed that we would drain it out of Mother's accounts. Mother had named us executors of her personal care. Neither of us had the inclination to be there when she needed someone. Neither of us wished to mention that we found the idea of perhaps having to change her diapers so utterly abhorrent, we couldn't even discuss it with each other. It hadn't actually come to diapering yet, but Nellie told us there had been a couple of "accidents."

"Who is Nellie?" Mother asked again.

"Your housekeeper."

"How are the children?" she then asked. She must have thought I was Gina. Odd how she switched on and off, from almost rational to barely holding on. She was gazing at the trees, still with that irritating, indulgent look on her face.

"Gina and I would feel happier if we knew you were in a safe place. Where there are people who know how to make sure that you are comfortable."

"Comfortable," she repeated.

"Where there are professionals who know what to do when you need help."

"Help," she said.

"Yes. You need people who can cook for you, put you to bed, and make sure you don't set yourself on fire," I said more harshly than was necessary. "It's easy enough to forget you have something on the stove and it can burn. You told me you almost burned your place down. Your doctor said it would be best if you had someone looking after you now."

"I think you are saying that I need a wife."

She was still smiling. Why did it have to be me telling her? Why did I have to try to convince her that it was for her own good? Her own safety? Why was I the one to make the arrangements?

We were both executors of her personal care, but Gina was the sole executor of her will. I had wondered about that, as I had wondered about many aspects of my relationship with our mother.

When I drove her to see the Fairview, I told her it would be for a short stay, that we were all going away on a holiday and the Fairview was a hotel with specially trained, dedicated service staff. I said there was a good restaurant, and when she said she didn't like restaurant food, I said she would have the widest choice of items on the menu.

We were lucky that Fairview was an old establishment with white pillars, wide stone steps, flowerbeds on either side of the entrance, and rosebushes along the path. It had pretty white-framed peaked windows. You couldn't see from the outside that there were bars on the windows.

We hadn't gone inside.

I lied. I said the doctor had insisted she try this hotel for a couple of weeks of relaxation, that he was sure she would like it, that it had special therapies to help with her forgetfulness (I never spoke to her about dementia) and her digestive problems, and that she would be able to come with us to the cottage the next summer, when she was better. I lied some more.

Gina, who had delegated the hard news about Fairview to me, could remain the gentler daughter, the one who listened to her ravings and didn't interrupt. She could pretend that they made some sense. I didn't.

Mother gave me the benefit of her half-smiling distant look, the one that used to denote that she knew something you had no idea how to discern, but that she was not going to share it with you because you were not ready. Or not worth the effort.

In the event, I wasn't there when she finally went to Fairview for good. February. More than a year ago. Nellie had packed some of her clothes ("She won't need much, though we do encourage them to dress up when they come to meals," the home's letter said), her festive bag of toiletries (a Christmas gift from Gina), a few photographs Nellie had chosen for her, a thin blue vase, her Bible, her new rosary beads, her brushed wool dressing gown and slippers. Nellie had spent more than an hour searching for her salamander, that long-ago memento of a trip Mother said she had taken to Tahiti. I don't know why that tiny carved wooden salamander had been so meaningful for her, but she always had it on her bedside table at home, later in her condo, and it traveled to the cottage with her when she came for weekends.

When I asked Eva about it, she said it had been a gift from her to Mother on the eve of their graduation from their boarding school, the one run by the Sisters of St. Joseph. She had brought it home from her last family trip with her parents and had given it to Mother because Mother had always admired it. Mother, she said, had never been to Tahiti, though she had always wanted to go. There was a lovely hotel, right on the beach, separate cabins with thatched roofs, big plush beds, pink drinks with umbrellas. Eva knew they would go there some day, soon.

Since Eva rarely mentioned her family, I asked whether she visited them as often as she visited us. My question had been intended to embarrass her, because I thought she was around too much, asking too many questions about James and whether he and I had split up, and whether I had thought I might abandon my "little books" and come back to my art. She had picked up Mother's habit of belittling my books and pretending I showed talent in art.

If she got my point, she decided to ignore it. "I never see them," she said, fingering the little crucifix on her chain. "They told me not to. Ever. Not even to call."

"Why?"

"I did something they disapproved of."

"What?"

"Something they considered unforgivable," she said and began to walk away from me.

"I thought the whole point of being Catholic is that nothing is unforgivable. You can just pop into the confessional, tell the priest, recite a bunch of Hail Marys, and all's well with the world again."

After a long silence, she said, "It's not quite that simple."

When Mother had moved to Fairview, the hall closets of the condo still contained dozens of unopened cardboard boxes full of her treasured books. She had kept very few photos (none of me). She said she had left most of them at the cottage. She hadn't bothered to keep and display even the framed ones.

18

IT WAS DARKER ON THE LAKE NOW, HEAVY CLOUDS gathering overhead, big waves surging over the shore. Whitecaps rolling in past the islands colonized by turtles, the water shooting up between the boards of the dock. I stepped outside for a moment and took a lungful of Georgian Bay. The wind felt pleasantly cool on my face. I don't know why I expected to see Mother at any moment, coming out of her room, hurrying out the doors and down to the lake. It seemed she was standing on the dock, taking deep breaths, letting the water slap her ankles, her dress fanning out behind her, hair flying in the wind. This was the kind of weather she really loved.

I had left a bloody trail all the way to the kitchen and back and there was now blood seeping into my mother's thin Persian rug—a small luxury for the summer, she had said when she unrolled it. I guessed that was at least ten years ago, long before dementia and before Father left.

"Silk. Knotted by hand as good quality Persians always are. The colors change depending on where you stand when you look at it. See?" She had directed me to the window, then back to the door. The colors did change: the reds turned dusty, the blues became turquoise, and the whites all but vanished.

"I got it in Teheran," she said. "I once gave a lecture there, at the university days before the shah was ousted. The subject was democracy."

I rolled up my pants and stuck several bandages on my knee (they don't make them wide enough). One leg of my jogging pants was now almost as bloody as my jeans. The blood on the back of my head had congealed around tufts of my hair, but it had stopped running down my neck and pooling at the waist of my pants. I went in search of kitchen towels and Lysol to mop up the blood from the carpet. In just a few seconds the Lysol changed the smell in the room from rank, decomposing to hospital. I knew this was temporary and that I would, eventually, have to find that dead critter, but not now.

The bottle of scotch, wrapped in a towel, nestled in the wooden crate. It was one of Father's more expensive single malts. Twelve years old. I wondered why he had decided to leave that here, since he was the one who had told us people broke into cottages once the lake froze and took whatever they fancied, and he was the one who selected the bottles to be left behind at the end of the summer.

I was surprised to see that the bottle had been opened and the towel smelled of whiskey. But not much was missing. Perhaps the top had come loose during the winter. The first two big blissful glugs were just the encouragement I needed to venture into the basement again.

I still couldn't budge the lever all the way to "open" and now I couldn't even find the piece of wood I had used to push it. The flashlight flickered out. Standing in the dark, I swore at the crazy system our father had installed and whacked the intake tank with my fists. Why would he have spent money on jetting to the Bahamas and, now that I had time to think about it, Nice and the Canaries and God knows where else but never updated this dumbass system? Not even the tanks, though one of them had leaked? Instead he had used a blowtorch to mend it himself. Took a full day to drain the bugger and then we had to wait till he filled it to see if it had worked, drained it again and filled it until, finally, it had stopped leaking. A man who could afford a bloody mansion for himself and whomever he chose to live with couldn't make this place easier to live in. Or wouldn't. "This place has character," he had told me. "My new house is just a house. It will never speak to me like the cottage does."

As for what the cottage said to him, I didn't know and I never would. But at least the tank finally did speak to me in hollow echoes when I stopped hammering away at it with my fists and at last thought I heard that light spatter of water dribbling from the taps upstairs.

This time I guessed correctly the position of the beam that hung down low from the underside of the deck and crouched to avoid hitting my head again.

During the years when he was trying to be useful on the island, James had knocked his head on that beam a half dozen times, much to the amusement of our father. And I thought he liked James, or at least he respected what James had achieved. Lawyer, investment analyst, later, director of a few public companies, but never a risk-taker, Father said. "Reliable. Always looking for the safe path, declining to choose the one less explored," he told me. "Mustn't expect to be surprised by this fella. He is exactly as he seems."

I assumed he meant boring, but he never said anything directly derogatory about James. He merely smirked when James emerged bloodied from the basement, but he laughed out loud when Sammy cut his shin with the chain saw. Mother, less reticent about expressing her opinions, would tell Gina that Sammy was too bumbling or too "cityfied."

I think she had always disliked Sammy. She thought he wasn't good enough for Gina, and she held him responsible for not earning more money to support Gina and the kids.

James, to be fair, had a lot to say about our father but never to his face, though a few times I caught him whispering to Sammy when they were on the dock together. He had asked me on several occasions some questions about Father. Did I have any idea how he had made his money?

Was I worried about it? Had he ever talked about the Wilson development to me? Had I heard him talking about it to anyone?

But the subject hadn't interested me and I hadn't asked Father about it because it was his business and nothing to do with me. I admit I was puzzled by the speed with which he had gone from being a not very successful architect to real estate to becoming one of the very rich. Not that he spent lavishly around us, or that there were luxury journeys for his family. His own travels to the Caribbean and Europe, he said, were linked to his business. Nor had he offered to pay down Gina's mortgage, though she kept up her regular complaints and had stepped up her barrage of entreaties after he told us he had made "a killing" on the Wilson development. She couldn't afford new clothes for herself and for the kids and she harped on about extra cash to "help" William or, as I saw it, keep him out of her way. She had put him into some all-day learning center, but what she wanted was a boarding school, one that would take him even after he turned ten.

Our father hadn't offered to help.

His wealth, James suggested, was unexpected because the Wilson development hadn't thrown off the kind of returns he had claimed. It may have earned him about a million or two, but the area was north of the city, hard to get to, and there was no public transportation at the time. Didn't I wonder where all the money had come from? How he had really earned it? Why hadn't I asked him about it?

Those were not the sorts of questions Gina and I asked. Nor would we have expected him to answer, had we asked. Gina was pleased to see his becoming, as she said, "a man of wealth, of substance" because she imagined some of his newfound money would trickle down to fill her own needs. I didn't care how he made his money.

Then, about five years ago, he had announced that he was moving out of the home he had shared with our mother. As simple as that. It was the winter after Mother told me she had dementia. Sure, there had been signs. But they had barely talked to each other for some time—I don't remember how long. On family occasions the silence between them had been so deep, not even Gina's noisy children could pretend it wasn't there. Father traveled a lot more. Mother was no longer busy with her lectures. Her dementia had advanced to a stage where she was often repeating herself. He pretended not to notice. When I told him that she would need more help around the house, he said I could hire anyone I wanted, long as they stayed out of his way. I assumed he didn't want to see her deteriorate, didn't want to have the responsibility for her care. He hadn't bothered to call either Gina or me to announce that he was leaving, but then we couldn't have expected that he would. Ours had never been the kind of relationship where you shared decisions or thoughts.

Still, I was surprised when he said he had bought himself another place. He mentioned it casually when I was at the house visiting Mother and he and a stranger in uniform—turned out to be his chauffeur—were packing suitcases and garment bags with his clothes. "Anything I forget to take, she can have," he told me. "Or throw it out."

We had assumed he would move to a downtown condo, or a semi-detached. He hadn't. It was the senior partner in his old real estate firm who told me he had bought a house in an area of the city where two or three million dollars wouldn't even buy you a two-car garage, let alone a house, so I asked Father if he was going to show us where he lived. He said he would when the structural changes were finished, and that seemed to take an inordinately long time.

When William was almost ten, Father finally offered Gina some money. Even then, it was not a gift but an investment. He paid off the bank and bought the house she and her family lived in. Then they paid him rent at the same rate they had paid the bank interest on their mortgage. If they ever wanted to sell, they would have to make sure he agreed, and he would take all of the money from the sale. "Not just the original investment, but all of it," Gina said. His lawyer had drawn up the agreement. Sammy hadn't wanted to sign it but Gina persuaded him. "It's a shitty deal," I said. "Unfair in every way. You get no benefit if house prices rise. You'll be at his mercy if he decides to sell it while you live there. And why wouldn't he? He hasn't been generous to Mother, why would he be any different with you?"

"I'm his daughter," Gina said.

"So?"

I was grateful he hadn't offered me anything. That's why I still lived in my old apartment in the Entertainment District, which was rent-controlled cheap. But booze in the area was expensive. I dropped into bars on King Street or Queen, near Spadina if I wanted to drink in public. Most often I bought my bottles at the liquor store. I had started hiding them when James was still living in my apartment, not so much because I didn't want him to notice but because I was tired of his lectures about the deadening effects of booze and the need for me to spend more time with the therapist.

When Father asked whether Gina and I would like to see his new house, we both agreed. Curiosity got the better of me, though I felt I was betraying our mother. Gina, for obvious reasons, was eager to please him. She always had been, but now, with his money in her hands, she couldn't decline.

The place was a mansion, with an iron gate, a long circular drive, a massive door with a clanging bell, a huge reception hall, ten bedrooms, a library with hundreds of real books—at least they seemed to be real, though our father was not known to be studious. He used to complain that Mother's books gathered dust. His study was bigger than the living room in our old home. There were two dining rooms, one for intimate dinners, he told us, the other, with a chandelier, a long table, and twenty-four chairs, for entertaining. I only ever saw the dining rooms when they were empty. The living room was almost the full width of the house, with tall windows, two large oil paintings of sea scenes by Manet or a follower of Manet, and mirror-polished floors. There were two long low tables and surrounding brown lounge chairs with wooden arms and cloth, detachable backrests. Everything was clean and tidy, no photographs or albums or small mementos to clutter up the space.

We ate in the kitchen with the cook. We hadn't been invited to dinner or to spend a night, and, though we had seen the warm indoor pool, Gina and I didn't have a chance to try it. Gina was not allowed to take her kids. "They piss in pools," Father said, adding that the house was not suitable for children. After he showed us around, he said we could come once a week if we wished, but I had not wished, so I joined Gina only a couple more times.

Once, when Gerry came to pick us up, we stuffed bathing suits into our handbags on the off chance that we would be invited to try the pool, but he explained that it had recently been chlorinated. It would be disastrous for our eyes.

I think he meant that the pool was not for us.

I assumed that our father had a girlfriend, maybe a string of girlfriends, but I didn't dwell on the thought because I couldn't picture him with anyone other than Mother, and even that, since they never seemed to touch, was a bit of a stretch.

That was before we met Gladys. She was very tall, young, maybe thirty-five, and pretty in a conventional high-cheeked, full-lipped way. Taller than Father and maybe even heavier, with powerful arms and shoulders that attested to her daily exercise routine. She wore black leotards and a cutaway T-shirt that flattered her long, muscular upper arms. He had installed weights, a rowing machine, high gym bars, a decathlon stepper, and a treadmill, and that's just the equipment I noticed the one time I successfully infiltrated the basement. She was there doing pull-ups on the bars. She had strapped weights to her ankles and looked like she was enjoying herself. Gerry said she worked out twice a day. She also swam lengths in the pool and ran around the neighborhood.

Apart from her weekly yoga and her penchant for standing on her head, Mother never exercised.

Our father hadn't worked out much either, though now he had hired a trainer to help him do leg lifts with rubber bands around his thighs and sit-ups with his hands clasped under his head. Gerry said Father hated his workouts and canceled them most of the time.

Mother was not surprised to find out about Gladys. She said that Father would, naturally, acquire a girl. Men like him, she said, always had girls.

Did that mean he had someone on the side during the years of their marriage?

"Certainly," she told us. "Women find him attractive. Always have." As for someone more permanent, she would be young, even younger than we were, she would dress well, walk with confidence, wear a lot of makeup, and enjoy the money in a way Mother had failed to do. She demonstrated how this girlfriend would stride across the room, head held high, mouth in a pout, hips swinging, back straight, a most unusual walk for a small woman with rounded shoulders whose natural disposition was to walk softly but with determination, her lectures usually delivered in a quiet voice that forced her listeners to lean in if they wanted to hear her.

We had this conversation before we sold the house and moved her into the condo. She still had her sense of humor then.

Gladys may not have checked all those boxes, she may have been older than me, but she was certainly more confident. She didn't even slow down her steady up-and-down lifts when I entered the basement gym, and the smile she gave me was cool enough to discourage my staying to watch.

When I asked Gerry about the girlfriend, he rolled his eyes. "Is that what you call them these days?" he asked.

The trickle of water from the taps had stopped.

I limped down to the lake and filled the red bucket from the other side of the dock, determinedly not glancing over to the side where I had fallen in. Or at Father's cabin, which looked even more forlorn than the basement. Gina had told me he hadn't come to the cottage last summer. In front of his cabin, I thought I saw some skid marks, which could have been left by the ice. Perhaps when the ice retreated, it had also left behind a dead animal I had no desire to think about, let alone see. I also did not want to see his cabin.

I felt the evening's chill, though the wind had died down, just the soft crinkling of tiny waves as they rolled to shore. There was a slight rotting fish stench and something else besides, sweet, but rank, like the wafting smell in Mother's room.

I hurried up the path. One small bucket of water would have to do for the night. I kept using the kids' red one because the big bucket in the basement looked like the one Father had used to drown the mice.

I collected an armload of firewood from the woodpile under the stairs. Though I was sure I would now have enough to last a couple of days, I worried about the wood getting wet overnight, because the tarp we had used to cover it had rolled off and lay limp and damp near the wall. I stood staring at the pile for a while, wondering whether the tarp had been there when I arrived or if it had been off all winter, or longer, perhaps since the last time I had been here. Almost two years ago. Could whatever it was last night have been digging and scratching in the woodpile? It could be a bear. They eat insects and larvae if they can't find something more appetizing. Perhaps it had swum over during the fall bear hunt and made its den in one of the large crevasses high up on the island. But wasn't it too early for a bear to come out of hibernation?

I slammed shut and locked all the sliding doors and turned on all the lights. They were dimmer than I remembered. Or were they? My head still ached. Could my fall have affected my eyesight?

"It's friendlier to have soft lights," our father had insisted, though he had long ago stopped any effort to make the place feel soft or friendly.

He had installed the lights when we were children, ten or twelve, I think, when we were still a family. He had been tinkering with the cottage, installing new stones for the fireplace, fixing the outdoor light, bringing in the new fridge, cutting the sumac and the raspberry bushes with his scythe.

I poured some whiskey into my wineglass to fortify me against the horrid smell in Mother's room and carried it with me. I wanted to see what else was in the bottom drawer. I wasn't keen about digging around in her private things, but I felt as if I needed to see what she had kept here. It's not that I expected anything startling, I had known her all my life, and we should have been well past extraordinary revelations years ago. Yet, perhaps we weren't.

Those photographs and papers must have been important to her or she wouldn't have kept them here.

Last February, on one of her "lucid days"—though it was not a whole day, maybe a couple of hours—she had told me I had to clear out her "hoard" at the cottage. I assumed she meant her clothes, the long summer dresses she favored during the hot months, clothes she had accumulated over the years and never given away, even those that had become frayed and gritty at the edges (she refused to have them cleaned because she thought they would disintegrate in the wash), those loose gowns she had worn to dinner in the evenings. I assured her that I had already packed them all into one of the large plastic boxes we used for winter storage and scattered rosemary leaves over them to save them from mice.

"My papers," she said. "You can jam them into a garbage bag. There is no need for you to look at them. None," she had added for emphasis, exactly the sort of instruction that made me want to see what else was in the drawer.

None of these photos was surprising—I had seen them all before— except for one: a somewhat creased picture of Gladys. She was marching with long strides, arms swinging, more or less the way Mother had demonstrated the walk. She was on a path with flowerbeds on either side. Maybe a park. She was coming toward the camera, though she didn't seem to be aware of it; she looked to one side, scowling, as if she were expecting someone she didn't like from that direction. She wore her tight-fitting yoga pants and a matching blue zippered top, Nike runners, a scrunchie keeping her long blond hair off her face. Not much detail in her face—the picture had been taken from a distance—but it was recognizably Gladys.

Now, why would Mother want, let alone keep, a photo of Gladys? How would she get such a shot? Who had taken it? Could Mother have been spying on her? I couldn't imagine Mother stalking Gladys. Would she have hired a private detective to take pictures of her? Why? She had declared she had no interest in any of Father's women, they were his business. Always had been his business. Her business with him, she said, had ended. As if their marriage had been a business arrangement.

I started to call Gina, then remembered that there was no reception at the cottage. "If you want to have a big social life," Father had said, "don't come here. This place is our family refuge. We come here to be away from all that." Once we stopped being a family he had bought a Wi-Fi hub for his cabin and managed to make his own long calls. Standing on the dock, I once listened to him shouting obscenities at someone. We were forbidden to connect to the Wi-Fi.

Briefly, I considered going down there, but the thought of it made me feel nauseated, his space, his belongings, whatever he had stored there for the winter was too depressing, as was the descending dusk. Instead, I got the fire started. The wood was winter damp, it hissed and smoked but did, finally, flare enough that I could confidently leave it while I went back to Mother's room.

19

BRACING MY FEET AGAINST THE OBSTINATE BOTTOM drawer and pulling with both hands on what was left of the handle produced no results. It was difficult to get a good purchase on the handle because it was too narrow and too short now for my hands. Only two fingers and one thumb of each hand managed to curve around it. My ass perched on the edge of Mother's bed, knees close to my ears. My fingers kept slipping off. I imagined my mother laughing at me. She would not be angry; my looking for that wretched will had been her idea.

It had been a long time since the two of us had laughed at something together.

I was on the point of giving up when what was left of the handle came off in my fingers. I fell back onto Mother's bed and rested. My efforts had jiggled my glass on top of the dresser, spilling some on the lacquered top.

Time for a refill.

I did not think my mother and I had ever had an easy time with each other. In memories of my childhood, she was always a little distant, not given to hugging, even after one of my falls, when she would hold me by my shoulders, keeping our bodies apart. I had the impression that she was anxious to get away from me and my pain. That was when I was five or younger; as I grew, she was less likely to touch me. Was she warmer to Gina? There was the time she had pulled her out of the water and hugged her. Was Gina already less judgmental, more accepting of whatever affection she got? Because Gina had been so clingy, she had been physically closer to Mother. Or was that my imagination? Mother once told me that I was more difficult; that, unlike my sister, I loathed signs of affection; that hugging made me nervous, or embarrassed. She said I resisted every attempt to embrace me, that I slid out of her arms and ran to a corner of the room where I thought I could not be reached. But she had said all that when we were fighting about something—I don't remember what. How would she have known I resisted affection when she had not tried it?

We had never seen our parents holding hands or hugging, they showed no obvious signs of mutual affection, so it was hardly surprising if I had refused her efforts to hug me. I certainly had no memory of her efforts.

Maybe Father had showed us he cared by teaching us to fish and teaching me how to handle a gun. Though I had been a disaster at both fishing and shooting, he had, no doubt, made the effort.

Was he marginally more affectionate than our mother? I didn't think so. That would be odd in light of everything that happened later.

Perhaps I shouldn't trust my memory.

I retreated from her bedroom, threw another log on the fire, and sat looking at the flames for a while. It was almost pleasant in the living room now. I boiled water for a box of noodles left over from last summer and, amazingly, untouched by the mice and heated a can of ready-made tomato sauce.

Another glass of whiskey to help me recover from the smell of the dead thing in Mother's room, or the stench near the dock. Or had I imagined that, too? I was starting to doubt my own senses. James had asked me whether I might consider going to A.A. We had been together for a couple of years by then and he was concerned that the therapist he had hired had not been able to slow down my drinking.

"You mean Alcoholics Anonymous?" I asked him. "Why?"

"Because I worry about you," he said. "I think it would be easier if you faced your demons—whatever they are. The alcohol masks their presence. It doesn't kill them."

"I like the taste," I said flippantly. Or did I? I knew I had started to drink more after we found Scoop's body, but I hadn't wanted to bring that up with James. It would have made me feel silly. Childish. Vulnerable. The same reason I hadn't mentioned it to the therapist.

I wandered over to the dining room table. It felt lonelier here than in the rest of the room. There had always been noise around here. Our childhood was noisy. Gina and I fought almost as much as we played together. Dinners, I thought, even later, when William insisted on counting all the knives and forks and rearranging them in two straight lines, had been fun.

Arguments had been heated, but they rarely deteriorated into fights. Our parents, while they disagreed vehemently, remained civil, even when the subject was the killing of elephants. Father had offered to show us data proving that elephants had destroyed much of Tanzania's savanna, tearing up shrubs and young trees by the roots, creating desert where there had been food for all herbivores, and Gina and I argued about stupid stuff, such as who had last done the dishes, which were rarely reasons to carry on battling beyond the first few minutes. I had been convinced that she disliked me, that she resented my being smarter. I think she even resented my writing stories, and she used to scrunch up my drawings and toss them into the garbage. She told me more than once that they were no good, that all I had to do to find out how stupid they were was to look at Eva's sculptures or even her sketches.

I think she resented me for not getting married, or just for not ending up with someone like Sammy.

As far back as I can remember, I had thought she was a whiny numbskull who seemed to know what buttons to push to get more of our mother's attention.

I took my plate next to the fireplace and ate off my aching knees. My reflection in the glass doors was frightening, my hair was disheveled, my figure shrunken, there was blood on my forehead from my adventures on the dock, and my shoulders were hunched. I hadn't brushed my hair since I got to the cottage. My head still hurt, and blood had caked not only into the back of my head, but also into the hair near my temple. I had a slightly crazed look.

I examined my hands. The knuckles were swollen red and scabbed, nails were broken, jagged. I thought the scar on my left hand was more noticeable with the dirt on my fingers. I usually took care of my nails; even when I didn't have time to have my hair professionally trimmed, I did make it to a salon for a manicure and sometimes shellac so they would be tough and shiny and last a long time. That hadn't been possible the past few months, and now, what with scrabbling on the dock and my battles with the drawers, my nails were like a child's.

I really needed a hot bath.

I poured some water from the bucket into a jug for coffee later, cleaned my hands and face in the rest, then poured it into the well of the toilet in the large bathroom (not Mother's). At least I should be able to flush once.

Two more logs on the fire, a few desultory sparks, smoke, and waspish hissing but I hoped it would last till the morning.

I went to bed fully clothed. Took my glass of whiskey and *Sapiens* with me to provide a scintilla of balance and maybe help put me to sleep. It might have been a brilliant book but it had begun to sag in the middle. I found it difficult to focus on "deterministic explanations of events such as the rise of Christianity." I was exhausted, but no matter how many pages I read, I was unable to go to sleep. I worried about having to tackle the basement again in the morning. I kept thinking about the hard, murky thing in the water, the slimy hairlike weeds, the blood on the floor from my wound, and the skid marks along the path, and I worried that the tarp was no longer covering the woodpile. If it rained, all the wood would be wet.

I placed Mother's bottle of diazepam next to *Sapiens* near my bed. I wasn't sure what the dosage should be, but I took three to make sure that I slept.

20

I WOKE WITH A START, INTERRUPTING A CONFUSING childhood dream about searching for my mother along the boarding school's long, echoing, barely lit corridors, my flannel nightgown winding around my legs, holding me back and tripping me as I reached out for the walls to steady my progress. Then I fell headlong into a black well, my cry echoing as I tumbled.

At first I wasn't sure I was out of the dream and had no idea I was at the cottage. I was still falling down the well. I landed with a thud, turned my face, expecting to feel pain, the wetness of blood, but there was nothing. I opened my eyes, saw nothing. I couldn't breathe. The darkness was so thick, I felt like I was being smothered in feathers. I raised my head from the pillow and gulped air. Still dizzy. But there was a dab of dim light dancing over the ceiling. A glance through the window told me I was in my room at the cottage. Scattered blue-lead patches whirled past so fast I couldn't distinguish the upper branches of the trees. Wind flinging branches at the deck. The booming sound of waves smashing onto the shore. Inside, there was a noise like thrashing or whipping something repeatedly against a hollow object, which gave off a whining or screeching sound. I lay very still. Rigid. Panting. Trying to guess where it was coming from. I tried to see past my windows—was there something near the front door? Solid darkness. Had I locked all the sliding doors and put latches on the windows? Surely, I must have. I remembered thinking about having to lock up before I went to bed.

The sound, I thought, was coming from the direction of Mother's room.

I slid out of bed sideways onto my knees and waited there uncertainly, thinking I should not lift my head higher than the blanket, so I wouldn't be seen—I definitely didn't want my head to be a target. I lowered myself to my hands and knees. It occurred to me that in years to come I would regale my friends with this story and everyone would laugh, me included. Then the thrashing started again and the screeching was louder. Slowly, I crawled to the living room. I hoped the fire hadn't gone out but I didn't want to crawl over to check if there was still a spark left, not with that noise growing louder.

I knew my way without a light. I had been here every summer for thirty-five years, and during some of those early summers I would have been crawling much as I did now, on softer, more tender knees, and no harm ever came to me. At least no harm that I could remember, though there was something niggling at my memory, a flicker of my fingers surrounded by flames.

Had I burned my hand in this fireplace once?

There were those scars on my left hand, running up to my wrist, thin lines, barely noticeable in the winter, but they stood out on my tanned skin in the summer. The scar on my palm was even less noticeable because no one tans on their palms, but my left palm was tighter than the other. The scar had pulled the tendon under my ring finger, making my hands uneven. Mother had said they were acne scars, as if anyone got acne on their hands. My father said he couldn't see anything, but if there were a scar, it had to be a result of one of our mother's cooking adventures. He said she was not only a dreadful cook but also a careless one. She often left food bubbling in oil and forgot about it. "Don't you remember the fire alarms going off on weekends when she decided to come down from her study and surprise us with a home-cooked meal?"

I did remember the fire alarms and that Father installed some extra ones in the kitchen area. They gave off horrific staccato shrieks, but luckily, they weren't connected to the fire department, so the firefighters didn't come every time she burned dinner.

Gina said I used to stand close to our mother in the kitchen, trying to see what she was doing, so it wouldn't be surprising if I had burned myself. She said Mother would tell me to go and play, but I persisted. Finally, she had to push me away. She had always pushed me away.

When James had given me the engagement ring, he had tried to put it on the ring finger of my left hand. "It's where my mother wore it," he told me in his hushed, emotional voice. "It would have meant a lot to her that I was giving it to you."

"Means a lot to me, too," I said, "but I prefer it on my right hand."

"Why?"

I showed him the scar then and how my palm didn't quite straighten out.

"I don't see anything," he said, examining my palm where the scar stood out even more than usual that evening. He tilted it toward the light, bent my fingers back just a bit, then kissed them one by one. "Even your hand is perfect."

He was lying, of course, but I liked it. Then.

I lowered myself to my elbows in front of the blue sofa, trying to blend into its coarse fabric. This way, if someone were throwing things at the cottage, or shooting, my head wouldn't be a target. My mother had bought the sofa at the King Edward Hotel sale when the new owners decided to renovate and redecorate and sold everything at, she said, "ridiculous prices." It used to be in the lobby, I think, and still sagged a bit on either side. When I was little, I would imagine impossibly elegant people wearing fancy hats, sitting far apart on the sofa, drinking tea from pretty porcelain cups, their little fingers pointing upward, exactly as Mother had told us never to do. "It's not becoming," she said, but never explained why.

I was about halfway to Mother's room when there was a crash and a flash of blue light that made the whole living room white. The edges of chairs and tables stood out, the frames on the family photos, the sides of the logs where I had stacked them, the top of the fireplace where I had left the poker last night. I lay with my face on the rug, still, waiting, holding my breath until I couldn't hold it any longer and choked on the rush of air into my lungs, too loud, hiccupping with the effort to keep quiet while breathing. From this position, I could see a patch of silver in the murky denseness of the sky and, through the sliding doors, the big oak desperately waving its branches. The sound of breaking glass from my mother's room. I crawled to the fireplace and grabbed the poker. The handle was hot, but comforting because the room was cold and damp. My clothes were clammy from the rug.

Still crawling, the poker in one hand, I made it to my mother's doorway. It was much colder here than in the rest of the cottage. And darker. Too dark to see anything. A compact darkness that felt like something solid, though I knew it couldn't be, and that noise, screeching, as if it were ready to hurl itself at me. Furiously beating against her walls, angry, persistent, and smashing, shattering things in the room.

I had to go back for the flashlight. Though aware that a flashlight would make me an easier target for whatever it was, I still had to know what was in there. I left the poker by the door and crawled back to my bedroom faster than I had come. I knew now that whatever thing or presence had invaded the place, it was focused on my mother's room. I picked up the flashlight from my bedside table, straightened up, and made my way back. A flash of lightning, another crash on the deck.

The trees waving their branches, as if they were asking for help. My mother used to say the trees danced on the island, that they were in love with the wind and bent this way and that at its behest. I thought they were in pain.

In the pale amber beam of my flashlight, my mother's room looked like it had been turned over by robbers, anxiously searching for something of value. Photographs were scattered all over the floor, the little glass figurines my mother had collected on her travels were all thrown around, my glass from the night before was shattered, and glass from her window had fallen across the bed. It had divided into long, vicious-looking sharp pieces that seemed to cut like knives into the darkness where my light glinted off them. The wind was howling through the long gap in her window, the rain came almost horizontally, pelting everything, pouring into her open drawer. It had soaked her duvet and the soft pillows she had loved so much. A couple of her long summer dresses had been wrenched from their hangers, scrunched up into sodden balls outside her open closet.

Just a storm, I said to the darkness surrounding my narrow light.

There, at the back of the closet, leaning up against the wood, for a moment I could see the blackened Ouija board and something else. White. Moving. Not a ghost. My imagination. Again.

My voice was unfamiliar, croaky, echoing, as if I were hearing someone else's. My teeth were chattering. The cold in this room was freezing my mouth. I reached for the light switch, hesitated long enough for one more lightning bolt to snap into the water near the dock. It lit up the cascading waves over the dock, spray shooting straight up, a deep rumbling as the water lifted some of the boards. Hadn't we bought longer nails to keep them firm in the storms?

No light when I jammed the switch up with my damaged hand.
The boat!

I struggled out of my mother's room, pulled on my jacket, stepped into my wet shoes, thinking that I could make it down to the dock and secure the boat. We have had so many summer storms here that we would run down to tighten the ropes. Once, when the boat got loose, we chased it, swimming and gasping, laughing in the wild, overwhelming waves, my father reaching the boat first and somehow holding it against the storm. His arms were so unnaturally strong, sinewy, the muscles long and hard, I remember when he hauled me up by my bum and threw me into the boat, my legs and arms flailing. "Start the motor, Jude," he yelled through the hurtling waves, and I recovered my footing somehow and did start the engine, so Gina and Father could scramble up into the boat. So long ago.

It took a while to zip up my jacket and tie my shoelaces with my frozen shaking hands. I stood by the sliding doors, waiting. Or not exactly waiting, but hoping that it was only a storm. Yet that low rumbling in my mother's room couldn't have been thunder. If it were thunder, it would have been all over, not in one room.

But I had to get down to the dock. I needed the boat to get off the island. I opened the door a crack. Lashed by the cold rain, I tried to pull the door open wide enough to let me squeeze through. The wind was a giant fist hammering my chest and pushing me back hard. It whipped my face and neck. I grasped the doorframe, desperate to hold on against the assault. Dammit, Jude, get a hold of yourself, I shouted in my father's voice. Or was that my father's voice shouting?

The darkness massed into a towering, looming shape outside, as if it were coming for me. Angry, impersonal, vile. A loud crack like a gunshot, those dreaded sounds my father's guns made when he was hunting. My wet fingers slid off the door and I staggered back.

It's just a storm, Jude, I told myself. Just branches torn from the trees. Nothing special. We've had storms here before, there will be more storms later.

I lay there for a minute or two on soaking floorboards. With a monumental effort, I stood up and threw myself at the door, yanking it shut. A few dead branches dropped on my feet. I knew I had to go out and hook the extra rope into the prow of the boat. But if I did I would, for sure, be swept into the lake. If the boat was gone, I could maybe get help in the morning, but no one could rescue me during the night in the lake in the middle of a storm.

I tried to find my flashlight. No idea where I had left it, or had it been torn from my hand by the wind? With my back to the doors, I waited for my eyes to adjust to the darkness.

Thank God, if there was one, for the few live embers in the fireplace. I threw on another log from the rack and thanked my father's wisdom for his placement of the logs, far away from the doors, because he had known about giant storms on the lake. Like my mother, he, too, had loved the storms when they came. He would sit on the deck for as long as possible and laugh into the wind. He had even loved the struggles with the boat. "Have never felt so alive," he had said when we rescued the boat for maybe the twentieth time. He had been standing on a rock, swearing, holding the boat at bay, sheet lightning all around us, Mother, Gina, and I huddled in the bow, and he was laughing maniacally, as if the whole drama of the moment had been created to entertain him.

When I turned away from the fire, I saw a weak, yellowish light beam moving near my mother's open door. What the hell! I really didn't want to believe in ghosts or apparitions, but there had been that damned Ouija board and the blue flame when it flew into the fire. No, there was a simple explanation. That was where I had dropped my flashlight and it was rolling with the wind. That was why it was so cold in there. Her broken window. That was it. Just a storm. Just a broken window. I would have to tape something over the window.

But what the hell was that sound? Scratching and thrashing and that high-pitched screech.

I didn't want to go in there, but I knew I had to. Mother would want me to clear out whatever was in her room. She was sensitive about her things. She hated it when Gina or I asked to borrow a shawl or a jacket on a cold day. "It wouldn't fit you," she used to tell Gina, who had always been a bit overweight and more than a bit after her last pregnancy. She usually said it with a genial, indulgent smile, but she was serious about not wanting to lend her clothes. She hadn't been here for some time, now, but her room still felt so much like her room, so exclusively hers, that I hesitated every time I entered.

I picked up the flashlight and tried to see the whole room again. Just one long narrow slab of glass, tapered to a killer point at one end, had fallen on the bed, not the whole window. It should be easy enough to repair, I told myself. But that would come later. The rain was still whipping in through the opening. Careful to avoid the smaller shards, I swept up the photographs from where I had left them on her bed the day before. Some of them stuck to my fingers, resisting, as I tried to return them to the drawer. Couldn't do that. They were wet. The drawer was soaking. All her photos would be ruined. I took them out to the kitchen in batches and spread them on the counter. I hadn't been careful enough with the glass, bits of it were now embedded in my hands, and there were tiny drops of blood over them. A photo of Mother and me walking toward the dock, both of us in shorts, carrying canoe paddles, talking to the person holding the camera. Strange that I hadn't seen this picture earlier, especially as there were so few photos of me in her room, or anywhere. She was shading her face with her hand, I seemed to be staring straight at him—I was quite sure it was my father and I even remembered the moment this was taken. Five years ago or more? She had already talked about her dementia, and he had told us that he could no longer live in our home, that he had bought another house.

That sound again. Louder. More insistent. Something repeatedly smashing into the chest of drawers, then slamming in her closet, the screech of her metal hangers. I held on to the counter. My flashlight was still in my hand, but I was too scared to lift it and aim it at my mother's gaping doorway. Whatever it was, it couldn't be let out of that room.

Suddenly, I had a memory of my sister screaming as her Ouija board flew off the table, ricocheted off the open iron doors of the fireplace, and bounced into the fire.

I think I had been steadying the thing, because I was sure Gina had been pushing it and I wanted to know how, when the board just flew off the little table. There was a sizzling sound as it settled over the logs and it went up in a shot of blue and white flame, with Gina screaming at me to reach in and get it. "You did that!" she accused me. "You didn't want to play. You threw it in!"

At the same time, she was excited about how it burned. I protested that I hadn't flipped the board into the fire, but she didn't believe me. I was sure that it was Gina who tossed in the damned thing because she didn't like its answers about the boy in her French class.

I reached into the fireplace and pulled it out, so angry at Gina, I barely noticed I burned my hand—my left, because I was still holding that infernal planchette in my right. Afterward I plunged my hand into my glass of orange juice, and laid the board on the stone surround, where it continued to smolder until I threw the orange juice over it. The smell was not unpleasantly sugary. Gina continued to yell that I had ruined her birthday gift from Mother and she threatened to throw my new swimsuit—a surprising gift from Eva for my thirteenth birthday—into the fire.

I didn't think she would really do it, but she did.

After we had gone to bed that night, she must have snuck out of our bedroom and flung the pretty new red bathing suit onto the embers. It was still smoldering the next morning when I pulled it out and showed it to Eva. I remember the shock on her face and how she hugged me and told me she would buy me another one. It was so unexpected, Eva hugging me to her stomach, stroking my hair, and whispering not to mind Gina's jealousy; I was so much more talented than she was. Like Mother, she had not been a toucher, never openly affectionate, or involved in my silly battles with my sister. That morning Eva took the planchette and told me she would never let Gina have it again.

I really don't know why I hadn't remembered how badly I had burned my hand and why I'd decided not to tell anyone about it. Eva had plastered salve on it and bandaged it all the way up the wrist. Gina knew, but she was so angry she didn't care.

I hadn't seen the Ouija board again until the night I found it in our mother's closet.

21

THE STORM WAS STILL SMASHING AGAINST THE
windows, the sound of thundering waves at the shore, the rain drum-
ming on the roof, and flashes of lightning beyond the dancing treetops.
Was it coming closer, or retreating over the roof and bearing down on
the middle of the island? I crept along the wall, feeling its reassuring soft
pine against my fingers. I didn't use the flashlight when I was next to my
mother's door, I just reached for where I knew the doorknob would be,
grabbed it, and yanked it shut. The door slammed on furious sounds from
the room. They gathered at the door, beating against it, again and again
till I thought it would splinter, but it didn't. This can't be just the wind.
Had some evil thing taken up residence in my mother's room? I told
myself that this was not real, that somehow my nightmare had invaded
my reality. I shouted at the sound to stop and it did for a moment, then
it began again.

I held the metal knob more firmly.

I had no idea how long I stood there, nor when the banging stopped,
nor when the storm ended, but I know it was very still and calm in the pink
early dawn when I went to warm my bent, swollen fingers at the fireplace

(yes, Mother, I have some arthritis). I didn't remember having gone to sleep, but I must have, since I was no longer holding her door shut. I was leaning over the kitchen counter, my hands clutching its edge, her wet, bloodied photographs spread out before me.

I had a towel around my head and a bandage around my leg under the knee. I didn't remember putting these on. I saw there was a light in my bedroom, though I didn't remember turning it on. I did remember deciding not to turn on a light when I crawled out of bed. Perhaps the electricity hadn't cut out, after all, or it had cut out only for a short time, or only in my mother's room. But I decided I wouldn't think about that room, let alone check if its light was on again. Not yet.

The sliding door I had such a struggle with the night before now opened wide enough to let me out. A branch had wedged itself in its runners, that's why it wouldn't open all the way. There were more branches scattered all over the deck, and a big one, torn from its trunk, lay miserably broken all the way from the steps to the door. It was the oak tree's longest branch that had landed across Mother's window, split the window and smashed through the glass. An upended bird's nest made of green shoots and old twigs had been hurled against the windows of my bedroom. The red roof of the outhouse had flown off and landed behind the cabins and the door was hanging by a hinge. I could see that the toilet seat was still in place. Good news, since I might have to resort to using the outhouse.

Dead leaves and broken branches were everywhere, a thick carpet of crackling, torn-off twigs with young buds underfoot, as I marched down the steps and out to the dock to see if the boat was still tied up where I had left it.

It wasn't.

I would have to call the marina for help.

Some dock boards had been torn away, though I remembered hammering them all down with new nails, replacing the rusted ones, only two summers ago. The dock was mostly pressure-treated spruce, replacing our old red cedar dock destroyed during successive November storms.

I couldn't remember ever having seen a spring storm like the one last night. Or was it just that we usually came up later, after spring had already settled in? In any case, there had never been one that had broken our windows.

There were pieces of dock among the stones along the shoreline. High water, white spume, suds, froth. Here and there, small dead fish. I glanced up at Father's cabin. The roof had held, as had the windows. Bits of boards from the dock and a dead squirrel under his deck. Must have been there when I arrived two days ago. Was it only two days ago? I was so very tired. The nightmares, the stench, the storm, the dreadful noises, and now the boat was gone.

I put off going into that cabin. Mother's command that I find Father's will remained less compelling than my desire to stay away from the place.

It was hard to walk along the shore because trees had snapped and dropped into the water, which was now much higher than when I'd arrived. I persevered for a while, picking up boards I thought had been part of our dock and could be put back in place later. There was something red rolling in the froth, a little farther out. It looked like a piece of thick cloth, maybe a sweater—it wasn't floating like a life jacket. I waded in to get a better look. Yes, someone's pullover, more burnt orange than red, the color both William and Father favored for their cottage attire. Perhaps it had been left on the dock and had fallen in last summer.

I couldn't place the memory. Two years ago? Longer? I stood in water that was over my calves, my feet slipping on the stones, but I didn't want to touch the sweater. I hoisted myself up, went to the end of the dock, and looked across at the turtle islands, where the waves were still mounting over the rocks. Our boat wasn't floating out there or knocking against that shore.

There would surely be someone at the marina after such a night. One of those orange helicopters was sure to check if someone had fallen overboard. They would help find the boat. If I was lucky, it wouldn't be too beaten up. Even if it had sunk, it could be salvaged. One thing about the *Hunt*, it was sturdy, designed to survive storms, completely functional, as Father used to say. Surely, someone would come and take me back to my car. I could help look for the boat later.

I needed a hot bath.

I tried my phone. Sometimes there was reception at the end of the dock but not today. I stood with my back to the cottage and the cabins for a long time, waiting for the sun to come out and warm me. When I finally turned and looked back at the cottage, my eyes were drawn inexorably to Father's cabin, but I knew that to get reception I had to go to the top of the island, almost on the other side, to the high point far above the cottage. I had to call for help, and that was the only place where there was usually some modest reception.

But not yet. I still had things to do.

22

I WENT UP THE STEPS WITH MY FACE TURNED TOWARD
the lake because I didn't want to look into my mother's room, but I
couldn't resist a glance. The branch of the big oak was leaning in through
her broken window, as if it had wanted to visit her. That oak was her
favorite tree because, she said, it cast a calming shadow over her space,
allowing her to relax quietly even when everyone was noisy. Oaks, she
told us, are famous for their endurance. The Green Man of legends
was made of oak. She used to watch downy woodpeckers climb up
the trunk seeking worms in the crevices of the bark. Yellow warblers
used to sit on its branches, waiting for their turn at the feeders—her
feeders, as we thought of them, because she had brought them up to
the cottage and had climbed up the wobbly ladder to hang them on
a branch close to her window. One summer a finch built a nest in
the oak and Mother would watch its engineering antics through her
binoculars. She took a broom handle to the red squirrel that tried to
shove its face into the nest. Of course, she couldn't guard it all day
and night. Something—Father had said the snakes—had eaten the
fledglings and destroyed the nest. "Snakes," he said, "are not particular

about what they kill. Birds, rats, mice, and they don't get emotional about babies. Eat them all."

I found the screwdriver in Father's red toolbox. The hammer was where I had dropped it, near the open door to the basement. Determined, I made my way into its murky depths, without a flashlight. I used the screwdriver to loosen the lever and hammered at the piece of wood that was still in place from my earlier efforts. I ran upstairs when I heard the gurgling sound in the pipe, and turned on the kitchen tap. Coughing and spluttering and giant hiccups, but the water finally gushed out, brown, muddy, with reddish pebbles, but it was such a great sight that I celebrated with a full glass of my father's whiskey.

I couldn't remember when I had drunk the rest, but it was hardly surprising, with the storm, the cold, the damage to my mother's room. It had been late and I had needed some solace.

I sat at the puzzle table and examined my injuries. The scratch on my arm was deep and red, but it hadn't bled during the night, nor had my legs. The back of my head was still tender but not bleeding, and the bandage on my forehead was still in place. The tips of my fingers, which had been scratched by the bits of broken glass, were still sore but not so painful, I hadn't even been aware of them when I worked on the pump. My right shoulder ached, I thought from the fall off the dock. The old injury on my left hand was sore and raised, as if I had just burned it. I even felt the handle of the hot tongs now, though I had not been aware of it when I grabbed them to rescue Gina's Ouija board.

The whiskey was delicious. I couldn't believe it was the same I had swilled into my wineglass when I'd opened the bottle yesterday. A tiny, pleasant buzz in my head, since I hadn't eaten in some time—couldn't recall when exactly. The whiskey tasted how it used to years ago when Father introduced me to his Talisker, back when I had only sipped a bit of wine at the dinner table. It was the day he decided I would learn to hunt.

"It will steady your hand," he had told me. "I don't expect you to get it the first time, but it's important you learn to focus. Focus is everything."

The therapist had told me that I used alcohol not to focus but to hide from my pain. "You have chosen this way of dealing with your life," she said. "It may be effective in the short run, but it won't work for long. You will, eventually, have to face the trauma or traumas that brought you here."

The short run had worked fine now for more than fifteen years, I thought, but I told her, "I didn't come here to solve a problem." When I had started with her, I was convinced that, since James had pushed me to go to therapy, the problem had been his, not mine. "I don't drink too much," I had protested.

"Denial is one of the hallmarks of excessive alcohol consumption," she said.

James used to ask me why I refused to see the effect it had on my system. Alcohol, he said, deadens your emotions. He couldn't understand why I needed to feel less, why I preferred stupor to clarity. The therapist's words about my drinking pretty much echoed James's.

Of course, I never told him that I had stopped going. There was no point. I wasn't ready then to deal with my grief over Scoop's death, nor to acknowledge that the little dog's sad demise was not the only reason for my needing the glue booze supplied to stay together enough to continue my day-to-day life.

Now, I was beginning to think he had been right. A couple of times recently, I had lost consciousness when I was drinking. And there had been those terrible mornings when I woke up in a strange bed with someone I didn't remember, after I had gone to one of the nearby bars and allowed some man to buy me drinks.

I had no idea what time it was. My phone had quit during the night, and I must have lost my watch somewhere. Looking up at the pale, overcast sky, I decided it was close to noon. A civilized time for a drink.

It was time to go back into my mother's room.

Whatever warmth the fireplace provided did not reach this room. The knob felt frozen, rigid, but it turned. The broken window would explain the cold air that hit me as I opened the door, like icy fingers wrapping themselves around my face. It was a shock to see the shards of glass glinting over the pink and blue duvet cover.

I stood still, listening for shrieks, or thumping, but there was nothing. As if making up for the eruptions of last night, the room was very quiet. Only a part of the window lay on the bed, the rest was still attached to the larger pane that had held on through the storm.

Three years ago, I had helped Mother pull that new duvet cover on, the two of us stuffing the corners of the duvet in first, then pulling down on the cotton cover until we could hold the corners, lift them, and shake the cover down. I remembered my mother laughing when she saw how much higher my side was than hers. "I must have shrunk," she announced. "I've been taller than you for at least thirty-five years. I keep regressing. Now, if this keeps going, I'll be able to sit on your knee and you can tuck me in early in the evening."

She wasn't laughing anymore.

I remembered gathering up her photographs and taking them to the kitchen counter, yet there were still a lot strewn all over the pink and blue cover, wet, peeling, and decomposing between my fingers. I picked them up, gently, carefully, by the edges, but even the edges crumpled. There was dark blood over some of them, more near the pillows where I thought I hadn't tried to pick them up last night in the dark. Her drawers were all at least half out and at an angle. Her blouses and nighties were layered in neat rows, but they were all wet, the bottom drawer almost empty. The small blue vase lay on the floor, it wasn't broken, though its dead flowers had scattered, soaked into the wet carpet. Her perfume bottle had also fallen, but its cap had remained in place. The smell of lilies of the valley was gone, but there was that other smell, maybe grown even more intense. More musty, wild. I knew I had to look for its source, but I loathed the idea of encountering some long-dead thing. It was bad enough to see the dead squirrel at Father's cabin. It reminded me of all his dead things on the island, all the animals and birds he had slaughtered. And Scoop. There were others I hadn't wanted to think about. Owls. Foxes. Canada geese. Minks. Two trumpeter swans that had recently been released from the Wye Marsh Wildlife Centre. When one of them hadn't obliged him by dying after being shot, he took the boat to where it was struggling and cut its throat. "There is no sense in bringing these back. When something is extinct, it should stay extinct."

That was another time I had wept and he had locked me into the basement with the dead and dying mice.

I had never volunteered to extract dead mice from the traps. Our Father used to do that every spring and even after he moved out of our old house—I hesitate to call it our "family home"—he still checked all the traps at the cottage. None of us offered to relieve him of the task. As no one asked him whether he was comfortable coming here long after he had stopped living with us in the city. He and Mother avoided being alone in the same space, and rarely exchanged words, but there was never a debate about his right to continue to be here when he wished. The one obvious change had been his moving his things to the cabin closest to the lake. He didn't mind using the outhouse—"It's built for comfort, not for style," he said. And he didn't need the shower, he enjoyed washing in the lake. "It's all the same water, isn't it?"

I did ask Mother about his coming and going exactly as he had always done, as if he owned the place, and she smiled. "That's because he does," she said. "It's still his place," she added. "He paid for it."

Father had come to the cottage only once that summer.

"If you got a divorce, it could be your place," I said.

She didn't reply.

"You're not getting a divorce?" I pushed.

"Don't see any need for that," she said. "If he wants to live somewhere else, that's his choice. If he still wants to come here on occasion, I am fine with that. He has always liked it up here."

"So have you."

"Not as much as he has. Besides, I have always traveled during the summers." That was true, she used to travel and give lectures and speeches, but those past couple of years, her regular invitations had been late arriving, or not arriving at all. I had no idea when we had this conversation, but it was after we had known about the dementia, so maybe three summers ago. She told me she assumed others had noticed she was no longer as fascinating as she used to be, and she wasn't surprised by the absence of invitations.

She told me how hard it was to find alternate words or phrases for ones that refused to come, that sometimes no alternative presented itself and she would have to stop and wait for that elusive word to drop into her mouth and how often it didn't. Hard to find an alternative for "Russia," for example, or "*détente*," she said.

"It will happen to you, too," she told me. "It's inevitable, like dying."

A few days ago I was telling a story to my editor about a skunk that had invaded the path between my apartment building and the entrance to the subway. A funny story I thought would distract her from asking me more questions about the next Kitty book. It was too soon to tell her that I was getting tired of the intrepid juvenile adventurer and thought I should start looking for something else to do with my life. But for some reason, I had forgotten the word *skunk* and found myself floundering about helplessly until I gave up and said, "the black-and-white animal that squirts stink at you." The editor laughed and said, "Skunk."

I had thought of my mother, whose brain had been so much more active than mine, yet she now had dementia. I could not imagine her becoming another person, one who, in front of an audience of a few hundred expectant faces, forgot what she had been talking about, had to stop and search her computer for clues, then resume as if there had never been a problem. Would she have easily replaced *skunk* with *smelly raccoon* and gone on with her story? She was so much more self-assured than I was. Surely, she would have been able to cover her anxiety better than I could.

Why is it we never get over our mothers?

I looked into the bottom drawer, noticed that whatever had held it fast had let go during the storm, a wad of wet paper, some white sheets folded over, with the type soaked through. Something small, dark, and solid was wrapped tight inside the papers. I thought she must have placed it intentionally at the back of the bottom drawer where no one would be looking for it. I took it to the puzzle table and tried to unwrap it to see what was inside, but it resisted, and I didn't want to risk the paper disintegrating. I could just read the heading on the top page without opening the wad. It was fancy brown lettering, official, a document she would have wanted to keep hidden. The words I could read were "Last Will and Testament." Presumably hers. I knew already that Gina was her sole executor, but I assumed that the two of us would get equal shares in whatever she had left at the end of her life.

Presumably there would be a copy somewhere. No one keeps only one copy of such a document. She would, of course, have had it drawn up when she was diagnosed. She would have assumed that she might not have time to do it later, after the disease had taken hold of her mind.

She had talked with both Gina and me about a "Do Not Resuscitate" order, but that was a separate document. Only two pages covering the possibility of her feeling unbearable pain and the "foreseeability" of her not sufficiently imminent death. She had met with two doctors she assumed would recommend her for "the final journey" when the time came. I wasn't there, but she told me that they didn't think she qualified yet. "Silly to call it a 'journey' when chances are you're lying supine in your bed and the only foreseeable journey will be to a slab in the funeral home," she had said. She was not in pain and was well enough to conduct a perfectly logical conversation. She was concerned that by the time she did qualify, it would be too late. That was why she wanted us each to get a large supply of Ativan.

She suggested that we tell our respective doctors that we were going on a long trip with our father on the Siberian Express and we were bizarrely anxious about it. She said if the doctors suggested a different kind of pill for our impending condition, to tell them that Ativan was the only one that worked, that we had tried some others, and they all had side effects. Heart palpitations with one, terrible diarrhea with another, and the herbal concoctions never worked. We had—yes, it was against the rules but we were on a trip with our father, far from home—tried one of her Ativans and it had worked brilliantly. We were to say that we would be on this trip for thirty days—we needed at least thirty pills. Gina's doctor, who was busy delivering someone's baby, sent the prescription directly to the pharmacy. My doctor insisted on seeing me in person and tried to dissuade me from taking Ativan. It was a strong sedative. It could make you feel confused or depressed. Thirty days could make you an addict. Fortunately, she answered an urgent call from someone with a situation much graver than mine, and while she stood with her back to me, talking on her phone, I took a couple of sheets of her prescription pad, and wrote myself two prescriptions, in case one was not enough.

"It's strange," Mother had said with remarkable clarity. "We exist in a world where advice books occupy the pinnacles of our bestseller lists. Did you know that more than a hundred million people have bought *Everything You Always Wanted to Know About Sex*? And do you know how many millions of copies of *You Can Heal Your Life* have been sold?"

No. I didn't.

"Fifty million. You would think that some savvy publisher would have commissioned a self-help book on how to die well. Or some enterprising writer would have written and self-published it. Not all of us want to heal our lives or are anxious to know everything about sex. But everyone, without exception, everyone dies, and a lot of us would like to do it without the fuss and the bother of lying about in excruciating pain."

"I thought you couldn't commit suicide if you're Catholic," I said.

"I don't consider it suicide," Mother said. "It's self-care and charity. You cannot inflict yourself on others if you have ceased to be the person you used to be. And you cannot commit a mortal sin if you are now somebody other than the Catholic kid who used to go to confession and take Holy Communion once a week."

"But you haven't changed much," I told her. "You are only becoming more forgetful."

She shook her head. "God will know the difference," she said.

Getting her the pills had been a solution to alleviate her concerns at the time. Unlike Gina, I had usually been good with practical solutions to problems. Not the kinds of problems the cottage had just sprung at me, but the kind I encountered on a usual day.

For some weeks after, we didn't deliver the pills. I kept mine, still sealed in two plastic bottles, on my desk. Gina said she had put hers in a brown paper bag at the top of her tallest bookcase where Mel couldn't reach it. She no longer had to worry about William.

We gave them to Mother only after her two doctors recommended that she should move to an assisted-living space. Assisted living, Mother had said, is assisted dying. "No one enters one of these hellholes with a view to 'living,' assisted or otherwise, in any sense at all that the word . . ." She had been searching for the appropriate ending to that statement for a while, and when I supplied "means," she nodded. A few moments later, she said, "Encompasses. I like that word better." Amazing, for a woman who was losing her memory of words.

Her memory had started to deteriorate sharply two years before that, when she moved from the house to the condo. It was spacious, two bedrooms, and there was that view I was sure she would like. Surprising, since she had been so fond of her lifetime collection of things, that she hadn't wanted most of them. They belonged to a different stage of her life, she said, and she didn't seem to care which pictures we put up. She had wrapped a few of Eva's tiny sculptures into tissue paper and stuffed them into her large purse next to her secret stash of Ativans. She didn't want her formal clothes, she said her formal days were over.

Less than a year later, she started to stay in her bed till late in the day and Nellie complained she couldn't talk her into going to the balcony on sunny days. During the summer, she wouldn't go to the island unless we were there, and I hadn't gone for almost two years. She said she didn't like being alone. She had begun to spend more and more of her time in her bedroom. Sometimes she forgot how to find her door, and Nellie told me she got lost on her way to the bathroom. "It's hard to get used to a new place," I had told Nellie.

"That's what she says, too," Nellie said, "but being in a new place is not the problem. It's the dementia."

I had booked her into Fairview for last December. The woman who saw us when we visited was pleasant in a hushed sort of way that I associated with people determined to show sympathy, or officials at funerals. She showed us the room with a view that we had been told would be available for Mother if she (or we) could wait till the end of February. It was spacious, sunny, a bit too warm, but the windows opened. The smell of disinfectant would evaporate in an hour or two. I didn't ask what had happened to the previous occupant. Gina did and she got the answer we deserved.

I shouldn't have been out of town when Nellie took her. Fortunately, I am not Catholic enough to be "blessed" with permanent feelings of guilt, but I had been around Catholics since I was born—both Mother and Eva kept their crosses and rosaries—that I did have twinges of it every time I thought about Mother.

Then, I had waited for a couple of weeks before I screwed up the courage to visit.

23

THERE IS SOMETHING PROFOUNDLY DISTURBING
about discovering that nothing was as it had seemed at the time. I think
this is particularly true of what you think you were observing and experi-
encing when you were a child.

I had thought of the cottage as a happy place. I loved the long warm
summers when we were growing up, the swimming, the tennis, the evenings watching the sunsets, struggling with the boats, the sudden storms,
the sound of rain on the roof, our experiments with cooking, Father trying to light the barbecue (when it didn't work on the fourth try, he threw
it out and then bought a new one), his sawing wood, the opening weekend with all of us pitching in. I even enjoyed the music. Both the classical
and the country.

Well, apart from the scything and Father's obsession with hunting, it
had all seemed idyllic. Even the debates over which music was played, the
arguments around the dining room table, the boyfriends' first experiences
of the family, watching our father giving them the gears, it had seemed
like fun, all part of summer. In hindsight, those summers were short, as
all summers are in the North, and there was a frantic pace about our daily

activities, an anxiety to cram in as much as possible because everything would be over too soon.

But I now knew that the cottage hadn't been a happy place for at least fifteen years. Perhaps it had never been happy. Those old photographs showed a couple who had been disengaged for a long time, and a few showed a scowling me and a puffed-up Gina. Father had enrolled us both in a tennis camp and on summer afternoons in the city, I delighted in beating her at tennis. Her inept fumbling and waddling to reach the ball made her an easy prey to my drop shots and forehand smashes. I used to laugh when she fell. Now, looking at those photos, I realized that I had been desperately jealous of her so-much-easier relationship with our mother and how proud I had been of my thin, muscular body. I had been so pleased when our father remarked that Gina, unlike me, had the wrong shape for tennis. She had cried in her bed that night, but then she cried a lot when we were in our early teens. How aware would she have been of her ballooning weight? How aware had she been that Father's remark had been meant for her, not for me? That he had intended to make her feel wretched? As his remarks about William had been aimed at Gina's failure to produce a perfect son?

Hadn't I noticed before that the only pictures of William in the cottage had been taken when he was a toddler? Before anyone knew that there was something wrong with him?

Even our parents' wedding photos, if I looked at them closely, showed two people reluctantly inhabiting rather than sharing the same space. In the photo in which Father had loosened his Harvard tie, he seemed to be staring into the distance, or just off to the right of the camera. Who had been standing there? Whom was he staring at?

Mother's voice, when she talked about the meaning of the flowers in her hair: Why the irony? Had she thought that he was only going through the motions?

I looked at the wedding pictures again. My mother's parents were standing to one side, close to the makeshift altar ("Anglican," of course). They looked like cardboard cutouts, arms at their sides, heads up, facing the camera, terribly uncomfortable, and there was that one shot where my grandmother, her mouth turned down at the corners, was looking across at the other side of the wedding party at someone, maybe the same person Father had been looking at in the other photo. Everyone must have noticed. She may even have said something. Her mouth was slightly open. She seemed close to speaking.

"What was she mad about?" I had asked Mother.

"She wasn't mad," she said. "That was her usual expression." She laughed. "Like yours."

They had disapproved of the marriage, she told me, and, looking closely at the photos, that was clear from their expressions. There had always been that problem with his not being Catholic.

But who had she been glaring at?

Mother said she wasn't glaring.

I scanned the pictures one after the other and put them in order of where everyone was for the group shots. That corner, off to the side, was where Eva had stood with that short potbellied man who may have been her husband. He had dark-rimmed glasses, his hair was plastered down, flat on top, his face was shiny, and he seemed not to fit his clothes. His belly poked out of his jacket. With his slicked-down hair, he looked sweaty. It must have been a hot day. Eva was pale, with long, lush hair over her shoulders. She stood far enough from him that their bodies did not touch.

As I studied him now, he seemed quite familiar. Not those glasses. Less hair. But where had I seen him?

I had no idea when Eva's husband had died, but by the time of the anniversary party, our mother had labeled her a widow. I had no memory of his ever coming to the island with Eva. My earliest memories of her are at the cottage drifting in and out of Mother's room and always keeping the door closed when she was inside. I could hear them whispering but couldn't make out the words. Often she drove up with Mother and stayed in the smaller cabin. After Father moved out of the family cottage, she started to occupy his room. Father and Eva rarely talked. But I have an early memory of her walking down to the water's edge with him, her arms behind her back, and his talking with her, softly and earnestly, his head bobbing as he emphasized words. When I asked what they had been talking about, she said, "Nothing."

There was always something strange about her. Soft-spoken, she moved so quietly that I never heard her entering a room. When I was still painting, I would be working on one of my layered watercolors and suddenly there she would be, standing behind me, leaning forward over my shoulder. She wouldn't say anything. Her smile could be read any way you chose to interpret it. When I was a kid, I thought it had been encouraging, that she liked what I was doing, but, later, I thought it could have been dismissive. She hadn't thought I was good enough.

I hadn't known then that Mother had wanted to be an artist. She had taken classes at the Avenue Road School, and Eva, it seems, had encouraged her to think that she, too, had real talent. I wondered whether that was true, or if Eva had been flattering her because she liked to be flattered. She had always craved reassurance, and her academic work rarely supplied as much as she needed. For such a person, the loss of her memory had to be fearsomely painful. Eva was, Mother said, "a real artist." Her tiny bronze sculptures had been bought by celebrities. "Elizabeth Taylor has one. The prime minister gave one to the queen for her Jubilee celebrations." That was the story Mother told. I had never read or heard about anyone famous owning an Eva Witmer piece, and her reputation at the art school, where she had taught, was more for aloofness than for success. I know, I had asked someone who had studied there. But I had never been curious enough to check what her sculptures fetched. I didn't believe the Elizabeth Taylor and prime minister stories. I thought Mother had invented them to send me back to my painting, suggesting that if Eva could be successful at art, why not me. Now, of course, I no longer thought that.

Now, I am not even sure that anyone had actually told me that Eva's husband was dead. Or that she ever had a husband. It's just that I had seen someone sort of with her in the wedding photos and there was no one with her at the anniversary party.

Why did our parents decide to have that big anniversary party? "Your mother's idea," Father had said. "She likes big statements, and there is no bigger statement than inviting a bunch of people, some of whom we barely know, to celebrate that after twenty years, we are still together. All evidence to the contrary."

I thought, at the time, that our mother wanted to show that, no matter what everyone thought, she did, still, care for him. She hadn't mentioned his "dalliances" till after the party. It was many years after he had quit architecture, a decision they had argued about so fiercely, I thought they would divorce. Or she would leave him. She didn't, and his choice of real estate seemed to have been the right one. He was happier and very much richer.

The cake was wheeled in on a covered table. The music stopped (it had been neither opera nor country: it was jazz) and we all stared at the melting wax until Mother stood up and raised her glass to Father and everyone cheered. Then, as he leaned over the cake to blow out the candles, she waved her glass over the wax couple in the center. When they fell, she reached in, I thought to set them upright again but, instead, squashed them, one after the other, face-first into the icing. She was laughing still when she told Father that he should have made a wish. He was standing near the open door. He didn't come closer even after she squashed the candle-people into the icing and he didn't say anything to her or to anyone else. He smiled. "I already have," he said.

The disaster of the cake was not the only scene that night. It was not even the strangest, or the most memorable. I remembered it now with such clarity because I had been looking at a photo of the cake with the candle-people still standing.

Gina and I had agreed that by far the most memorable event that night was our mother pulling the long white tablecloth off the table. The glasses and plates flew in all directions, guests tried to jump up and out of the way of flying cutlery, the plates falling into their laps, some landing on the floor as the guests leapt away from the table. Eva, who had somewhat recovered after her nap over her plate, had tried to stop the whole thing, but Mother shook off her hand. They stood facing the shocked dinner guests—flecks of food on their jackets, some with plates in their laps. The glasses had flown farthest because, Mother explained later, they were not real glass, they were plastic.

"Fake," she said. She was still laughing. "The thing with the table-cloth," she said, "it's a party trick. You do it so everything lands back where it came from. Look it up online if you want, there are lots of people who have done it. Even clowns. Often clowns. And I tell you it works. Except perhaps for the cake. I haven't seen it done with a cake before, but nothing ventured . . ."

Father had remained standing, he watched everyone scramble to remove the spilled food from their clothes, a few of them were embarrassed, trying to pretend it was some sort of joke they hadn't quite managed to follow, waiting for an explanation that, other than Mother's declaration about a party trick, never came. Nor did she apologize.

There was some forced laughter, Mother thanking everyone for coming as they hurried to grab their coats. Since she went to the door of the restaurant to say goodbye, most of them made fumbling attempts to hug her. Still smiling, our father stayed back and waved at the guests as they escaped. I was sorry that the photographer hadn't managed to capture that grand finale to Mother's idea of a celebration.

It had been obvious that Gina and I were no longer needed. I wasn't sure we were ever really needed, then or before, other than as an audience for our parents' acts of reciprocal, low-key nastiness. The magic trick with the tablecloth had been Mother's most obvious attack on Father's sense of dignity, if you could call his seeming indifference dignity. Though our mother had said he was aggressive, it was not a side we had seen much, except, I suppose, killing things on the island. That must have shown his aggressive side.

Later, she told me about his "dalliances," that he had "women on the side, he had always had them. Most of them didn't matter because they lasted only a week or so, but there were a few stragglers who stayed longer." When I had asked her how she knew, she said it hadn't been much of a secret. Everybody knew. He was famous for his little affairs. The periwinkles he had planted were, she thought, harbingers of a new affair.

I assume she would not have been surprised when he set up a separate household in another part of the city with Gladys. I was. No longer just a dalliance, and his setting up a whole gym just for her was certainly a sign of her planning to stay.

"You two," Mother had said to us at the party, dismissively, "may as well leave. The show, as you can see, is over."

The cake had managed somehow to dodge the fate of the other plates and made it to the restaurant kitchen, a little worse for wear, but almost whole, though it had sort of collapsed in the middle, and the icing and candles drooped off its sides. Happy to be released, we ate some (it tasted delicious) and packed more pieces into paper napkins to take home. We were both still hungry. Neither of us had eaten our dinner of overcooked chicken, chopped limp salad, and bland white rice with peas—a dish neither of us liked and our father had always hated. He called it "too Rosedale," meaning that it had been cooked for so long it had become tasteless.

When we left, the manager was talking quietly with our father (I assumed there would be no extra costs for the broken plastic glasses), the restaurant staff was cleaning up the considerable mess, and Mother and Eva had retreated to the bar for nightcaps. They were both laughing. I thought Eva was drunk again.

I was almost twenty-one, Gina a year younger, but that night we both felt like children. We were nursing memories of our own, aches we had never discussed. We walked home. Each of us alone. Both of us needed fresh air.

What I had found inexplicable was that our father came to the cottage the week after that disastrous reception. And continued to come, unexpectedly, every summer, even after he had bought himself the new house and traded us in for Gladys. I didn't know whether Gladys didn't come to the island because she had no desire to be with our family, or because she thought she couldn't. Since he didn't care what we thought about his new life, I doubted that her absence was the result of any sense of discretion on his part, or his desire to spare our mother the embarrassment. He had been cheerfully open about his new life and Gladys's role in it, even when we had visited once and found them naked in the hot tub. She hadn't bothered to cover up, continued to lean back, looking at us, a rolled towel under her head, her breasts flowing down on either side of her chest, one leg flat on the boards, the other knee slightly up displaying a thick thatch of hair. Father had a pleased look on his face, a small smile, as if he had been expecting us to stop by. He had certainly known that Gerry had picked us up and that we were in the house.

Gina shrieked, and we retreated quickly. We both had thought the sight had been too disgusting though later, the memory made us giddy with laughter. I thought that maybe our father's new house, his silly relationship with Gladys, Mother's dementia, and, of course, all that happened later, should have drawn Gina and me closer. We should have been able to repair the damage of our mutual jealousies. The therapist said I could still make it happen—if I wanted. But did I?

I didn't go to that house again until the day I had asked Gladys if she knew something about Father's whereabouts. I refused to believe he had simply vanished.

Our parents had, as far as we could remember, never shared a bedroom in our house. His bedroom had been fairly spartan, no soft coverings, blinds not curtains, polished floor, rough carpet, a single closet, and one square chest of drawers. His walls displayed photos of his real—or imagined—hunting expeditions. Her room was all pastels and throws, a Persian carpet, a long dressing table with a gilt-edged mirror, paintings, a soft wooden armoire from somewhere in Quebec, long drapes. We had seen him in her bedroom a few times early in the morning, carrying empty cups, but we hadn't seen her coming out of his room except when he wasn't there. I wondered whether she had been looking for something, but when I asked, she just shook her head. On the island, he had slept in his study.

Here, though there were many rooms to choose from, Gladys and Father shared a bedroom.

Another bizarre thing about his new house was his collection of clothes. When we were growing up, he had maybe four or five suits, all more or less the same color: gray. Maybe one of them had little black stripes in with the gray. His new life seemed to require blues and blacks, maroons, beiges and whites for the summer and bright green jackets and light blue pants for his travels. He must have had five hundred ties and at least fifty pairs of shoes, some with tassels on them. And a couple of dinner jackets. Gina thought it was Gladys's influence. I thought it was the company he kept. Less old-fashioned, more adventurous. Our father had never before been interested in clothes. Her own generous assortment of clothes joined his in the massive walk-in closet off their bedroom, hers on one side, his on the other, facing each other, with a full-length mirror at the end of the passage.

With such a wide choice, it would be impossible to figure out what he had worn when he disappeared.

24

CAREFULLY, USING ONLY THE TIPS OF MY FINGERS, I
unfurled the Last Will and Testament on the puzzle table. The small solid
thing I had felt before it fell out of the wrapping and rolled down into
my lap. It was the tiny memento Mother said she had kept from her trip
to Tahiti—where she had never been. A black salamander with startlingly
yellow spots, it was made of wood, chiseled to a smooth finish. It seemed
to be straining to lift its head high. I had read somewhere that the salamander's skin is poisonous. Obviously, it had some special significance
for her, since she had always kept it close, but when I had asked whether
she wanted to take it with her to Fairview, she asked, "What's the point?"
Then added after a few moments, "Now?"

I tried to read the words of the will, but it was difficult with the letters running into one another. Water had turned some of it into the sort
of pâpier-mâché Gina and I had once used to make our Halloween masks.
When I tried to separate the pages, they started to dissolve between my
fingers. But there was enough of the first page left that I could see the
word *wife*.

I took a swig from my glass and strode back into Mother's room. It was very quiet now, hushed, as if it had been waiting for me, so still that I began to think that I had imagined the furious noises of last night. I focused on putting one foot in front of the other, gently, avoiding bits of glass and twigs, making sure I didn't step on the scattered pictures that must have dropped onto the carpet.

A scraping sound near the broken window.

A face, pale, grim, hollow-eyed, stared straight at me.

"Shit!" I yelled at it, my hand bashing the chest of drawers that had been so reluctant to divulge their contents. "What the . . ." Noise was coming from the floor on the other side of her bed next to the broken window. But that face!

It took a few moments of petrified silence to remember that there was a small mirror hanging on the wall between her windows and that the face staring at me with such horror was my own. My eyes were swollen and dark-ringed, with those deep lines under the eyes—but where had my eyebrows gone? Their place was bare, like my mother's, but I had never plucked them, though Mother used to tell me to. She would say they looked like a man's, bushy and curly—had I seen those old black-and-white movies with Groucho Marx? If I bought myself a stick-on mustache, I would look like Groucho.

Why would she say such things? I had once asked her.

"It's for your own good," she told me. "You'll want to replace James one of these days, though God knows you can't do that if you see only librarians and kids who read your little kids' books." I didn't bother to tell her that I wrote for teenagers or that some librarians were men. "If you had kept up your art, you would have met interesting, artistic types, who knows, maybe even a wealthy collector. It's the one talent you had and you decided to fritter it away."

The mirror was angled upward, broken in half, the bottom still attached to the frame but the top gone, so that my forehead and most of my eyebrows had vanished but appeared as I lowered my head. A little closer and I could see remnants of those offensive eyebrows. "When you are older, they will be grizzled," Mother had said. Her own eyebrows had been plucked and "groomed," as she called it, by a professional. They described neat little arcs a bit higher up than they should have been, lending her face a somewhat quizzical look, halfway between surprise and disbelief.

We stared at each other, my reflection and I, still shaking but with a sense that the room had returned to normal, or as normal as it could be since last night, when those noises drove me out of here. I held my breath, the better to listen to whatever it was that had been in her closet, my hand slowly letting go of the chest of drawers that I hadn't realized I had been grasping. The stench of something wild, and could it be chalk? And still the decomposing thing. The room was very quiet again. As if we were both holding our breaths, waiting.

In the end, I was the one who gave in. My breath returned with a rush as I stepped closer to the closet. The source of those infernal noises thrashed against the plywood walls and screamed. It was a desperate, high-pitched shriek that sounded both frightened and threatening. Last night it hadn't occurred to me that the thing itself could be as terrified as I was. Now, with light streaming into the room, I could see through the open closet doors: the muddy feathers, the bloody head, and two yellow eyes looking at me, furiously flapping its wings, exhausted, frantic to escape. A seagull. Its neck feathers were pink, blood-splattered, as was my mother's floor, her shoes, the long dress that had fallen, and the ceramic pot broken in half with Scoop's ashes spilling out. There was chalky green bird shit everywhere.

It took a while for me to notice that one of the seagull's legs was bent at an unnatural angle. That would be why it couldn't escape its corner. Perhaps it couldn't walk, or it had lost its sense of balance.

I was thinking that I could try to urge it to go outside and hope it would find its way to the lake, then I remembered the time when James attempted to save a seagull with a hook stuck in its beak. It had been circling our dock for some days, unable to feed, or to fly. The protruding hook was preventing it even from drinking. The day had been hot and James had been determined to let the bird drink. He had waded into the lake, grabbed it by its back and folded wings, its head safely away from his face. He suggested that I hold the bird while he used long-handled pliers to remove the hook. It was hard to transfer the bird to me. It fought with its feet and its beak, tried to extricate its wings while we had it out of the water.

When James turned it around and pushed the pliers towards its beak, it struck out at his eyes. Luckily, its neck wasn't long enough to reach, but it did cut a nasty gash on James's chin. "No damned gratitude," he had mumbled, holding his bleeding chin with one hand as he wrenched the bird out of my hands and tossed it back into the lake.

The next day its corpse floated to the shore. Its eyes had been pecked out.

"It's what they do," Father had said, "always go for the eyes. They are mindless beasts with only one purpose: dispose of garbage."

He rarely shot seagulls. He said he hated to see their dead bodies in the water.

I would have to get the gull out of the cottage before nightfall, I wouldn't be able to sleep if I had to listen to its thrashing about. Although it must have come in through the broken window, the gap didn't look wide enough to allow it to escape. I got a pair of my mother's rubber gloves from the kitchen (they were too tight, her hands were more delicate than mine), climbed over the bed, and pushed the long cracked shards outward. A couple of them slid down and smashed on the deck. The gull hopped a little way out of its closet and glowered at the window, its bloody head turned to one side. I didn't think it was encouraged by what it saw because it retreated. I thought of throwing one of my mother's blankets over it, wrapping it up to take it outside, but the sight of its sharp yellow beak dissuaded me. I went back to the kitchen counter, poured another glass of scotch, and decided to sort wet photographs and dissolving papers. My second bottle, but the first one hadn't been full when I opened it, and it had been a stressful time. The therapist had said something about making sure I didn't seek relief from my anxieties by drinking or popping tranquilizers. But the therapist had never been in a storm in Georgian Bay and she had never seen the sorry cadaver of a much-loved dachshund.

Perhaps the bird would try the window when it couldn't see me.

There was a clump of old black-and-white photographs with deckle edges featuring clusters of people I didn't recognize. There was a man with a fedora, a woman in a tidy belted dress and lace-up high heels, another woman in what could have been a 1940s evening dress, and two small boys with tricycles. In another, the small boys were on the floor playing with blocks and grinning at the photographer, and in a garden with a water fountain and a white dog, a man in overalls—he could have been the same man who was in the other photo, but here he didn't have a fedora and was holding a spade.

It occurred to me that neither of our parents talked about their own parents. When I asked what they looked like, both Father and Mother said I should look at the wedding pictures because, of course, both sets of their parents had been part of the wedding party. She pointed out her mother in the picture, the one where she is staring, or glaring, at someone at the other end of the group, the person I thought was Eva.

"No," she had said when I asked whether her father had given her away, "we decided not to have a traditional wedding. We went to Bermuda to get married. Your father liked the Coral Beach Club, and it was perfect. There was this large outdoor patio with a bar, overlooking the beach, rolling waves, cicadas, tree frogs, the whole tropical experience without the wet heat and the sunburn. Bermuda is cooler than the rest of the Caribbean, and the club has large white umbrellas over all the tables and imitation marble paving to keep your feet cool."

"But all our grandparents came?" I insisted.

"Obviously," she said with her usual look of detachment.

"Did they approve?"

"Approve?" Mother seemed amused by my question. "They must have. We were such a perfect couple." I was too young when we had this conversation to detect a note of irony in how she stressed "perfect."

"Haven't you seen your parents since the wedding?" I persisted.

"Not very often," she said. "They were Catholic, as I am. They would have preferred I marry someone who shared our faith. But they came to our house when you were little."

"I have no recollection of ever meeting them."

"Well, I said you were little."

The story was they had died before I was four. In an accident. Or separate accidents. "What are the chances?" I had asked Gina after we heard about the accidents.

It seemed odd that other children had lots of grandparents, and Gina and I had none. Our father's parents had moved to New Zealand. Too far to travel to meet them, he had told us and too far for them to come before they died. He also had a cousin in New Zealand. I found his name—Jordan Bogdan—at the top of the first page of a book about New Zealand, all lovely scenic photographs of mountains and meadows. There were no photos in the book that included people. I looked Jordan up in the Auckland online directory and called him after Father had disappeared. He seemed surprised to hear from me. "We lost touch years ago," he said in what I assumed was a broad local accent. "It's the distance, you know."

I did know. I had lost touch with the only person I had been genuinely fond of at school. Annabel. The two of us used to retreat to the art room during the afternoons when the other girls played basketball or soccer. It's not that we couldn't have played sports, we just chose not to. That decision gave us a sense of superiority we otherwise couldn't lay claim to.

We were mediocre at sports and mediocre students. But we both loved art. The art teacher gave us paints and charcoal for sketching but otherwise left us alone to experiment.

After we had graduated, she decided she wanted to live in France "where real artists lived," and she asked me to come along but I stayed. I liked her art but I didn't like my own. At first she wrote me from Paris, telling me about all the wonderful people she had met there, the cafés full of artists, and that she was taking lessons from some guy she said had already succeeded in selling his work. She carried on writing for a while, though I had stopped replying. I found I had nothing exciting to tell her. She wouldn't have been interested in Kitty's adventures or my readings at libraries.

Jordan Bogdan took his time checking my credentials. He was suspicious that I was about to scam him, ask for cash or a money transfer. When I explained that Father had disappeared and we wondered whether he might have gone to New Zealand, he protested that he had heard nothing from his cousin for more than thirty years, and that would make him about the least likely person for Father to visit, or for him to know where our father was.

At the end of the conversation, he asked me to let him know if his cousin had died. I thought it odd that he hadn't asked me to let him know when our father was found alive. If he was found alive.

Mother had a brother in California. I had found a dark-haired man in one of the wedding photos who seemed to resemble Mother—the same rounded shoulders, the oval face, the way he held his head to one side, as if trying hard to listen. He had an open-necked shirt and no jacket. He stood near her and he didn't look into the camera. He was looking at her. I took the picture out on the deck, into the light. Yes, he was looking at her, and he had an odd expression on his face: disbelief, I thought. But that could have been my interpretation. The longer I looked at the wedding photos the less likely I thought my parents' marriage had been a good idea, and the more I remembered of the two of them together, at any time, in any place, the less I thought their marriage had ever worked.

I counted twenty people in the wedding pictures. They must have been close enough friends to spend the money on a trip to Bermuda, and a few of them had been invited again to celebrate the anniversary. Then, the men had less hair, the women were sturdier. A couple of men had acquired new wives and one of the women had a new husband. Eva was the only one who had come alone.

I thought that if they had stayed friends for twenty years, some of them might still be friends and one of them could know where our father had gone, assuming he had gone somewhere on his own.

I had spent some time looking online for the Donavans, only to discover that they were both dead. The Johnsons said, sadly, they had lost touch with our parents, though Mr. Johnson said he had done quite well with one of our father's investment schemes, the Wilson development, but he was now retired and very careful with his money. He didn't take any "flyers" on new developments. He said he hadn't seen or heard from Father in at least five years. He wouldn't go into details about the Wilson thing because, he said, it was confidential and, besides, it wasn't relevant to wherever our father had decided to go. He said that he was certain Bogdan (he called our father only by his surname) would reappear when it suited him. He was not the sort of man who would just vanish. Kovacs said he wouldn't be surprised if our father had moved to the Bahamas or the Canary Islands. They had more favorable tax treatments for men like him. His tone clearly disapproved of tax dodgers.

I had spread most of the damp pictures out on the puzzle table when the seagull hopped out of Mother's room. I had been certain I had shut her door but maybe with everything going on around the cottage, I had forgotten. The seagull couldn't have opened the door. It was hopping on one yellow foot, the other was still hanging at a slight angle, backward. It had stretched out its wing on the same side. The wing swayed out, then in, as the bird hopped toward me. Was it looking at me or at the screen door? Hard to tell with birds, their eyes are on either side of their heads, but there was no doubt it was moving in my direction. Slowly, I stepped away from the table and its direct path to the door. It flapped both its wings and squawked, hopping, thrashing, and almost crashing into the puzzle table before it righted itself and whammed into the screen.

I should have opened it when I had a chance. Now, I had to back up, go out to the deck through the door by the dining table to open the living room door from the outside while the bird was thudding against it from the inside. I slid along on my bare feet, trying to avoid the bits of debris, careful not to make any noise, or a sudden movement, keeping an eye on it all the time, in case it discovered the other door and came after me. I was almost at the door, reaching for the handle to pull it open, when I saw the second bird. It was standing on the deck balustrade, feet planted, neck, head, and menacing yellow beak stretched forward, its red-rimmed yellow eyes looking at me. There was no question this time: the bird looked at me, intently, focused on my face, as if daring me to make another move.

I didn't. I wondered whether it saw me as a threat or as potential food. It stretched up its neck and cawed at the sky, once, twice, and flapped its wings. Meanwhile, the bird in the living room was going crazy against the screen door and it occurred to me that if I didn't open it, the screen would be shredded and the inside bird would land on the deck with the door-frame and bits of screen under it. I slid my hand closer to the handle and pushed the door away from me. The bird on the balustrade let out a shriek and launched itself up onto the roof, giving me a chance to yank open the living room door. The inside bird flapped out of the opening, its head and wings already outside, its broken leg dragging behind. It yanked itself all the way out as I backed away. Jumped in the dining area door and slammed it behind me loudly enough to bring the seagull down from the roof to inves-tigate. They were staring at each other when I raced to shut the living room door and then went back to the puzzle table.

My hand was shaking so much I almost dropped the whiskey bottle when I poured more into my glass. I was surprised to see the bottle was half empty.

Had the second gull been waiting for its mate to come out of the cottage? Do seagulls mate for life? I would check that when I had access to the internet. If they mated for life, would they defend each other when they were attacked? I remembered the dead body of the seagull James had tried to save floating into shore. We assumed that it had been killed by other gulls because its beak had been wedged open and it couldn't fight them off. It had also been weakened by lack of food and water. Perhaps it hadn't had a mate to protect it.

The two gulls were still nearby, one back on the railing, the other on deck. The one that had been in my mother's room was listing sideways, one wing still not at the same level as the other. It must have been using it as a crutch because of its broken leg. Its mate flew back up to the roof and walked about, making a lot of noise with its feet on the asphalt shingles. It was also growling from deep in its throat. It sounded impatient. The one on the deck flapped its wings but didn't take off. Instead, it retreated to the far end of the cottage, near my mother's broken window.

I don't know why exactly my sense of urgency about making a call to the marina had deserted me. It could have been the whiskey. The "deadening effect." I told myself it could wait while I looked at the will. Mother had been very clear when she asked me to find it. I had been surprised that she hadn't been concerned about Father's whereabouts, only his will, as if she had been sure that he was dead. How could she sound so composed and rational when she had been showing signs of advanced dementia for a few months, "such a rapid decline," the Fairview doctor had said, "which is unusual, but so little is known about this disease . . . ?"

To regain my own sense of balance, I opened *Sapiens* again. Since I couldn't remember where I had stopped reading the last time, I went to page 170, under the heading "The Global Vision." Harari was writing about a "practical perspective" of the "last few centuries," as if such a perspective really existed, but it might be useful to know how chili peppers made it into Indian food and how evolution got people to divide into "us" and "them."

25

I SPENT MUCH OF THE AFTERNOON TRYING TO decipher the slowly drying will. That the paper had become a malleable mass made the effort largely pointless, but for some reason—perhaps because the alternative was going to the top of the island, or worse, checking Father's cabin for signs that he had been here—I had fixated on this project. I had managed to flatten the lower parts of the papers, but they were still stuck together, and even gentle prying threatened to tear them apart, but at least I could now make out the words near the top.

Smudged but legible name right under "Testament": "Murray Bogdan." Our father had never bothered with a middle name, so I hadn't expected to see one now, but then, I hadn't expected to see his will coming out of our mother's dresser. What I had expected was her own will, the one that designated Gina as sole executor. She had told me once that she kept some of her private papers in a drawer at the cottage. I don't know why she hadn't treated Gina and me equally. She had no illusions about Gina being more reliable. I was the one, not Gina, she first told about her dementia. She had appointed both of us executors of her "Living Will," responsible for her personal care, and I believed she trusted me to ensure she would die before the disease robbed her of her ability to make decisions. She hadn't discussed with Gina what it meant to be Catholic when planning your own medically assisted death, only with me.

"If all else fails," she had said, "you'll have to do it with the pillow." We were on her condo balcony, watching one of the city's falcons circling in search of a slow pigeon. "You put it over my face and sit on it," she explained. "Pay no heed if I'm struggling, it's not me, it's animal instinct. You can read all about it." She had been composed and focused that day, giving me reasons to doubt our decision to consign her to Fairview.

She had been equally lucid when she told me to find Father's will. That was a couple of weeks after Gina and I thought he had vanished. She hadn't been concerned that he would show up and demand to know why anyone would think they had the right to dig into his personal affairs. She said a will was personal not only to the person who had made it but also to his beneficiaries. We had a right to know if he had made any changes. She said he hadn't given her a copy, but she remembered seeing it years ago.

Gina had offered to help search his house, his office, his car, and even Gerry's own home where, it turned out, our father had kept a few documents in a wooden box. These, he had designated as "sensitive." Gerry claimed he had no idea what they were, he had never looked. He was eager for them to be gone. "Mr. Bogdan," he said, "liked to keep secrets. I don't. Never have. I used to say to my wife not to share anything with me that she doesn't want me to tell someone. He sealed the envelopes, in case, he said, I would get curious, but I didn't. I know I would want to tell someone about them."

I doubt he would have understood what they were, had he opened them. They were details of complicated financial transactions between numbered companies, and many of them were in French. I had labored through one of them, only to find that it referred to some other transactions named but not included. Not only that, I told Gina, but all the transactions also had the same code name, though not a file number, as I would have expected with something obviously concocted by a lawyer. The English language documents included words like *Notwithstanding* and *Heretofore* at the beginnings of paragraphs consisting of lists of long numbers. There was even one *Hereinunder*, which was not even a word, and it appeared directly above the last set of numbers.

The code name was "Silver." I had looked up the name on business sites, in case it referred to a mining interest of our father's, but there was nothing named "Silver," and nothing on the long list of his securities that his broker had sent to our mother. Strange that, despite her memory loss, she was able to convince him that she was entitled to a copy. She had handed the paper to me soon after Gerry said he had last seen our father, and that was the same day that she started worrying about his will. I was surprised to hear that she had searched the broker's lists and even more surprised when she remarked that the Wilson project was no longer listed. For a person with impaired memory, she had no trouble remembering the Wilson development.

The will was not in any of the envelopes.

He didn't invest in mines, his broker told me when I visited him. "We didn't like mines," he said. "They are exhaustible."

I liked the way he said "we." "Exhaustible?"

"Sooner or later, they run out. We don't like predictably diminishing assets, you can't tell how long mining deposits will last. He didn't like gold, diamonds, or coal either. He didn't even like oil. Whatever Silver is, it couldn't be a mine."

Instead, Father's "holdings" were mostly in financials and pharmaceuticals. But the broker seemed eager to assure me that he managed only a small portion of our father's investments. He said he had a tiny corner of the whole—about fifteen million dollars—and, though he was proud of the "compound growth" of the account, he said Father claimed his other investments returned a much higher yield. He claimed he didn't know what the rest was invested in or with whom, though he knew enough to warn me about it.

"Downside of that kind of investment, Miz Bogdan, is it's high risk. You have to like living on the edge. You have to like the danger of it," he said. He was a cheerful man, jovial, with silvery hair and a round, open face. His suit looked expensive but not as expensive as our father's suits in his new walk-in closet. His office was designed to inspire confidence: airy, wood paneled, comfortable, with a couple of large paintings of summer scenery. "My kind of investing is safe and, I think, sound. I may not ride the highs but I also don't suffer the lows. You can pretty much count on the returns, Miz Bogdan." He consistently prefaced my name with "Miz," making sure I understood that he was all about feminism and dealing with both—or all—sexes equally. "I eliminate the headaches. Leaving you in peace to write your kiddy books and live your life as you please." He was obviously pitching me, in the event that our father didn't return, to leave with him whatever portion of my father's wealth came my way.

"Do you know anything about my father's other investments?" I asked.

There was a long pause before he answered with a definitive "No."

"Then how do you know they were high risk?"

"I was assuming. Wasn't it mostly real estate?"

I had called James, then. He already knew from the newspapers that Father had disappeared. It wasn't big news—page six, I think—because the police were sure he would turn up sooner or later. He may have had, they told us, reasons to take time away from the city.

Gladys, Gerry had told them, had grown demanding. There had been loud quarrels in expensive restaurants where the norm was hushed conversation and respect for other diners. The police had gathered testimony from witnesses that the arguments were nasty. A man was entitled to take time by himself, the lieutenant said. Had we heard that Gladys could become violent?

We hadn't. Neither Gina nor I had ever heard her even raise her voice to him, but we were rarely in his new house, and while we couldn't say we had observed them fighting, we were sure she would win any physical battle. Our father was a slim man, sinewy, his broad shoulders had become thinner, his chest narrower, and he had always had prominent collarbones. When we were little we used to put salt and pepper into his clavicles while he slept in the hammock. We thought he hadn't noticed until he hit me across the face, just once, but it stung. The hammock was usually at the far end of our property, strung up between two maples, close to the water. It was his private place where he could rest and drink his light summer drinks—scotch and soda—and get away from us. He often had an open book lying facedown across his belly. Mother used to say that he only ever used books to cover his belly; he didn't read them. "His only reading is the financial pages," she said. "He starts early with the *Financial Times* and ends late with the *Wall Street Journal.*"

But he had never discussed what he found in those papers, or whether he made his investment decisions based on what he had read. Mother was not interested in the market, and he was not interested in political thought or philosophy, only in the politics of the moment in countries he had some reason to visit. Our parents' debates were never about money.

Yet now, Mother had focused her remaining mental energy on persuading me to find his will.

James had read some of the same news—the *Economist,* the *Financial Times,* the *Wall Street Journal*—and that, James told me, gave the two of them something to talk about. They had often taken their conversations to the dock, and when I asked James why, he said they talked about things that wouldn't interest the rest of us.

When I told James that the police had a theory our father had gone away somewhere to escape Gladys, he laughed so hard, he started hiccupping. "That's the dumbest reason for anyone to vanish that I have ever heard. Gladys loved to be with your father. If she knows where he is, she would want to be there, too. Their relationship may have begun as a quasi-business arrangement, but it had become a lot more than that. As for their battles, she may have wanted more information than he had been willing to share, but no chance their fights could have become violent."

"What do you mean a business arrangement?" I asked.

"Just that. It had begun as business but it was no longer just that."

"How come you know that about her?" I asked, because I realized that I had known nothing, had never been interested enough to ask.

"They met on one of the islands. Nassau, I think. She'd been a close friend of one of your father's investors, a wealthy American, lives on Lyford Cay. He bought her a villa on Paradise Island."

"And the business arrangement? How?"

"In the beginning, she was supposed to be watching over the real estate purchases. Report on whether they were good quality, make sure they were resalable at good prices. Your father's new associates wanted to be sure their money was safe."

"That changed?"

"I think so. Surprising that she had fallen for your father."

"Surprising?"

"She's much younger, and given the world she moved in, she would have had more choices. Some of them may have had even more money than he has."

On the other hand, James hadn't found it the least bit surprising that Father would vanish. He had suggested I come to his condo on Bloor Street, where we could have a private discussion. I am not sure whether he thought I was with someone else when I called him. I wasn't. I hadn't been inclined to invite anyone else to take his place. He hadn't been back to my apartment since I bundled his stuff out the door.

His condo was the place he had bought when he imagined we would be married and that there would be room for children in our lives. I think it was the mention of children that had ended the relationship for me. Children brought back memories of my childhood—the uncertainty, the fear, the loneliness—and it had reminded me of William. Yet, because I was sure James would be able to help, I went.

His place was on the twenty-fifth floor, blue marble bar, designer furniture, flocked wallpaper, thick carpets, wall-to-wall bookcases, and a fabulous view all the way to the lake. I had been here before, but only in the dark, when I had met James for dinner, after we had broken up, and those times, we had headed straight to his bedroom. Now, the place made me uncomfortable. That he had bought this spacious apartment thinking that the two of us would live here, that there was a special room for a baby, added to my feeling of general misery.

I remembered pulling his ring off my finger when I had told him our engagement was off. Around four years ago. At the cottage.

"Off?" he had asked.

"I'm not ready for that kind of commitment."

"Or any other commitment?"

"Not sure what you mean," I said, holding the ring in my fist.

"It seems we're living in the same apartment. Should I consider that a temporary arrangement?"

I hadn't responded to that question because I hadn't thought about it yet. Somehow I had assumed that while he kept his own place, no matter how much time he spent at my grungy home, my place would remain mine. I shrugged, and James turned his back and marched out of the living room. It was becoming too dark for him to leave by boat. No one would take him to the marina. He spent that night sitting in my mother's chair on the dock waiting for daybreak. Sammy drove him in before the rest of us got out of bed.

He settled me into one of his Larkin leather club chairs—he told me he had bought two of them for "only" $10,000, one for each of us.

He mixed an excellent manhattan in a squat crystal glass, threw in a sliver of ice, and handed it to me. I was surprised because James used to lecture me about my drinking. When our relationship was new, he used to experiment with complicated cocktails, kept a range of ingredients in a glass cabinet that came with him when he moved into my apartment, but then he never replenished it when I emptied the bottles. All that was left at the end were lemon juice and a bottle of bitters. I included those in the stuff I left outside my door for him.

After preliminaries, which included his telling me I should eat more and rest more (meaning: you look gaunt and unkempt), he asked, "How long do you think he's been gone?"

"About a month. Hard to be sure, since we didn't live with him and rarely visited and he never calls."

"Did you ask Gladys?"

"Of course. She said she'd last seen him at night, at least six weeks ago. They had dinner at the Four Seasons, Café Boulud, and went to bed late. She mentioned they'd had an argument. He wasn't there in the morning, but she didn't think that was unusual. He often left home before she woke up."

"Had she seemed concerned?"

"No. But she wasn't in the habit of confiding in me. Why should she? Did she talk with you?"

"Not Gladys. Your father asked me for a legal opinion on his deal with the Lyford group, and he told me about Gladys moving in with him for a while."

"He told you about her?"

"Yes. And he came back to tell me that she was no longer working for his clients, that she was staying with him."

"It never looked like a business arrangement to me," I said, thinking about the two of them in the hot tub and the unmade bed in the master bedroom.

"Did you talk to his secretary?" James asked.

"No. Not sure he still has one. The offices are fairly basic. A couple of his old design tables, a coffee table with some chairs and an uncomfortable sofa, wilted plants, a TV. No filing cabinets. A little dusty. I don't think anyone had been there for a while."

"A computer?"

"No. Nothing. It seemed more like a movie set than a real office."

James nodded. "Makes sense," he said.

"Why?"

"The sort of business your father was engaged in didn't require an office."

"Where did he meet the people he was in business with then?"

"Barbados, the Caymans, London, St. Petersburg, Paris. Wherever they were. But there has to be a computer somewhere. Did you ask his driver?"

"Gerry said Father always had his laptop with him. MacBook Air. Never left it in the car, not even when he just popped out to pick up something. Took it with him wherever he went. To restaurants. To his doctor's for his checkups. Even took it to the gym."

"You take a good look around his home?"

"Gerry said he locked the laptop in a safe when he went to bed. When we insisted, the police opened it up. It wasn't there. And I went through all the rooms." Gladys hadn't been particularly welcoming, but then she had never been pleased to see Gina and me. We noticed that her clothes now took up most of the space in the bedroom and there was some brand-new leatherette furniture. Father had hated leather furniture. I had even explored Gladys's domain, the gym, over her taciturn insistence that Father hadn't been down there for months. "He didn't like to exercise," she said.

I checked our mother's still unsold condo, in case he had decided to leave his laptop there. No reminders of their marriage there. He hadn't visited her; never even called, according to Nellie. There was nothing of his at her place.

Next I was going to check the cottage.

"Men like my father don't just vanish," I told James.

"You'd be surprised," he said. "It is exactly men like your father who do vanish. Or haven't you worked it out yet? He was in a dangerous business."

"Buying and selling houses?"

James smiled. "He wasn't buying and selling properties for himself, he was doing it for others. People who had reasons to hide the sources of their money. Do you know anything about money laundering?" he asked.

I didn't, so he told me.

When he was still in real estate, Father had met a couple who needed to hide their "gray" money from the tax authorities in Holland. He invested their cash in a condo development in North Toronto. He then helped sell the development to a corporation that already owned land in the area and wished to own more properties. The Dutch couple got their money back with a handsome profit. That money, unlike the original money, was "clean." No one, least of all our government or the bank that had facilitated the transaction, was at all interested in how the original cash was made. The Dutch couple were happy, the bank got its percentage, and Father got his share. Better than that, he was now known to be in the business, and others came to him with problems similar to the Dutch couple's.

"That, in a nutshell, is how he got rich," James said. "Didn't you ever ask him?"

"No."

"Weren't you even curious?"

I shook my head. "I assumed he'd become a developer. It's an easy enough switch from selling real estate." Frankly, I knew very little about money laundering.

"Long as you can use other people's money."

"How did that Dutch couple make their money?"

"I have no idea, I didn't want to know, but I assume it was something not quite legal."

"And the others?"

"Drugs, mostly. The Nassau man had made his money in gambling. I did make some discreet inquiries about him. He also ran an agency for expensive call girls."

"Prostitution?"

"Obviously."

"My father told you all this?" I was reeling. I couldn't wrap my mind around his having made his money from drugs and prostitution—even if once removed. That he would be eager to get involved with these people. That Gladys had been sent here as their spy.

"A couple of times he asked for my advice. He was concerned about his clients having to pay his commission, legally, even if the kinds of transactions he was involved in were beyond our set of laws. When I told him that his clients' activities were largely illegal, he asked whether he could retain me to draft the contracts. I think he assumed that if I was retained, I would have to preserve what we call client-lawyer privilege—in other words everything he told me would be 'off the record.' He offered me a very handsome retainer."

"And you said?"

"I declined," James said with a little moue that he used on distasteful occasions, such as when I told him he had to leave my apartment. "That's what he wanted to talk about in the cemetery when you buried William. He'd brought some papers with him, but I didn't want to look at them."

"How much money was involved in his scheme?"

"From the little bit he told me, I guess a few billion."

"Billions of dollars?" I squawked.

"There's no point in laundering small bits of money. With laundering it's always massive sums, and your father had a reputation for discretion and cleanliness." James chuckled at his own joke.

"So, he'd have a bank account somewhere with a ton of money no one knows about?"

"Probably a bunch of bank accounts. Though don't be fooled by the billions. His share would have been only a percentage."

"You mean millions."

"And much of it would be somewhere offshore. He was allergic to paying taxes."

"What happens," I asked, switching topics, "if someone dies without a will?"

"Someone?" James chuckled. "Intestate? There would be a probate. It would take a long time, but usually, the court would deem that it all belongs to his closest relatives, such as his wife and his daughters."

"I wouldn't want anything from him," I said and I thought I had meant it. I hadn't. But it wasn't the money I wanted but some sort of validation, an acknowledgment of my value or "usefulness" in the world, as Father saw it.

I wondered then whether I hoped he would not be back. Whether, just like Mother, I, too, secretly wished he were dead. That he had chosen William's funeral to discuss his disgusting business with James was no longer surprising. In hindsight, leafing through my memories of childhood, there had always been the underlying reality of the sort of man he was and that he had always been not the way I had chosen to see him at the time.

26

GINA AND SAMMY HAD TAKEN THE NEWS ABOUT Father's money laundering in stride, especially after I quoted James's opinion that members of his family, unless they were directly involved, could not be held responsible for his actions. Gina's main concern was whether someone else could call in Father's loan or the mortgage on their house. She had said she planned to repay him when our family home sold, but there were always new expenses and, surely, there was no sense in rushing the repayment now, while he was God knows where. Of course, she meant when there was a good chance he was dead.

I hadn't been sure whether Mother wasn't interested in Father's financial shenanigans, or whether she couldn't follow what I was telling her. I had simplified the matter in a way she would have found insulting only a year before.

Her memory had seemed to be slipping a bit each time I visited her at Fairview. The staff said she no longer knew what day of the week it was. When I asked her, she said it didn't matter. "Here, every day is the same."

But she had spoken surprisingly clearly when she asked me to find Father's will. She said he had never discussed it with her, not even when they were still sharing our home, and he would not have had any reason to discuss it after. "If he isn't found," she said in her old, decisive voice, "we will need that will."

The only person who had admitted to knowing something about a will was Gladys, and she hadn't been interested in discussing it with me. "Suffice to say," she had told me, "his main concern would have been to take care of me."

But when I had visited Mother last week, she had brought it up again. In a whisper, looking past me at the open door, as if she were expecting someone would be listening, she had asked whether I had met with his lawyer yet. Acting like a spy in a John le Carré novel, she slipped a bit of paper into my hand, closed my fingers around it, and said, "He has an office on Bay Street."

I told Gina that Mother was losing her tenuous grip on reality—something her doctors had predicted would happen in time, but we had assumed not so soon.

"What was on the paper?" Gina asked.

"A name I didn't recognize." But I had called anyway. His name was Harold Spiegel. I had asked his secretary whether I could come and see him about our father's disappearance. His secretary said Mr. Bogdan hadn't been a client, but Spiegel called me back anyway, and we arranged to meet.

His office was one of those big glass-encircled ones at the top of a downtown bank tower. He was elderly—in his seventies, I thought—and he had kept adjusting his hearing aid most of the time I was there. He kept his back to the enormous window with the sun glinting off the gently shaded glass, so his face was difficult to see, but I thought there was something familiar about him. He said he had done a couple of real estate transactions for our father, but he didn't usually practice estate law. If Father had made a will, he would have gone to a different lawyer. As for my inquiries about Father's whereabouts, they hadn't spoken in at least a couple of years, he said; he flipped the cover of his fake-leather-bound black diary back and forth, as if whatever was embossed on it would reveal something.

He wasn't sure when he had started working for Father and he was sure other lawyers had also been engaged.

"2012," he said, when I kept pushing. "He was buying that development north of the city."

"Wilson?"

He shuffled some papers on his desk. "That may have been the name on the file. I did the applications for zoning approvals, I dealt with the city, the parking, the building restrictions . . ."

I asked him whether he had been involved in another deal or series of deals my father had referred to as "Silver."

He shook his head rather more vehemently than necessary for a simple "no." "No idea. After my time," he said.

They hadn't kept in touch after those property deals closed, and as far as he knew, Father had stopped dabbling in real estate.

"That's weird," I said. "Because someone else told me he not only continued to invest in real estate, but that he also increased his investments. Perhaps he hired another lawyer?"

"Unlikely," Spiegel said. "I would have known about it." But he was rubbing his hands together, and his knee was jittering where he had crossed his legs. He looked at his watch several times, got up, and announced that there was another client waiting. He opened the door for me and stood there, watching as I walked past the receptionist and stepped into the elevator.

With the sun no longer at his back, the two of us shared the fluorescent lights of the corridor, and it dawned on me that he was the man next to Eva in one of the wedding pictures. I wanted to go back to ask him whether he had been married to Eva. Instead, I asked rather too loudly whether he had been at my parents' wedding.

"Of course," he said as he closed the door to his office.

I WAS AMAZED MOTHER HAD understood what I said about the lawyer and the broker. She even asked whether James had said how much money Father had handled and how much he would have kept as his fees. But in the middle of my explanation, she lapsed into her usual faraway look, gazing at a fixed spot in the garden, barely present. She perked up only when I mentioned what Gladys had said about the will. "She hasn't been with him long enough to be entitled to anything," she said, decisively. "A couple of years."

"Much longer than that," I said.

"How do you know?"

"I don't. But I am pretty sure it's about five years."

"Not enough," she said.

"If he isn't coming back . . ."

"If he is dead, you mean?"

"Yes."

"Depends on whether he has made a new will. And if he has, whether anyone can find it."

"A new will?"

"Yes. Just keep looking," she said with a smile. "Why don't you ask Gladys again?"

After talking with the police once more—I assumed they hadn't mentioned how Father had made so much money, because they didn't know—I had asked Gladys whether she had a copy of a new will.

"I don't think he's bothered to do one," she said, "but if he did, I doubt he would have left much to you or your mother. I assume that's who sent you."

"Why?"

"Why do I assume she sent you?"

I nodded.

"She can't get me out of her mind—what's left of it," Gladys said. "She thinks she's entitled to everything he's ever made. She's not, you know."

"They are still married," I told her. "And you're not. So, why shouldn't she assume she's entitled—"

"Because she had no idea how to make him happy."

"And you do?" I asked.

"Obviously," Gladys said, lifting her arms and stretching, as she often did before a set of serious exercises, though at the time I thought she stretched to display her shapely assets for me.

Following James's advice, I had called on Spiegel for a second time. I hadn't bothered with an appointment, I didn't care whether he was busy with another client (he was), or how outraged his receptionist became when I barged past her and threw open his door.

"Mr. Spiegel," I said, louder than necessary, since he was sitting behind his desk, not six feet from me. "It's been more than four weeks now since we last heard from my father. The police have begun to wonder—as have we—whether he is likely to reappear. Don't you think you owe us some sort of explanation?"

He stared at me.

"You were his lawyer," I shouted. "And you may also have been his friend. For God's sake, you were at his wedding!"

"No need for that tone, Ms. Bogdan," he said. "You can see I am with another client . . ."

I glanced at the nattily dressed man in the chair facing Spiegel. He was visibly uncomfortable.

"He can leave," I said. "I doubt if his father has also vanished. Whatever reason he has for wanting your services, it can't be as pressing as my need to know more about my father's business partners and whatever deals or contracts you have prepared for him . . ."

The nattily suited man stood up and left without a word. "You know he didn't stop his real estate business after the Wilson development. I am sure you know he had a bunch of new investors lined up and you know—"

He put up his hand to stop me. "I prepared some pro forma papers, that's all," he said.

"His deal with Nassau?"

Spiegel nodded.

"Were these the Silver deals?"

"I don't know," he said. "He didn't tell me, and he filled in the names of the other parties himself."

"And a new will?"

"Not a new will."

"How about his old will? Did you do that?"

Spiegel took a deep breath before he answered. "I gave him the forms. Like the Silver deals, he filled in all the details."

"You mean all the names?"

"Yes, Jude," he said, suddenly using my name, "he always kept his own secrets. Never one to share. Not even with his lawyer. And I was not his friend."

"The wedding?"

"I was asked to accompany a young woman. That's all."

"Eva?"

"Yes. That was her name."

HAVING FINISHED THE BOTTLE OF scotch, I opened a bottle of vodka I had slipped in among my shoes the last summer I was here. It was for extraordinary circumstances, such as if I had run out of everything else and didn't have the energy to take the boat into town to replenish supplies. I liked vodka only on warm days and mixed with something sweet, but today I needed it to settle my nerves.

I was thinking about that almost illegible will. Why would Mother have hidden it at the back of the drawer, and why had she said she didn't know where it was? Was she worried that a new will would leave us nothing? Or was that her dementia talking?

To put myself into the right mood for sleeping, I took a couple of Mother's pills and delved into *Sapiens* and vanished empires. Useful to contemplate Sargon the Great, great and fearless ruler of the Akkadian Empire, when you were alone at the cottage and determined not to be scared.

27

THAT NIGHT I SAW WILLIAM WALKING NEAR THE edge of the lake in front of Father's cabin. There was a sheen of moonlight on the water, there may have been some satiny clouds over the moon but I could see him clearly, with the trees bending over in their humbled after-the-storm stance. Then he was slowly stooping to pick up something in the weed beds where Mother's July lilies used to be. Trying to clear my eyes, I closed them, and opened them again, rubbed them with both hands, but he was still there. I ran my fingers through my hair, scratching my scalp to make sure I was awake. My hair was soddened, the skin on my face was puffy, it felt like plastic, as if it didn't belong to me. My clothes were damp, too, watery, unreal.

The moonlight made the figure oscillate, almost dissolving into particles.

Though I did remember trying to read another chapter of *Sapiens,* I couldn't remember actually going to bed. It must have been late, because it was dark, too dark to see whether the seagulls had left the deck. I hadn't put a light on because I was worried about being seen from the outside, even if only by birds. Where did seagulls sleep at night? On rocks? In the water? I was pretty sure they didn't sleep on roofs. I remembered dropping the flashlight somewhere in the living room.

I was still wearing the clothes I had pulled on after I came out of the lake. A hazy memory of wanting to wear James's shirt again, but where had I put it?

I watched William moving toward the dock, his arms swinging, as they used to when he was happy and getting ready to play one of his games with his sister. In the city, Mel rarely paid attention to her brother, she found him embarrassing in public and uninteresting at home, but she was always happy to play with him at the cottage, where there was no one else to play with and no one except us could see them. She was a year younger than William, but she was older intellectually and more developed physically. She would race him to the end of the dock and they would take turns jumping or diving, swimming back to the ladder, then back into the water, laughing, shouting for us to watch. This time there was no sound. No laughter.

I knew I must have been dreaming. William couldn't be here. He was dead.

He was ten years old when he died. Same age as my father's Talisker when he first offered me a taste, at the time he was teaching me how to handle a gun. It may have been the memory of holding it and aiming at those crows that started me crying about William. I didn't think I had even liked him very much. Was I wrong about that, too? For sure, Mel and Sammy liked him. He was born a year after Gina and Sammy were married, and if twenty-two was too young to be married, caring for a baby at twenty-three proved to be too much for Gina. And William had not been an easy baby. Gina had expected everyone to pitch in, but Mother was busy with her lectures and she had never been interested in taking care of babies. She had been lousy at taking care of us. "It's not one of my strengths," she had told Gina. She had held William for only a moment, at arm's length from herself, and handed him back. "He is too wriggly," she said.

I was working on my first Kitty book. Besides, as I had told Gina, I would be about as useless as Mother. But when no one saw us, I used to pick him up and hold him close to my chest, so I could feel him breathing. There was something about his softness and warmth that made me want to cry. And that was another reason I hadn't offered to take care of him. I had been afraid of how I'd felt. I had managed to convince myself that, like our own mother, I wasn't cut out to be a mother.

Sammy took time off work and lost his seniority at the bank. Father used to joke that if he continued in this way—"babysitting is not a man's job"—he might make it to senior teller by the time he retired.

William was an awkward child, demanding attention, loud, anxious. He was possessive of everything he decided was his, including other people's clothes, his sister's shorts, Gina's bikini, and my red running shoes with the white laces he had tried on when he was nine. Another year and they would be too small for him. He had hidden them under his bed where he imagined no one would look. He made a terrible keening noise when I tried to take them away.

He was quiet unless he was reading for his father or playing with his LEGO set. He loved to build elaborate structures, always using pieces of the same two colors, so if he ran out of reds or yellows, his building would remain unfinished. When I showed him how he could fit in a few blue bits to finish something he had been working on for hours, he refused. He watched me doing it, and when I walked away, he took the whole thing apart.

At ten, he had grown into a large, knock-kneed, big footed, pudgy boy with big blue eyes, uneven teeth, sparse hair, a concerned frown that divided his forehead into two uneven parts. He walked with his chin up and his arms loose at his sides. He was surprisingly agile in the water. He would leap off the end of the dock and swim out toward the turtle islands, his arms skimming the waves in an easy crawl, his face coming up for air every third stroke, exactly as he had learned at swimming classes.

I remembered how proud he had been of being faster and stronger than his father. It was Sammy who had enrolled him and Sammy who drove him five times a week to pools where he had been promised first-rate instruction.

Gina had said it was all a waste of money, but she, too, was impressed that William had become such a good swimmer.

That's why everyone was surprised when William drowned.

I watched his oscillating shape move easily through the darkness between the birches—where he couldn't be.

I tried lying down again, but the room spun. Tried to focus on the spot of moonlight on the ceiling until it disappeared. Slowly breathing in the cool air from the lake. There couldn't be cool air from the lake! Surely I must have closed the doors. Did I remember closing them? Had they even been open? I tried to piece together everything from last night. There had been the broken glass in my mother's room, the wet pictures, my father's scrunched-up will. And that damned seagull. I got up slowly, without glancing at the lake and looked through the glass door to see whether the seagulls were gone. Had I opened the doors then, or had they been open all night?

Obviously, I couldn't be seeing William.

My dreams were leaching into my consciousness, making it harder to distinguish what was real. That's all. I had to focus.

I tried to see the dock. It was too dark now, clouds had covered the moon. I listened for footsteps. There were none. Then, piercing the silence, there was a big splash, as if someone had just jumped into the lake. No. Not William. Had to be a big fish. April was carp mating season, and they usually became passionately rambunctious, sometimes leaping into the canoe when we paddled near their spawning area at the back of the island, and a few times they even flopped onto the dock.

I don't know why I had been thinking so much about William since I came to the island. I remembered most of the funeral, but not all of it. I had needed two swigs of wine to dress (luckily, I had a lot of black clothes), and another to propel myself out the door and into the car. At the church Gina had sat in the front pew, twisting a white cotton handkerchief around her fingers. She was crying gently, not the hiccupping cry that our usually composed mother exhibited or even the rage of Sammy's tears. Mel had perhaps been the saddest. I watched her leaning into her father, her narrow shoulders shaking. She had always been a sensitive child, smart, perceptive, unlike her brother, sometimes even helpful. At the cottage she often helped with the dishes. She used to watch Father when he made remarks about William's lack of coordination. Once, when he said it was amazing that Gina would have a second child after William, she spoke up defending her brother. "At least he is kind," she had said, and she was only about nine. "Someone in this family has to be . . ."

Father, as usual, ignored her.

I am not sure whether the priest spoke much. I could see his mouth move, but I definitely hadn't heard him. Father had offered me a swig of whiskey from his hip flask in the parking lot of Our Lady of Perpetual something, a name that had made him chortle, and then he launched into a speech about how corrupt the Roman church was and how the pope's banker had been found hanging from Blackfriars Bridge in London.

But at least Father was there. Sort of.

He didn't actually go into the church, he waited outside on the well-cut grass. Even that had been a major concession from him. He could still hear the music and the words.

He told me after the whisky but before I joined the others inside that if Mother tried to give him some sort of mumbo-jumbo priestly ceremony after he died, I was to "whack her on the beak." Since I was the older of his two daughters and, I liked to think, the most like him, he promised his will would contain a clause disinheriting me if he had a Catholic funeral. I would be responsible for the cremation, for having his ashes scattered in the Bay, no fuss, no whispered words, no pretending that there was some kind of afterlife.

Afterward, he came to the cemetery, too, but stood a few steps back from the rest of us.

Sammy was one of the pallbearers, and I thought I recognized a couple of guys from his office helping him shoulder William's weight all the way. I had assumed that the funeral people would take over and roll the coffin to the edge of the grave, but Sammy had insisted that he wanted to be part of William's last journey. I thought he had felt guilty for not being there for him when William swam that day on the lake, but it had been such a calm day, and William had become such a good swimmer, there had been no reason for him to always be watched. "He is becoming so independent," Sammy had said with pride. "He's gaining more confidence every day. It's why I like to come to the cottage," he added, assuming he needed to explain why he kept coming.

"A great relief for her," our father had said to no one in particular as William was lowered into the ground. He was still standing apart from the rest of the family, but I think most of them, except perhaps for Sammy, would have heard. Sammy was so close to the edge that I worried he would fall into the grave. He watched as the ropes lowered his son's coffin and wiped his hands on his trousers, crying.

"Don't act as if you don't know," our father said. "Just look at her." Gina had stopped crying and, as I turned toward her, I saw that she had just the tiniest grimace. If I hadn't known her better, I would have thought it was the effort to hold in her grief, but I knew Father was right. She was smiling. She was relieved.

She hadn't liked William much since she had been told he was "on the spectrum." At first, when he was about four, she had tried to hide that from us, saying he was extra bright but awkward in social situations. "Sometimes, he's preoccupied, that's why he doesn't respond to what you're saying." I had grown used to his staring at something in the distance when I was talking to him. She assured me, as if I had asked, which I hadn't, that he would grow out of it. She hadn't wanted to take him in for an assessment. Sammy did. He told me a developmental pediatrician had diagnosed William. He was hopeful that William's case would turn out to be mild, but he couldn't tell yet.

It was pretty clear by the time he turned seven that the case wouldn't be mild. Long before then, Gina's complaints about her son's behavior had become the opening phrases of most of our conversations, and I could tell that Mother had stopped listening long before she had lapsed into dementia and before Gina had decided she needed someone to blame.

"Everybody knows it's in the genes," she had said over dinner at the cottage. "It doesn't just happen. It's even predictable. Runs in families." She was staring at me, as if I were about to confirm that my genes and William's were very similar. "Sometimes, it starts late, with erratic behavior, a sudden onset, but usually it's there from the beginning." Looking at me again, she said, "You were a screamer, weren't you, when you were a baby?"

I said I had no idea, but Mother confirmed that I had been a difficult baby, that she had to hire help so she could get some sleep at night. Also, she said I had a habit of rocking myself from side to side, as if I were learning a dance step.

"Classic," Gina said.

"Quite normal," Mother told her. "A lot of kids do that. It gives them comfort if they are feeling miserable, and Jude was not a happy child. Nothing to do with autism. Lots of kids are miserable. They grow out of it."

I know from the way they were both looking at me then that they thought I hadn't.

James had come late to the funeral. He had missed the church part altogether but caught up with us at the graveside. He was in his business suit, jacket unbuttoned, and he carried the briefcase with his laptop that he used to leave at the office when he came home. Home, to the apartment we used to share.

I hadn't realized I had been crying till James put his arm around me. He said something about William, then he went straight to our father's side and whispered to him while the priest waved some sort of silver dispenser, dropping holy water over the coffin and spoke about William, whom he hadn't known, and our mother, whom he had known for some years, since she had joined his Bible study group after Father left. Mother had recently joined his congregation at Our Lady. She had held on to my arm and studied her shoes, her head moving from side to side, as if trying to understand whose feet they were. He was effusive about her steadfast virtues and how these would help her and her family through the crisis of losing one so young. He smiled benignly at Gina but didn't mention Sammy, the parent who had really loved William, the one who would miss him the most.

I buried my face in my long silk scarf and tried to pretend I had a cold, but I knew Mother had looked at me, and judging by her expression, she was surprised. All the years I thought I had found William annoying, I must have been fond of him. Fond enough that I was furious with my sister and found it hard to look at our father.

Father had become louder as he talked with James, and he had taken a sheaf of papers from his inside jacket pocket and tried to give it to James, whose hands were palms up at shoulder height, refusing to take them. They stood side by side a while longer, Father still holding the papers. He glanced around the cemetery, then at our small group of mourners, nodded to me once, turned his back to the grave, and left. I watched him marching along the paved path toward the exit or his car. I lost sight of him when the path veered left.

We threw handfuls of earth over the coffin, then waited while the cemetery workers ladled in more earth, which thudded on the wood and made Sammy weep louder. He didn't care that Gina was glaring at him with obvious distaste. I held on to our mother.

"I'll drive you home," I suggested.

"Home?" she said. "Do I still have a home? Hasn't he destroyed home, too, along with everything else he has ever touched?" She had refused to use the fold-up chair she had been offered, and though she was leaning heavily on her cane, she continued to ignore it during the whole burial ceremony. "Now, that I have arrived here," she continued, "I wonder whether we have ever had a home. Was it an illusion? Something we manufactured to fool ourselves even before he changed?" A very thoughtful speech for someone with impaired memory.

The funeral was three years ago, and she had been showing more signs of dementia by then, the gaps in memory shifting and becoming wider, and her awareness of them diminishing together with the rest of her. Her back was bent forward a little, shoulder bones poking up under the thin skin, she was painfully thin. From behind, I thought I could count the vertebrae holding up her neck. Her body had lost much of its substance. But her voice was still strong enough to be heard even as the wind graveside picked up. "You remember my little dog?" she asked.

"Scoop."

"Strange, I had forgotten its name. His name, right?"

"Yes, it was a male," I said, thinking about Scoop hoisting one hind leg rather balletically at tree trunks when he pissed, holding his tail even higher. No mean feat for a dachshund.

"Your father hated dogs."

"He hated Scoop. He might have liked a hunting dog, one that could fetch his duck kills and lay them at his feet," I said. "He thought dogs, like everybody, had to have a function. Be good at something."

Mother snorted her derision. "Scoop was good at giving me love. He was soft and he cuddled up to me at night. A function? What function does your father have?"

I sidestepped the question because our father was making so much money now that there could be no sensible question about his function. His function was making money. He hadn't loved architecture. Money seemed to have provided him with a reason to exist. The rest of us, especially William, I thought, had been given fewer reasons to exist. Instead, I said, "You could have bought another dog."

My mother shook hands with the priest, thanked him, and leaning on her cane, started to walk slowly and deliberately away from the grave. I offered her my arm, but she refused to take it.

I looked behind us and saw Gina, Mel, and Sammy, still standing at the grave as the workers piled the earth higher and patted it down with their shovels.

"He would have killed that, too," Mother said.

28

MY HEAD FELT TOO HEAVY FOR MY NECK. IT WAS crackling with pain. Pinprick lights flashed before my eyes when I moved. I tried to remember details of last night, of William walking along the shore and jumping into the lake; it must have been a dream, a weird kind of nightmare from drinking too much vodka or reading *Sapiens*. I tried the bedside lamp. Nothing. And nothing in the bathroom. The kitchen seemed too far away. I took two crumbling aspirins from the bottle I had left here two summers ago, groaned, and dropped back into bed, pulled the blanket up around my neck, and tried to think about nothing.

A wedge of sun between the branches, it must be close to noon. Still not enough light in the bedroom. I dragged myself to the kitchen, listening for the happy drone of the fridge. It was silent. OK, so there must be an electricity pole down on the island. Or on the mainland. When the power cut out on the mainland, we always got blackouts here. There was a remote possibility that I would be able to pull the generator out of the basement but no chance that I could start it. It was just another thing only Father could handle because, as he pointed out, there was a right way and a wrong way. I had never bothered to learn how it was done.

It was intensely cold in the living room. The fire had died during the night. I scrunched up old, somewhat wet newspapers and bits of kindling, laid a couple of birch logs over that and spent a long time striking damp matches against the fireplace before one finally caught.

I found my phone in my bag. Hadn't searched for it recently because the only way we could use a phone in the cottage was to connect to my father's hub and, obviously, he would have taken it with him the last time he came. He always did.

I could try the end of the dock again, I thought, but it was probably useless. I had to go up to the middle of the island—close to where Scoop had been found—and call the electric company and the marina. I needed help to find the boat or get someone to ferry me back to my car. The reasons I'd had for coming here on my own had withered during the last couple of nights, though I still felt the need to find things in my mother's room, things that would make sense of the present and maybe even a few unexplained bits of the past. The shared past, because I wanted to find photos of myself as a cute kid, held on my mother's knee, being hugged, her gazing at me with love. It was true: we never get over our mothers. I certainly hadn't gotten over mine.

Not even in her diminished state had she ever held my hand. Had she held my sister's?

The two gulls were not on the deck. I listened for the sound of their feet on the roof, but there was nothing. No shrieking when I opened the living room door.

The sun was shining benevolently on the deck's bitty glass slivers, bunches of soaking wet dead leaves, thin sharp twigs, and Mother's broken birdfeeders. I pulled on my bloody jogging pants and an old sweater for comfort, stuck my feet into my stiff (dried blood) running shoes, tucked my phone into my back pocket, and headed down to the dock. The storm had left a lot of debris on the path, broken branches, slippery stones, thousands of acorns. The dock was missing several boards, and it had tilted to the left a little, but the metal girders had held. The end of the stern rope was still tied to the hook, frayed where it had been attached to the boat. The dock line was missing. There were gulls shrieking overhead and diving into the water near me, but they were not threatening. There were whitecaps rushing toward the shore, but they were not cresting over the dock.

I looked as far away as I could along our shore, in case the boat had capsized on the island, but I couldn't see it. I started to walk east, close to the water's edge but avoiding the slippery rocks the water had turned green and slimy. I found a couple of our dock's boards, slapping against the rocks, some pieces missing, warped but still serviceable, worth hauling back. I pulled them out of the water and leaned them up against some brush to dry. Near the eastern tip of the island there was a big white half-submerged dead fish, a hook still in its mouth. It was drifting in and out with the waves, its white belly exposed to the sun. Maybe a pike, but it was hard to remember what dead pike looked like, and this one had been partly eaten by the birds. Our father had showed me once that the whole catch-and-release program in the Bay was useless because most people had no idea how to do it right, they pulled the fish's guts out with the hook and killed it anyway. He had spent a weekend pulling dead fish out of the water. "Sportfishing," he said. "What's the sport in landing the thing and putting it back in the water, half-dead, and you know it won't live more than another day or two."

He didn't release the fish he caught, though he wouldn't eat them— "carp are too oily," he said, he preferred to bury them.

"Passive resistance, or civil disobedience," Mother suggested, though we found nothing passive, civil, or sporting about burying fish.

He didn't do the actual digging and burying. He stood at the appointed spot, the place he had chosen to dispose of the fish, and supervised our efforts with the spade and the rocks we put over the top to cover the site. A couple of times, after Gina was married, he ordered Sammy to bury the fish. Sammy, being good-natured, fearful Sammy, never protested. Father never asked James. I wondered now whether it was respect for James or fear of whatever James knew about him. His so-called business. Silver. He also didn't insist that James learn his fishing or hunting techniques. Years ago, he had offered Sammy one of his shotguns for a tryout at the back of the island, but all Sammy did was waste ammunition.

Sometimes the raccoons dug up the dead fish during the night, and the stench would greet us with our eggs in the morning. Only Scoop enjoyed the smell. He would roll in it and try to share his delight with us by rubbing up against our legs.

Another reason for Father to hate the dog.

Farther along the shore, there was a red life jacket, frayed at the seams, the back covered with seaweed. The front looked like it had been scraping the bottom for some time, it must have been in the water long before this storm. But surely not so long ago that it could have been William's. He drowned the last summer I had come to the island and that was almost three years ago. It must have belonged to someone else. Someone whose boat had capsized and he or she had drowned during the last storm.

Every summer there were people foolish enough to tempt fate taking their boats out during rough weather on the lake. Some of them drowned. We would see the orange search-and-rescue helicopters flying low over our island, looking for debris or bodies.

After William had drowned, there were helicopters all the time. Even at night, their searchlights scoured the shoreline. Sammy had told them about William's bright red life jacket, that it would stand out, that the reflective strips on the shoulders would glow in the dark. He had bought the jacket at a store that specialized in gear for deep-sea mariners. Fishermen who might fall off a schooner wore jackets like this, Sammy had told them. He had talked so much and with such earnestness that the rest of us thought he had prepared his son for exactly this sort of situation, but of course he hadn't.

His preparations had been for choppy days when he took the boat out and William, though he was scared, insisted on going along for the ride. He liked to sit in the stern; he enjoyed the sound the propeller made, he liked the hull smacking into the wake, and he loved the roller-coaster feeling of the boat riding the waves. Sammy worried he wouldn't be able to keep an eye on him when he was driving. But that day, they had not been in a boat.

It was a calm early August day when William drowned, one of those lazy, balmy summer days when nothing can go wrong. We were all in and out of the lake, Father's music playing softly in the cottage—he had come up again to the island, unexpectedly, and was staying in his cabin. At dawn, he had marched to the back of the island with his gun, but we heard none of the usual popping sounds that proved he had found something to slaughter. Now he was at the lake, enjoying the sunshine. Sammy was getting the barbecue ready for an early dinner of burgers and franks, I was cutting up potatoes, Gina was making her signature all-vegetarian salad with kale, arugula, baby tomatoes, avocado, pine nuts, and pears. Mel was painting a picture for Gina's September birthday. Eva, still in her bathing suit, had stood behind her, watching. Mother, who seemed almost her predementia self, was setting the table and grousing about my leaving bits of my papers on various surfaces in the living room. I used to think up plot twists for the Kitty novels while I was doing something else and often left them for later collection.

Father had taken the *Hunt* for a fast run to the turtle islands. He was concerned about the boat becoming sluggish. He said he would be back in time for supper. He returned at the time we were shouting for William to come and eat.

William had gone down to the lake, wanting so much to have a swim before dinner that no one argued with him. His life jacket was dangling from one hand behind him as he loped down the path, singing some song about "swimming, swimming in the swimming pool, when days are hot when days are cold . . ." Sammy had shouted that he should make sure to be back for dinner, so only a couple of jumps, and no swimming out from the shallows.

None of us had any idea when William disappeared. I had heard him splashing and whooping when he jumped in, and I know he was still laughing and shouting when I put on the water for the potatoes. It was such a mellow evening, I had almost forgotten that we were no longer a family, that Father had moved into his own house, that Gina had sold our childhood home. I set the table outside; Father came up to the deck in his bathing suit, a towel wrapped around his waist; Sammy, ignoring Gina's disapproving looks, laid the hamburgers on the grill; Gina brought out her salad and called William. We were all gathering at the table, Gina getting angry that William hadn't come out of the lake yet, so Mel offered to go and get him. I still remember the tone of Mel's voice: annoyed that she would have to take care of her brother, again. I still remember the smell of onions and garlic, the sound of spitting fat from the grill.

William wasn't anywhere near the dock, and no matter how loud we shouted, he didn't emerge from the water. Sammy dove in from the end of the dock, William's favorite swimming spot because he could run down the length of the dock and jump in, feet first, windmilling with his arms and yelling his delight. Sammy swam out almost as far as the small islands where the cormorants nested, turned, and screamed William's name. Father took the *Hunt* west, then around the island. It took him fifteen minutes. He returned, shaking his head. The rest of us were still in the lake, searching and shouting. Gina had already called the Coast Guard.

The Ontario Provincial Police were there in less than an hour. Our parents were known to them as longtime cottagers with local influence. Father had contributed to the area's Conservative Party funds and to several candidates in the district's local elections. I think that was the reason they turned a blind eye to his out-of-season hunting and fishing adventures. They could hardly have pretended not to know.

It took almost a week to find William's body. It had floated to the surface near Christian Island, about fifty miles away. The police said they were amazed that it hadn't been spotted before by the float planes or the search-and-rescue helicopters, or one of the cottagers along the channels it must have traveled. But it wasn't in the area where they had been searching.

He hadn't been wearing his life jacket.

His chest and hands had been cut by propellers. He had lost his green shirt, and his striped shorts were in tatters.

Seagulls had pecked at his face.

He had been entangled in a rope that was still dangling from his arms and around his neck when they brought him to the dock, wrapped in a canvas sheet, only his feet sticking out at the end. Sammy screamed. Father glared at him, as if he had committed some nasty social error. Gina was mumbling that she didn't want to see him like this.

I knew even then that police procedure should have prevented the body being deposited here. But Father had insisted. He was very calm. He said other people drowned in the Bay during August and he had to be satisfied that it was William.

My mother stood at the end of the dock, close to the policemen who had brought in the body, not moving all the time while they were talking and Sammy was screaming. She just stared at my father.

29

I COULDN'T PUT IT OFF ANY LONGER. I CHECKED that my phone was still charged while I waited for the coffee to brew. I needed to call the marina to get help searching for the *Hunt*. Or someone to take me back to the mainland and my car. Then later, I could borrow or rent a boat. We hadn't been overly friendly with other islanders, but we had chatted with a few about the weather, and when Gina and I were kids, we helped some of the older people lug their grocery bags from their cars to their boats. I think the main reason we were helpful was that our parents discouraged fraternizing.

I tucked my phone into my back pocket and marched up the narrow path, glancing behind me all the way in case I saw a boat coming in. Jim's guys would know that I had taken the boat out and they would worry about me here on my own. Or would they? The past couple of years had made everyone less likely to lend a hand. More concerned for their own safety than for others'.

My head still felt like I had run into a wall, face-first, the pain like a vise around my forehead and on top of my head. My teeth ached. Tight like a bridle—horse's or witch's. Father had suggested once, when I was criticizing his hunting animals on the island, that I would benefit from a scold's bridle. My eyes were vibrating, everything seemed hazy, distant, undefined. I would have to be careful where I stepped. There were still some rattlers on the island.

Sometimes one of the other cottagers went around after a storm to see if anyone needed help, but they didn't like to come to Gull Island. In addition to Father's unfriendly attitude, which had surged to rudeness the few times one of them had tried to land, there were too many barely submerged rocks around the island, and in rough weather it was hard to see them. Even a sturdy metal boat would be in danger. After the 1990 hurricane, there had been police helicopters searching for survivors and cottage roofs that had flown far from home, but last night's storm hadn't been a hurricane, just an ordinary Georgian Bay gale with forty- or fifty-knot winds and three-meter spouts, the kind we had seen several times in the past. Besides, no one would be particularly concerned about me. No one had actually watched me take the *Hunt* out. How long before someone noticed that it was gone? A few days? It had already been more than three days. It would take longer, if the marina hadn't fully opened yet. Most cottagers didn't come up till the long weekend in May.

The path looked like it hadn't been cleared for at least a year, but I could still follow it all the way up. White pines, junipers, raspberry bushes, and some desultory red oak grew over much of it. Inland, far from the lake, clouds of aggressive blackflies circled my face and settled around my neck and my ankles.

Two big oaks close to the top of the island had taken direct lightning hits, their black, outstretched, leafless branches reaching for the sky. The electricity posts had held through the winter, but some of the wires had looped down low to the ground, and there were broken trees over them. That would be why the power was off. I would have to call and report this. The storm had strewn branches over the path, birds' nests had crashed down. But I could still see the hard shale rock underneath, with patches of glowing white that looked like quartz, overgrown with yellow and green lichen. The poison ivy was already knee high, stretching out of cracks in the rocks.

"Nothing much grows on this island," Mother used to say, "but we're sure to have a grand crop of poison ivy again this year."

When we didn't know any better, we would wade into the poison ivy, chasing a ball or trying to catch a dog—yes, I now remembered the spaniel, but not how it had choked on fish bones—and we would suffer terribly from those itchy red welts covering our legs and arms and spreading over our whole bodies if we scratched. Once, Gina had wiped her eyes with a hand that had touched the ivy, and her eyes swelled and she couldn't see for a week. I think she was about four years old, and Mother had tied her hands to her bedframe at night to avoid her scratching her eyes. Strange, she hadn't told us to stay off the path if we weren't wearing knee socks, long pants, and running shoes. We learned. As Mel had learned when she was only three, running up this path after a monarch butterfly, stumbling and falling. Sammy had taken her to the hospital in Barrie because she was feverish and hyperventilating. It had taken William a dozen falls to learn, but once he did, he avoided all leafy greens, no matter how benign.

I jumped around and over the high growth, though my body still hurt and my head felt like my brain was sloshing around inside. Still, it was good to be away from the cottage.

I hadn't realized how intently I had been listening for sounds until I heard a faint cry from a dense copse of white pine near the crest of the island. It was a thin wail of a sound, long and pained, as if something had been broken or caught in a trap, but far enough away that I didn't want to investigate. I told myself that it could be the wind brushing against dry leaves. I didn't need to know.

I stopped near the crevasse where Scoop's little body—or what was left of it—had been found. Had it been crows that pecked at it?

I thought about the seagull that had come out of my mother's room and how big and angry it had seemed when it looked at me with its cold eyes. And James trying to save that other gull and being attacked for his trouble. "They always go for your eyes."

It was wonderfully comforting to finally get a signal. I input the marina's number. It rang and rang and continued to ring without switching to voicemail. They were probably busy with the boats. Some boats may have been swept off their moorings in the storm, and there would be trees down. The men would be out there with chain saws. No one to answer the phone.

I ended the call and waited a while, listening. The sound came again, I thought closer this time but couldn't be sure, perhaps more of a moan than a wail. Almost a human sound. A kid caught in a trap. But I was pretty sure there were no traps on the island now, our father had stopped trapping after the mink were gone. Still, it could have been left three summers ago when he was excited about trapping a muskrat. It had been caught by its hind leg and had tried to bite it off before we found it and he killed it. "One shot in the head and all its troubles are over," he told us with a smile.

"Why would you want to kill a muskrat?" I asked.

"Had no choice. It wouldn't survive without its foot. Stands to reason."

"Why would you trap a muskrat?" I persisted.

"Maybe it was rabid. It shouldn't have been so far from the water," he said, as if that would explain the whole miserable thing.

Mother didn't say anything but just stared at him, as if he were a sorry example of another species. I remembered the look on her face. It was the same look she had later, after William's body had been brought to the dock.

I called the marina again. Still no answer.

I thought about calling Gina but I wasn't sure what I would say to her. I wouldn't want to tell her that I was scared. And I wasn't going to tell her I thought there might be ghosts on the island. She knew I didn't believe in ghosts. And our family avoided talking about emotions. Even when she was a child, we didn't talk about how we felt in that house as it became less and less like a home. When she was about three or four, she would cling to our mother's legs, wanting her to stay every time she left for one of her lecture tours. One by one, her fingers were pried open. Mother didn't try to console her, she said Gina would have to learn to let go. She did learn. By the time she was six, she cried only when she had fallen or when her hands were tied down so she wouldn't scratch her poison ivy welts.

I don't remember ever crying. Not even when Father hit me for prying into one of his bags—I was looking for paper to draw on—so hard that I smashed into the wall of his room. Mother was standing in her doorway and she saw but said nothing at the time or later when I was in the bathroom stuffing wads of toilet paper up my nose to staunch the bleeding.

Our mother had ignored our father's absence. She never talked about his moving out, and I didn't ask whether she had been glad he was gone, or whether she missed him. Her dementia didn't really account for her seeming indifference. I hadn't ever asked Gina if Father had been right about William's death being a relief for her, that she no longer had to care for him or worry about his special needs and his education. Neither of us had ever asked our mother about Eva. Why she had become her companion after she had been one of our father's lovers. Or even whether that was true.

For all the endless talking at the cottage, we never talked about anything that mattered. To any one of us.

I picked my way carefully over the tall bushes of poison ivy and around the fallen trees. The sound was closer now. I was sure this time. Could a child have wandered away from its parents and been hurt? Sometimes boats anchored off the back end of the island, people spread their blankets and picnics on the long slabs of smooth Georgian Bay rock near our father's blind. He used to scare them off by shouting, and if that didn't work, he fired his gun into the air. But it was unlikely that someone would picnic here after that storm.

There had been that life jacket in the water. Maybe a capsized boat had been swept up here and a kid had gone to look for help, got lost in the woods?

There was just enough wind for the branches to rustle last fall's dead leaves. You couldn't get lost in these woods. Not enough trees and too much rock. You could see through what trees there were to the other side of the island. I thought I saw Father's boat, *Limestone*, tied to the tree near the blind, but I could no longer be sure of what I was seeing. If it was a boat, it couldn't be his boat. Or could it?

As for that plaintive sound, perhaps a kid had given up hope of finding someone on the island and settled down for a nap.

I yelled "Hello," my voice crackling with disuse. There was no response. I waited. The wailing sound didn't come again. There were some burned bits of wood near the first of the trees, itself singed by fire but no longer smelling of smoke. More lightning, maybe. I yelled again.

Nothing. A few more steps brought me around the singed tree, just in from the edge of the woods. I didn't want to go farther. So many broken branches obscured the way, it now seemed too thick to walk through. No one, least of all a kid, would have gone in there. If they were looking for help, they would have followed the path.

I phoned the marina again and, at last, it did go to voicemail. I explained I was stuck on the island, I thought there was no power and the boat had gone off in the storm. I needed help to leave . . .

I hadn't finished when the signal cut out. I was on the point of calling yet again when I heard that cry again.

Hiccupping between sobs or what sounded like sobs, then quiet when I ventured deeper. I stopped and waited. Blackflies settled around my eyes again, and I kept hearing, or thought I was hearing, that buzzing sound because it was hard to tell—and even harder to see with my hands rubbing my eyes—but I thought I saw William sitting on a log, leaning forward, his head down, studying something on the ground. He wore his favorite green shirt and striped short pants and he was weaving from side to side. Or was that my eyes throbbing? The pain in my head was so intense now, I had to take deep breaths, trying to focus, but failing, William oscillating, his green shirt blending into the leaves. Then my foot landed on something soft that gave off a pungent dead smell.

It was on its back, whatever it was, mouth gaping open, its tiny teeth gritted, blood on its nose and whiskers, blood splattered on its white chest hairs, legs up, toes stretched out, as if it had been trying to hold on to something and had refused to let go. Scoop! No. A red squirrel. The wailing had started up again, so close that I thought for a moment it was the dead squirrel, though I knew it couldn't be; it was dead. A flash of something huge, back in the woods. I froze. It was thrashing. Shrieking as it rose. Close by. Black arms beating against the branches. Some kind of bat? Bird? It was coming straight at me. Yellow claws outstretched, its bald red head stretching toward me. Yellow beak. Hissing. Something foul spewed out of its beak, stinking bits of it landing on my face and on the front of my shirt. It was looking at me, sideways, and hissing. It stopped for a second, then rose, wings outstretched, bashing the trees, its claws still extended.

I turned and bolted down the path, ignoring the poison ivy, almost tripping on the rocks. Stopped near the cottage and looked back to see what it was. A huge turkey vulture, rising awkwardly above the trees, still flapping its immense wings, a bit unstable, maybe drunk on whatever it had been eating, up higher until it stumbled onto the top branch of a tall spruce and maneuvered its wings to steady itself, folded them, and neck outstretched, it sat.

Oh God, it was ugly. Brutish. Disgusting. I had never seen one close up before.

I ran into the lake to try to get clean. My shirt was covered in bits of stink, some as big as quarters. I held my breath while I pulled it over my head and dropped it into the water. I leaned in to wash my hands and my face, and threw up last night's booze in a thin stream of acid. Nothing I had ever smelled had stunk so much. The bandage on my hand had come loose, and there was blood coursing down my fingers. I bent over, undid my shoelaces, the stench unbearable. I splashed icy water over my arms and my chest, cupped more in my hands and washed my face. Some of its spew had landed in my hair. I dunked the top of my head into the water. Despite the pain, it almost felt good, as if the vise was coming off with the water.

I looked in the water for the thing with the thin reeds I had seen earlier, but it had disappeared. Perhaps I had dreamed that, too. A nightmare of a floating head, its face turned up. Had I passed out for a moment at the top of the path and imagined William sitting there, where I had once found him waiting for his mother after he had rolled in the poison ivy?

I left all my clothes in the water and crunched, naked, up the stony path to the cottage. I swallowed a couple of diazepams, washed them down with a bit of vodka.

30

DURING THE WINTER, THE MICE HAD EATEN MOST
of the rice we kept in plastic containers and spread the rest over the
shelves. We haven't been able to figure out how they did it, since the boxes
were closed, but they had managed to pry off the lids, extract enough rice
to sustain themselves, and scattered the rest to prove that they could do
it. Odd how they kept coming back every year, as if to spite Father in his
relentless efforts to kill them.

Packed in at the back of the shelves, there were always some cans
of soup. They were rusted on the outside, but I assumed they would be
okay inside and I needed to settle my stomach. What I hadn't thought
about was how canned asparagus soup would look and smell when you
opened it. I threw up again, this time over the kitchen counter and down
my breasts. Luckily, I was still wearing no clothes. I wiped the vomit off
my chest and belly with an old kitchen cloth. Propitiously, it smelled like
yesterday's wine mixed with bitter herbs.

I would have to go back to the dock and rinse everything I had been
wearing. But not yet. I couldn't face what I had left there.

My head was still throbbing. My eyes felt like they had been soaked in vinegar and reinserted into their too tight sockets.

I swore I would drink less today.

I took a couple of old aspirins—not ideal, given that I hadn't eaten all day. I had to eat before I went back up the path to call the marina again and find whatever had been making that plaintive noise. Or was that the vulture?

There was the loaf of sliced white bread, still pristine in its plastic wrapping, untouched, sitting in the bread basket far from the counter, in other words, safe. I stuffed a slice into my mouth, chewed slowly, as the therapist had suggested back when I was still going to the therapist. Her advice had been to chew at least thirty-seven times before you swallow.

"Doesn't matter what the food is. This will help you focus on what you're doing, not what you are thinking or remembering. Keep you in the moment."

This might not have been the kind of moment she had in mind. I didn't think even she could have pictured this particular moment, with my mother's ruined bedroom, the storm that swept off the boat, the seagull lurking somewhere close by since it couldn't fly, the snake, the snickering squirrel, the thing in the woods, the hissing, puking turkey vulture, all my bleeding wounds, the stinking body on the path and whatever was still in the woods near the crevasse where my mother's little dog had been found. I thought that the sound I'd heard had been crying or whimpering. It sounded like William when he was miserable. But I couldn't have seen William. He was dead.

I struggled to keep the bread down, splashed more water over my face, and shoved my hair into the bathroom basin. I hadn't intended to glance into the mirror over the basin; it was one of those automatic movements imprinted over time. I had always looked into this mirror and checked whether I was still managing to seem presentable.

Not this time.

My body, at least what I could see of it, looked like I had been in a fight and had lost. Flecks of blood and bits of what I assumed was vulture vomit still in my hair. A livid red-and-blue bruise just inside my shoulder where the stock of my father's shotgun used to wedge. How could it still be there? I had quite forgotten that I had bashed my head on the dock or on the rocks the first morning after I arrived. I had every reason to feel real pain in my head. It wasn't only the usual alcohol headache that James had referred to as marginally healthy—"So long as you still have a post booze headache, you know your system is resisting the drinking. It's healthy. It means you could still stop."

I now knew that the main reason I had stopped my living arrangement with James was his getting too close to my well of despair. Instead of finding comfort in his affection, I felt I was suffocating.

My face was thinner, even more haggard and less familiar than the face I had seen in the cottage mirrors before. It resembled only the face I had seen in my mother's room. Dark lines like furrows ran from the corners of my mouth all the way to my chin, and those thin knife-edge lines on my forehead had deepened into a permanent scowl. There was loose skin under my chin, the beginnings of wrinkles that would only sag more with each year. I was not yet forty but I thought I looked older than my mother at eighty. In fact, I didn't look like Mother at all. Gina had been lucky. She had inherited her blond hair, her round, youthful face with those arched eyebrows. I was darker.

I hoped it was a good sign that the light came on in the bathroom. Perhaps the electricity company had fixed the problem or it had been something temporary. Lots of temporary blackouts around the Bay.

I had a hot shower, washed the stubborn lingering gunk out of my hair, fingered stuck-together strands that came apart only reluctantly. The bump on the back of my head was excruciatingly painful when I touched it, and I was too absorbed in my aches and in watching the blood coursing down the drain to feel the water becoming colder. Had the tank run out of hot water or was it the dread of the day that made the water feel colder than my skin? I wrapped myself in one of the big, fresh beach towels from the cedar chest and decided I would now start feeling better, or at least more like myself.

I went into my mother's wrecked room, put on her fluffy blue, seagull-smelling dressing gown, still slightly damp from the storm but comforting. I pulled on her blue also-damp socks—her shoes were all too small for me—and I wound one of her fleecy scarves around my neck. I wanted, desperately, to lie down on her bed, put my head on her pillow, and weep. But her bed was a mess of broken glass. On the way out I resisted the temptation to look into her closet because her presence was so powerful in this room that I was afraid I would see her. Father, the last time he spoke to me, said that I was turning into my mother—and he hadn't meant that as a compliment. Perhaps he thought I was just as tiresome and judgmental.

I thought the therapist would tell me to stop doing whatever I was doing that made me feel depressed. "Think of it this way," she had once said. "You keep whacking your head with a baseball bat, taking painkillers to dull the ache, not realizing that if you would only stop whacking yourself on the head, the pain would stop."

My depression had started with our finding Scoop's body. I had known, even then, that my father had shot him because he had been deemed useless.

"Abnormal," Mother had said when I visited her a couple of weeks ago, "that you had taken his death so much to heart, yet didn't feel anything when William died?"

"I did," I protested. "I used to play with him and I thought he liked that. I liked being with him. I really did. It's just that he hated being hugged, so I didn't hug him." I was going to add "nor did you," but it would have been pointless. She didn't hug anybody.

"Your father thought Gina's life was going to be much better without

William," she said. "Mine was much worse without Scoop. But he was my dog, not yours."

At Fairview she had a photograph of Scoop on her bedside table.

In this case ceasing to beat my head with a baseball bat started with leaving my mother's room.

I sat in the chair near the puzzle table and tried to take control of myself. That thing up at the top of the path had been killed by some other animal. It couldn't have been a hunter, it was not hunting season, and the locals made sure no one hunted in the spring. It was when the babies were born, and if they were killed, there would be no hunting season in the fall. Our father was the only person who thought he was above that law, but even he was careful not to admit to shooting something in early April. When questioned, he denied he even owned a gun, let alone two of them. He was questioned only once, and he said that was a mistake by a new officer, too young to know better.

Could he have come here this spring to hunt?

I tried to breathe deeply and focus on the sun glinting off the lake. And on chewing.

Time for another glass of the vodka. The bottle was almost empty. I would have to face my father's cabin to find his expensive whiskey. He had always kept his supply there to discourage me from grabbing for it when we were out of wine. "It's for sipping, not glugging," Father had warned when I had tried one of his even rarer bottles of Talisker. That was some years ago, when he would still sleep up here in the main cottage and sometimes, in the evenings before dinner, would offer me a drink.

Aware of that awful post-retching pressure in my head, I sipped slowly, finished chewing the bread, and took another slice.

Obviously, I would phone the marina again. Obviously, I would avoid coming close to that morbid little body, so I wouldn't have to contend with its stench. Obviously, that vulture was just doing what it's meant to do: clearing away the dead. I would not go near any vultures. I would try to walk deeper into that grove of trees to see if there was really someone back there needing help. I was fairly sure that the noise I heard had come from there, or was it the vulture warning me to stay away from its meal? If that's the kind of noise vultures make, I couldn't have heard it before. While I have seen many of them during summers on the Bay, they were usually circling in wide arcs at a great distance overhead, floating on air currents, searching for their next meal. The closest I had been to one was watching it eat a dead carp on a smooth rock near the turtle islands the last time I'd been here. They didn't attack humans. At least not live humans.

Obviously, I couldn't have seen William in that clearing. Yet I was still postponing the walk up the path. Could I have seen a boat near the hunting blind? The headache, I thought, would have to be gone before I set out again.

A last glass and the bottle was empty.

I decided to make another attempt to find what was under the wall where that thing had been scratching on my first night here. I grabbed the flashlight because it was darker under the trees by the side of the cottage. The storm must have cleared away some of the leaves from one little patch more or less under my bedroom window, and in the beam of the flashlight, I saw there were small mounds of earth, as if they had been shunted back from a groove. I used the end of the flashlight to move the rest of the rotting leaves and dig under them. It was too easy.

For sure, someone or something had dug into the earth here and maybe uncovered a cache of what? Termites? I scooped the rest of the soft earth by hand and felt the base of the wall. The first thing I found was my missing engagement ring; the second was Gina's planchette, still recognizable from that long-ago game we had played. How could they have been put here? And by whom?

I remembered taking the ring off and holding it in my hand when James went slowly down to the dock. The next day I hadn't remembered where I had left it but hadn't spent much time looking for it. Perhaps Gina had picked it up and buried it here with the rest of her secret possessions? But why would she have picked it up and why would she want to keep it? She had never shown any interest in James, nor in any of my other fleeting, long-ago boyfriends, with the fleeting exception of the boy who had asked to take me to the prom. If anything, she seemed to agree with Mother's assessment that I could do better.

Now, I wasn't sure I could. I missed James. I missed his large presence, the sense of security it offered. I even missed his smell. I wondered whether our relationship could have continued had I been less secretive, more willing to accept his desire to be part of my life and for me to be part of his. Why had I found that suffocating? I should have asked the therapist about that instead of dwelling on Scoop's death and William's drowning.

I forced the ring back onto my finger. I knew I could manage the pain.

The planchette was less of a mystery. Eva must have hidden it here after the accident with the Ouija board falling into the fire. Had no one looked for it since? Gina had said she never wanted to play with it again, that it might as well burn, but perhaps she hadn't meant that. The planchette had been here for more than thirty years. Amazing that it hadn't rotted in the damp soil. I brushed the earth off it and held it up to the light. Its varnish was cracked, but it had held its shape and its little wheels were still attached.

There was a muddy little velvet pouch next to it. With my cold, aching fingers it took some time to open the drawstring and pull out the folded paper inside. There was an official-looking stamp at the top of it and something written in the middle, but it was faded and hard to read and I had a lot to do before I could settle down to decipher it. There was a tiny silver charm bracelet next to the paper, so small it had to have been a baby's or a very tiny young child's. There was only one charm on it: a miniature silver salamander.

I dug down under the pouch, my broken nails scratching at the muddy soil and decayed leaves, and brushed against a small, hard, angular object. It was a plastic card, bloody from my hand and even bloodier after I tried to clean the dirt from it. I rubbed it against my mother's fleecy gown and took it and the folded paper down toward the dock where it was sunny. I spat on the card to clean it some more. It was issued by the Province of Ontario, it said at the top of the card, and in capital letters in a box at the bottom: BIRTH CERTIFICATE—CERTIFICATE DE NAISSANCE. The name at the top was: "Judith, Marie Witmer." Sex: F. Birthplace: Toronto. Date of birth: July 15, 1986. Registered, Sisters of Mercy, August 1987.

Does it usually take a year to register a birth?

The sunlight was too bright. The end of the dock was weaving in the vibrating light. My ears were buzzing again, as if a cloud of mosquitoes had colonized my head. I went back to my mother's massive oak and leaned against it. Holding on with one hand I slid down to sit on the acorn-strewn ground at its broad, scaly base. "The oak," my mother had told us, "signifies strength and endurance. It used to be cherished in the ancient world." That word *cherished* had stuck in my mind. I did not think I had ever been "cherished" as a child. By anyone.

I felt no pain, but I could see the blood trickling down my fingers, seeping into the oak's long vertical fissures, some of the skin of my palm having been shaved off by the tree's rough bark. Do oak trees like human sacrifice?

July 15 was my birthday. I was born in 1986.

The only Witmer I knew was Eva.

She must have given me up a few months after I was born. Sisters of Mercy must be a Catholic convent that took in unwanted babies.

I was adopted. Or I was just handed over like a bundle of discarded clothes.

I looked up at the sky through the oak's branches. They were all, except for the one big branch that had attacked my mother's room during the storm, sprouting young spring leaves. They were gratingly bright green against the blackness of the bark. Where the first two branches stretched out over the path, there was a deep chocolate brown, round, elevated fault in the trunk, like a giant stamp, its outer rim raised higher than the rest. In its center a woodpecker had made holes that looked like eyes and, if this were a face, its big downturned mouth gaped open where some animal had made a home for itself in another cavernous hole the bird had dug.

Mother used to tell us a story about the Green Man, whose face was made of oak leaves and branches. He was a pagan deity who liked to appear in the early spring and seek out a female goddess to have fun with. Some religious zealots, she told us, tried to make him seem evil, but he couldn't be either good or evil because he would not have known the difference.

One spring when I was about ten, I had asked her whether the Green Man ever got angry. I had been up to the middle of the island and heard the trees swish and crack, though I hadn't thought it was windy.

"Of course, he gets angry," Mother said. "Every spring your father takes a scythe to its saplings and everything else that could grow up to his knees."

I used to try stopping Father's destruction. I remember standing between him and a pretty little spruce he was about to cut down. He had shouted for me to get away, then whooshed the scythe so close to my neck I felt its blade, but it was only my imagination. He hadn't cut me.

I complained to Mother that he had almost killed me.

She smiled her benign little superior smile (yes, she had it already then) and said, "If he wanted to cut off your head, he would've done it."

Now, I thought the Green Man must have been very angry to have broken through her window and scattered glass and debris all over her bed. Or did he think she was some kind of goddess and he wanted to lie down with her?

Looking up at the tree was a whole lot easier than looking down at the plastic card in my hand.

If this were my birth certificate, Mother was not my mother. She may have been Gina's mother, but she certainly wasn't mine. It had always seemed strange that there were no baby pictures of me, only of Gina. When I came here, I had wanted, dreadfully, to find some cute photos of me and Mother holding me against her chest. Obviously there would have been no baby pictures of me if I weren't her child.

I had often wondered why they had sent me but not Gina to boarding school, why they said I was difficult when she had been much needier, less inclined to play by herself. She was more clingy. At least she tried to cling to Mother. I had not. When Gina was little, she cried easily, whereas I kept my tears to myself and fought hard to maintain a straight face when I was hurt. I had a small soft pillow I used to bury my face in at night, and during the summer, I would walk down to the dock and talk to the lake.

Gina had been resentful and envious of my escape from our home, but I had thought of boarding school as banishment. No one had wanted me around. Now, I realized that Gina's early marriage was her making her own escape.

The place by the wall had been Gina's special spot for hiding her treasures. She must have known about me. Perhaps she had already known when she said William and I had both inherited the gene that made us different. I had always been different. But if William and I had inherited that gene, we would have shared at least one parent. Father? No. Gina couldn't have known anything. She had never been one to keep secrets, and a secret like this would have given her the advantage she had sought since we were children. She would have used it.

If not Gina, who else would have used that spot to hide something? Eva? But why would she put this here for me to find? Or was it Father?

The card and the tiny bracelet had been buried next to Gina's planchette. What had been there longer? Perhaps I had been wrong all along. That place under my window hadn't ever been Gina's secret hidey-hole. The spot where she had hidden my sketchbook was farther along, under the steps. It was Eva who had found it for me. Eva had known where to look. Maybe because this is where she had hidden her own secrets. Such as my birth certificate.

Up past the top of the oak, a vulture floated in wide circles on the warm air currents, its black wing tips tilted elegantly upward. I could almost make out its red head.

31

THE INJURED SEAGULL WAS BACK, LIMPING ALONG THE deck, its white head held high, as if on guard duty. It didn't slow down when it saw me, in fact it gave no sign of seeing me until I was directly in its path, then it leaned forward, lowered its head, and growled or grunted, as if to assert its right to the place. One of its wings was still slightly lower than the other, but apart from that, it looked remarkably healthy. Maybe its mate had been bringing food?

I wanted to see where the other gull was, but I was afraid to look away from the one on the deck. We stood glaring at each other until a crow landed with a loud caw on a long branch of the oak, flapped its wings, lowered its head, and moved closer to our deck. The gull backed away from the crow's direct view and retreated to the wall. I went inside as quickly as I could with my still-bloody hand sliding the door open, then closed behind me.

I wrapped a paper towel around my hand and sat down by the fire. I needed calm to gather my memories of Eva, no matter how inconsequential some of them seemed, and none of them seemed significant because I had never considered Eva herself significant. She had been a vague presence near the periphery of our lives. I realized how little I really knew about her. If she had been a lover of our father's before he married, by the time of my earliest memories he had certainly stopped paying attention to her. She had hovered around our mother—well, perhaps not-my-mother—like a protective ghost.

There was that short, somewhat disheveled, potbellied man standing near her in the wedding photograph. He had barely made it into the picture. I began searching through the photos I had saved from the storm and found it, still intact, near the bottom of the pile. They were not part of the family group. Nor were they standing together. They were not touching. He, too, seemed to be by himself. Looking at him closely, for the first time, I saw that his suit didn't quite fit. The sleeves were too long, the jacket too tight, his shirt gaped a bit. Maybe it was a rental. He was already balding. His hair receded at his temples, leaving the middle portion—thin, longish, but not combed over—on its own. He had a round face and a goofy smile. He definitely bore a resemblance to Harold Spiegel, a decidedly younger version but the same forehead, the same pursed lips. But if Spiegel were my father, wouldn't he have said something when I was in his office?

Also, if he were Eva's husband, she needed to take self-regard pills. Why on earth would a woman as attractive as Eva was in these wedding photos pick a man as unprepossessing as this?

She seemed prettier even than the bride. Long dark hair sweeping her shoulders, slender waist, slim hips, a pale oval face, tear-shaped eyes staring straight into the camera, her mouth slightly upturned but not really smiling, more of an amused look, as if she had found the occasion somewhat bizarre. She had well-defined, thick eyebrows, but unlike mine when they had been thick, they suited her face perfectly. Mine were a couple of shaggy caterpillars seeking to connect over my nose. Still, the shape of her face was mine as was her hair. Her upturned mouth, that amused look, was one I had been accused of by teachers in the classrooms where I had read Kitty's adventures. Disengaged. I had always thought it was a look I had copied from Mother, the airs she gave herself, her sense of superiority. It certainly wasn't how Eva seemed. She was usually trying hard to fit into our lives. Asking questions, volunteering to clear the table, offering me art lessons, bringing food from the delicatessen at Honey Harbour, later, helping Mother get up from the table when she seemed to need help but protested that she didn't.

I wished I had magnifying glasses.

I took a closer look at the photo of my grandparents, "Mother's" parents. If the photographer had swept around from the line of guests at one side to the group on the other side, the person my grandmother (or not) was glaring at could have been Eva.

I couldn't remember who had told me that Eva's (never named) husband had died. Mother had mentioned she was a widow by the time of the anniversary party where she was drunk, though not as destructive as Mother or, to be accurate: my not-mother.

Could the repulsive little fellow be my real father? I couldn't accept that. There was nothing about his features that was remotely similar to mine. I had always thought I looked like the man I had thought was my father. It was a resemblance that people remarked on when we were seen together. Something about my mouth? No one had ever remarked on my resemblance to Mother. Both our faces were thin now and my mouth had shrunk into a straight line of anger, or was it fear? And hers had all but disappeared with age. She had those fine eyebrows, and mine, while they lasted, had been bushy, unruly, wild, like Father's. Though Eva's eyebrows were, like the rest of her, beautifully groomed. I remembered when Mother told me to have mine groomed, I thought she was kidding. Whoever invented that word for eyebrows must have been a horse lover.

Gina, as Mother had often told me, looked like her. It wasn't a contest I had been interested in entering. I couldn't win.

Earlier, when I had glanced at my face in Mother's (?) mirror, I thought I had seen her—not me. But was there any similarity? Really?

Holding one of the few close-up wedding photos of my perhaps Father, I went into the bathroom. He had really been a beautiful man. With the light on and the picture and my face side by side, I thought I discerned some similarity in the outline of our mouths. The rest of my face was so drawn and bruised, there would be no sense in comparing us unless his face was also bruised—and I didn't want to think about his face the last time I saw it.

When Father said I was beginning to resemble my mother, had he meant Eva?

I finished the last sip of the vodka and tried to think about Eva.

Had she been interested in me? I hadn't thought so, but I did remember her hovering when I painted. She used to make suggestions about how to mix paints and what effects I could expect if I mixed certain ones. She had suggested I switch to acrylics from oils because I was too impatient for oils; the base coat needed time to dry before you could apply a second coat, acrylics didn't require a long wait. She had given me a lesson in perspective once, but I hadn't been interested. I was planning another Kitty novel by then.

We had the same hair color, and if I had worn mine long, it would have been fine, soft, and wavy like Eva's. Gina had blond curly hair, frizzy in the summer, a lifelong struggle for her to straighten and smooth down. Exactly like her mother's. Mother had pulled hers into a tight bun, but curly bits escaped. Eva and I were slim, perhaps too slim in recent years, but well proportioned, I thought. Narrow hips, fine breasts. Because I hadn't nursed babies, mine were still their original shape, "a young girl's," James used to say, while Gina had put on a lot of weight when she was pregnant, and despite all her efforts in the gym, she had remained quite heavy. She had started to sag after Mel.

Five of Eva's miniature sculptures were still on the mantelpiece. None was bigger than my thumb, but now that I finally looked at them closely,

I could see that they were finely proportioned, lifelike. There were two little animals; the others were little people, smooth, silky to the touch. One of them, a tiny, long-legged girl with long wavy hair, hands held awkwardly at her sides, I thought looked like me, but I was probably imagining things.

I wondered how Eva's rough, square, short-fingered hands had made those tiny sculptures. They were hands more suited to hard work, machine shops, factories, digging in gardens—as were mine. Mine were filthy, my nails stubby, with dirt under them from digging under the window, and they still had dollops of dried blood. Mother had beautiful smooth, soft hands with long tapered fingers that hadn't been visited by arthritis. "One of my best features," she had said, spreading her fingers in front of her. She had loved manicures and usually wore light pink nail polish. I didn't. I didn't like to attract attention to my ugly hands.

Father had mentioned once when Mother was opening one of Eva's elaborately wrapped Christmas presents that her sculptures wouldn't even be worth melting down. Then he had banged on about the price of bronze on the market. Eva hadn't been there for Christmas, but Mother's face had reddened, and she put the gift back into its box and the box under her chair. Later, after Father had moved down to the cabin, she arranged them in a straight line on the mantelpiece.

Perhaps she had invented the bit about Elizabeth Taylor and the royals owning Eva's sculptures to counter Father's dismissal of her work, but it could have been true. The pieces were exquisite, perfect in their diminutive way. Eva had a good eye for detail. She had also been able to draw in a way I had been trying to learn years ago. Eva had told me once that, after she graduated, she had gone to art school in Amsterdam, and that was where she had learned to use sharp pencils for fine drawings and how to use oils. In those days, they hadn't taught acrylics. She said watercolor was the hardest, but I had never inquired why because I hadn't been interested in her advice or in learning new techniques.

I used to think that I had liked painting only because it had given me access to the art room at the boarding school, a place for connecting with Annabel in our own space where we could be alone, and we could share stories and gossip about the teachers. But it hadn't afforded me an escape from people at the cottage; everyone could look over my shoulder and make comments. Eva had been particularly keen to make suggestions. I hadn't wanted them. I had found her intrusive.

At home and at the cottage, writing offered me the escape I needed. Kitty lived in my notebooks and on my computer screen. I could make her anything I wanted, all it took was words, and I had always been good with words. She turned out to be braver, tougher, and funnier than I was. She faced her enemies with style and confidence. She had been my near-constant companion through the last year of boarding school, when Annabel was slipping away from me. She had already applied for residency at a Paris art college. Kitty stayed. She had been a fierce opponent of a man's hunting expeditions, she had confronted him (or someone like him) in Africa, India, and even on a Pacific island. Though she had been bullied, threatened, and followed, she never backed down. She could outwit bullies. She excelled at martial arts. She always won in hand-to-hand combat. In the second-to-last book, the one I had been reading from on my most recent tour of schools on a government grant, she had acquired a dog.

I told my editor that having someone or something to care about would make Kitty less remote for my YA readers, most of whom could only aspire to her audacity, toughness, and sense of adventure. They could more easily identify with a pet owner, especially if the pet was cute and had a bit of attitude—for example, a dachshund.

"A what?" my editor asked.

"A dachshund. Black and brown, short legs, long body, you know . . ."

"A wiener dog?" she asked, sniggering.

"Exactly. Small, friendly, plucky."

"Useless," she said, echoing Father's views of dachshunds. "Couldn't chase down bad guys; couldn't defend Kitty if they went after her; would never grab a bad guy's arm if he was about to shoot—"

"I thought you said no guys with guns, it would scare the kids. Triggering, you said. And a dachshund could distract a bad guy chasing Kitty."

"How?"

"For one thing, he'd have to stop and laugh. A dachshund attack dog would be very funny."

Unlike my fictitious bad guy, Father had never been amused by Scoop. He was rarely amused by anything, though he said he found most of us funny but not in a laugh-out-loud way, more in a perverse, incredulous way, as when his face had twisted into a wide-eyed, mouth-down-turned grimace watching William trying to hit a tennis ball. Or when he taught me how to handle a gun.

It was one of his handguns, a Remington—he said they had a long history. It had a polished wood handle and two barrels for multiple shots, useful in case you missed your target with a single shot, which, he said, was likely to happen with me. The gun was very heavy. At first, when I lifted it with both hands, my hands dropped down and it smashed into my knees. He showed me how to stand, legs wide apart, somewhat sideways to the target, lifting the gun with one hand, holding up the other, easy, fire, then let it drop down gently before lifting it again for the second shot. At first, we practiced on soda cans. His gun had a longer, single barrel and some fancy drawing on the wooden handle. He used to tell us it was a collectors' item. He said he had chosen the single-shot Remington because he wouldn't need more than one shot. I had the double-barrel. When I got the hang of that, he took me to the back of the island and showed me how to shoot crows.

He took my gun and demonstrated how easy it was to kill them, since they had not been expecting to be killed. "They don't fear us," he said. "They should, but they don't. Stupid. Useless birds."

"Do you want them to fear us?" I asked. That was when he gave me his mirthless, amused face and switched our guns.

"They make good targets," he said when I protested that I liked shooting cans, not birds. "They travel in mobs. Sometimes, you can get three or more of them in a row."

I tried but didn't get the hang of shooting crows. Worse, after I shot in the air a couple of times, they flew too far away for Father to have a turn.

When we returned to the cottage after my shooting lesson, Mother (?) shouted at him that I was a child, I was only fourteen, and I didn't need to know how to kill things. She took the Remington I had been carrying and threw it into the lake.

I had never seen our father as enraged as he was that day. He hit her a flat back-hander across her face. She almost lost her footing on the dock but held on to her chair and straightened, glaring at him. Silent.

32

I HAD NOT BEEN IN THE BACK ROOM FOR AT LEAST two years. During most of my childhood, it had been Father's—a good reason not to go there. He hated intrusion into his space. He kept his guns and his special fishing rods there in a gun cabinet, all his private papers were a small safe to which no one else had the combination. Once, when I was about ten, he had found me poking around his desk drawer, and he whacked me so hard, I flew across the room, and then he locked me into the basement for two days and nights. During the day it didn't make much difference but at night I begged Mother to give me a blanket so I could hide from the mosquitos. It was Eva, not Mother, who had slipped me a blanket after the cottage lights went out. Luckily, Father had left the key to the basement door in the outside lock. When I asked why Father had rarely hit Gina, and never locked her in the basement, Mother said it was because I was older and should know better. Eva said it was because Gina showed little resistance. She just did what she was told.

After he had moved all his stuff to the cabin, Eva slept in the back room. It gradually become her room. It was not even on my household chores list because she always vacuumed, swept, and dusted before she left. She would take the sheets and towels she had used with her and return with them fully laundered, ironed, and smelling of lavender. The room still smelled of lavender, but there was something else there as well, sweet, rotting, like the mice that might have died in Mother's closet during the winter, or that infernal stench up in the middle of the island. The bed was covered by a red-blue-brown quilt that used to be Mother's, as did the cushion with the happy dachshund that used to be on Mother's reading chair in the living room. She would tuck it behind her when she curled up for a rest in the late afternoon.

There was a large painting on the wall facing the bed, a crowd scene with a crucifixion, the people all in garish colors, the cross dark, Christ with big nails sticking through his hands and his feet, the sky darker with a single bolt of lightning in the distance. I couldn't imagine why anyone would want to look at this every day. Though I didn't think Eva had ever talked about it, I had always known she was Catholic. She wore a gold cross on a chain around her neck. It used to dangle down near my face when she hovered over my shoulder to see how my painting was progressing. I had discovered that Mother had encouraged her to teach me techniques. Why? Was it because she thought I needed a new way to see things, a way I didn't find threatening? Or was it because Eva was my mother?

I opened the drawers. The top one was empty. The second drawer had a soft black leather-bound book with gilt page edges and HOLY BIBLE embossed in gold foil on the cover. Eva had pasted a photograph of a baby on the inside cover. She—I knew this was me—wore a white onesie, her legs kicking the air, her hands covered by tiny flaps. It must have been cold that day. She had a little tuft of dark hair on the top of her head and she was smiling—a happy toothless baby smile that lit up her face. There was a gold chain with a tiny gold cross around her neck. She was lying on a shiny pink and blue duvet that must have been Mother's when it was new. It was impossible for me to imagine someone—anyone—giving up a baby like this, but that was precisely what had happened.

The bottom drawer had Eva's thick, padded gardening gloves, a flash-light, a screwdriver, a black rolled-up fleece hoodie, large silver cross, a pair of cotton panties, and a photograph of someone who looked like Gladys.

It couldn't be Gladys!

I held it up to the light from the skylight Father had put in when this was still his study.

There was no doubt it was Gladys—a more flattering shot of her face than the one in Mother's room. There were palm trees in the background and a sandy beach, blue sky, and a powerboat in the distance. She wore a yellow bathing suit, and she was looking directly into the camera, her mouth was open, she seemed to be speaking. Perhaps asking a question, such as, Why are you taking a picture of me?

I went to Mother's room to look for the photo Mother had—equally inexplicably—in her drawer. Of course, it wasn't there. I must have swept it up with the other pictures I had tried to save from the storm. The room still had that dreadful stink, despite the new bird shit odor and the wind pushing through the gash in the window. I would have to check for its source. But not now. Later.

The photos I had spread out on the kitchen counter had mostly dried. Their edges were curled up and the tiny glass shards shone brightly in the sun. I wrapped my hand in a dish towel to search for the one I had seen earlier. It wasn't there. I couldn't find it, even when I picked up each picture by its edge and held it up to the light.

Could I have taken it with me?

I went back into Eva's room to make sure her Gladys photo was still there. It was. And there was a large manila envelope with several sheets of official-looking paper with *Starline Insurance Company* embossed at the top, and *Subject Name: Gladys Somerville* underlined several times in red, then *aka Gloriana D'Ange, Lyford Cay, Bahamas* followed by a list of dates and times, starting with *March 11, 2018,* and ending with *March 21, 2021.* Each entry had a place-name, and several had added names of people I didn't recognize, except for one: Harold Spiegel. There was another photo of Gladys in the middle of the second page. This one was taken close-up, by someone sitting across a table from her—I could see a bit of the table edge and the top of a glass—someone she obviously knew because she was leaning in with a smile on her face.

The last page ended with the words *submitted by,* a signature I couldn't read, and a line under that: *Starline Insurance Investigator.*

Mother or Eva must have hired this person to check up on Gladys. Since the photos were taken in the Bahamas, she and Eva must have known about Father's shady deals, and how he had come to be with Gladys. She was part of the money laundering package. I remembered telling my "mother" and Gina about what I had learned from James and how indifferent they both seemed. Clearly, "Mother" had known for some time. Now I began to wonder about her dementia. Had it been real in the beginning? Or had she been preparing for the time when there would be an investigation and the dementia gave her an excuse not to have known how Father had made his money?

I stuffed the envelope into my pocket and took out the Bible. It felt spongy and warm and smelled of lavender. As I lifted it to my nose, three photos fell on the floor between my feet. Two were of a chubby baby in a pink outfit and a pink knitted cap. The third photo was of the young Eva with long dark hair over her shoulders. She was holding Mother's black salamander toward the camera. My father's hand was on her arm, and he was grinning. I couldn't see much of her face, but what I could see was sad, or resigned, unless I imagined that.

I remembered our conversation about her parents, that Eva had done "something unforgivable." Was that me? Had I been the reason her parents had disowned her? Because she had been pregnant and unmarried? Had she given me away reluctantly to make up for her Roman Catholic transgression? Did the woman I called "Mother" take me out of friendship, or because her husband was my father?

There was a soft sound from the other end of the room, from the closet where Eva kept her dresses. Her blue summer wraparound was swaying in the faint light from the window. I had closed the room door behind me and checked the windows. They were all closed. Yet the robe continued to sway, as if something was propelling it gently from side to side, the light flashing on its terry cloth folds each time it came toward the window.

I froze.

Trying to see if there was something or someone in the darkness behind the robe, I leaned to the side, without moving my feet, but there was nothing to see. "Is there someone here?" I asked, my voice cracking, because of course there couldn't be anyone else here. Surely, I would have noticed a person coming past me. What about the back door?

We never used that door. The steps had been removed. But someone could . . .

I repeated my question, trying to make my voice stronger, more commanding, but all I could hear was the hook of the metal hanger grating on the rod in the closet as the robe kept swaying. It could be an animal. Came in while I was putting a log on the fire.

Keeping an eye on the robe, I backed out of the room, slowly.

When I stopped and looked back at the closet, the robe was no longer moving. But the smell still lingered.

There had to be an explanation. Maybe air coming through the windows. It was cold in the room. I had been shivering. The windows seemed to be closed, but there could be cracks at the base. These windows had been among the first ones installed when the cottage was assembled from prefab pieces and, unlike those in front, which had all been replaced over the years, these were still the originals. The front ones had become clouded, they collected a lot of condensation, but back here they had stayed clear. No idea why. I stared at my father's skylight. The sky was weirdly bright, no clouds. No cracks in the glass that I could see.

Could this strange woman, who had attached herself to our family and clung on over the years with barnacle-like tenacity, be my mother? Could there be any other reason for her name on my birth certificate? And those baby photos? Were they the missing baby photos that I had been searching for?

I still couldn't remember who had told me that Eva had once been Father's (if he was my father) lover. If she were pregnant, she—being Catholic—would have had the baby. Devout Catholics didn't do abortion. She could have given me up for adoption by her best friend, the woman I had thought was my mother. But she apparently wasn't my mother. That would explain why I'd always had the feeling she didn't like me a whole lot, though she relied on me to find the will she assumed would give her what she was entitled to have.

Then, there was still the question of who my father was. I don't know why I was still clinging to the possibility that it was the man I had known as my father, the man who rarely noticed my existence, who beat me when I made him angry, the criminal money-launderer, who murdered animals for sport. And what about William?

Was it because he was handsome and I had always hoped I was beautiful? Or because I was resisting the notion that Harold Spiegel might be my father? Or was I just clinging to the last vestige of belonging to people I had assumed were my family?

One of Father's colleagues had said he felt sorry for Eva when she got drunk at the anniversary party. At the time, I had assumed she got drunk because Father had married Mother and not her. This could have been *her* anniversary. But then there was that moment when she and Mother made their exit together, laughing. I think the arrangement could have served both of them well. Eva would be free to pursue her art and Mother could afford babysitters and a private school. They were best friends. And my existence was something my not-really-mother could hold over Eva.

But why would she have accepted the gift of a baby, if she thought that her husband was its father? Could friendship stretch that far?

I was desperate for a drink. The only option now was to face my terror and look for whatever Father had left behind in his cabin. I dreaded the thought, but I had to go there, while it was light. I could not confront it later when the light dimmed. I checked the fire. I don't know why but I cleaned my hands and my face again. I unfurled more of the drying will on the puzzle table. I could read now most of the first page and the top half of the second. As she had hoped, Father had designated Mother his chief beneficiary, leaving her the house and all the furniture she no longer had, also all his stocks and shares. His one caveat was that she not give him a Catholic burial, no church service, and no cross on his grave.

And, so far, no mention of me. Perhaps on the next page . . . but I didn't want to risk rolling out more of the will because it was still damp and might be shredded by my hands. Smears of my blood had already marked the first page.

I headed for the door, only to be met by the injured seagull cowering against the screen, and a gathering of noisy crows on the long branches of the oak. A gathering of crows is known as a "murder of crows," and in ancient times, they were thought to be harbingers of death. I had used them in my Kitty books to send a little frisson of fear down the spines of my young readers. I had read from those sections in a couple of my Kitty readings and loved watching the kids' faces when I got to the "murder of crows." They would all know crows are black and noisy, and maybe a bit scary, but they wouldn't know that crows were a bad omen. Only Kitty would know that, but she would also know how to get away from them and whatever they purported to mean.

Thinking of intrepid adventurer Kitty gave me a bit of courage. That the crows shrank back a bit, though they didn't stop their infernal noise, added to that feeling, my sense of gaining some control over my situation.

"It's not real!" I shouted at the crows as I stepped onto the deck, staring at them with determined hostility. "It's just a turn of phrase. There is no murder of crows!" They gronked at me, raising and lowering their heads three or four times, all of them ending in a grating rattle. I straightened my back and marched to the end of the deck, fast but not too fast. I didn't want them to think they had scared me. Looking back through the shimmering light, I thought the seagull had squeezed past my feet and was now back inside the cottage.

I would chase it outside later.

33

THE PATH TO FATHER'S CABIN WAS SLIPPERY BITS OF shale and pebbles with small tufts of green lichen in the cracks. The dead squirrel lay close to the first step, its belly ripped open. I thought it had been moved during the night. Do vultures feed during the night? Seagulls? Crows?

The cabin was about fifteen feet off the direct route to the dock. It was on concrete stilts, high off the ground, so close to the shore November gales often swept water under its platform. The steps were high, but Father had installed sturdy wooden railings on either side, so he could climb up easily even if the waves took out the lower steps. The building was too high up to see inside when you walked past, even though its big window looked out on the lake. I know, Gina and I had tried when Father was out on the lake in his boat.

We had been curious about what he did in there. But I had not been allowed inside. James and I had used the other cabin many summers ago when our affair was new and we were still pretending we didn't share a bed. I would sneak out of my room after dark and spend the night with him, making sure I was up in time to see Father going for his early morning swim. One morning, when he was sitting on the deck, sipping his coffee, he told me I had fooled no one with my antics. Everyone knew I was sleeping in the cabin with James.

"Even Mother?" I asked.

"Especially Mother."

That was before he lugged all his clothes, his guns, his favorite fishing rods, the lures box, blankets, and sheets—the dark brown ones—down to the cabin and, without an explanation, established it as his new residence—his, not shared, as the cottage had always been. He used to lock it when he packed up his hub, stuffed his papers into his leather bag, and left.

Somehow I already knew that it was not locked now.

The afternoon light was streaming in through the big window and flooded the room with such deceptively cheerful brightness that I was tempted to sit on the long window seat and relax a while. Try to gain some perspective on the day. And on the night before. And the day and night before . . . Had I really been here for only three days?

The therapist had said I had an unhealthy tendency to personalize everything. It would be much better for me, she said, if I decided that not everything that went on around me was, actually, about me. Sometimes, she said, it was about someone or something else. Knowing that would give me perspective.

On balance, I thought, I would chance postponing perspective until I'd had another drink and curled up with *Sapiens* in front of the fire. I wanted to go back to reading about flourishing European empires gaining an advantage over China and the Muslim world because they believed in science. Physics and biology. Not random apparitions that made no sense in science and had no biological bodies.

On a sunny day like this, I could see that the window, though lovely, didn't fit perfectly. There were tiny gaps on the sides for the cold air to come in. Father had installed it himself, as he had built the cabin himself. The window seat was still wet from the storm.

His printer, an HP Color Laser Jet, was covered by a gray tarp. His laptop computer was on the white night table. Open. Gerry had told me that Father always had it with him. How could it be here? Had he been here and left before I arrived?

The bed—a king, with a raised mattress—was set back from the window. The blankets were tossed aside, the sheets were rumpled. It looked like someone had just got up, though I thought Father hadn't been here since last summer. There was a coffee mug on the table with coffee still in it and a thin stack of papers. I smelled the coffee. His favorite Colombian blend.

The head of a white-tailed deer with antlers was mounted on the wall above the bed. He had never mentioned having taken one of his kills to a taxidermist, though he had shown me a photograph of himself grinning over the raised head and shoulders of a dead deer. It had staring eyes and blood on its face. Luckily, the mounted head had neither.

The Remington he had used most often was, I assumed, in the metal box on its own stand, near the chest of drawers. Locked. That's how he always kept it. "Responsible gun ownership," he had told us, "means always knowing exactly where your guns are and always keeping them locked so that no one can take them from you. There have been too many accidents with guns." The other Remington, the double-barrel shotgun, was kept in its own soft brown leather and canvas case with the Remington logo in white on the front. He had rescued the gun from the lake after Mother's attempt to get rid of it. He'd spent days drying it in the sun, then polishing it and buffing up its wooden handle before putting it away and clipping a lock on the zipper that went around the case.

That case was lying open at the end of the bed. It was empty. A sudden flash of memory: my fingers fumbling with the zipper. I had been trying to open it.

Guns would be the first things the locals would steal, Father had told us. "Good ones are expensive and these guys hunt year-round." He had never left his guns here for the winter. If they were here, he would be here.

Could he have come up alone after the lake froze? A couple of years ago, he had purchased a snowmobile, so he could come when no one else was at the cottage. He enjoyed the quiet, he said, but more often he talked about wanting to shoot coyotes or wolves. When we were children, there had been wolves here in the winter, some staying over till the early spring. We could hear them howling at night after we opened the cottage. But they had been driven north by the coyotes and the nighttime howling was replaced by their yelps.

Father had said, "The best time to get them is the winter. You can see them running on the ice. Easy to shoot." But, surely, he would not have come here during the winter only to kill coyotes. Or would he? Could he have come in February and got stranded when the ice thawed? When had the thaw been this year? Early March. Could he have been here for five or six weeks and no one knew? Impossible. He would have called for help and someone would have picked him up with an iceboat.

I would have seen the snowmobile on the island.

Of course, he could have come by boat. The *Limestone* . . .

My breath came in short spurts. I was shaking so much I almost dropped the Talisker. It had stood next to his laptop. The gold foil top and cap had been twisted off and thrown into the reed wastebasket. About a quarter of the bottle was missing. The bottom of his glass had remnants of amber liquid. I held the bottle with both hands and took a long swig.

I didn't want to use his glass. Didn't even want to look at it.

There were small piles of leaves—dark green, orange, burgundy, brown—on the blond pine floor of the cabin, which must have blown in when the door was open, flying on the wind from the lake. The knotted rug I remembered from his cottage room was near the bed. It felt damp to my touch. When I started to pull it away from the bed to see if there were footprints underneath, wet mud stuck to my fingers. The stench coming up through the floorboards was fetid, as if something had rotted under the cabin—like the smell in Mother's bedroom and Eva's closet. As if the whole island had decayed.

I had to reach someone at the marina.

I needed to talk with James.

The light seemed unnaturally bright in the cabin. The tile washbasin glowed, as if lit from the inside. It must be the headache I woke up with, the one that followed drinking too much the night before, and went with the anxiety that I always felt when I was hungover. I knew I should be taking deep breaths to dispel the feeling of terror, but I didn't want to breathe in too deeply because of the stench.

It could be blood. Something dead and still bleeding had been laid on that rug. Something Father had killed and brought back here. But why would he do that? Why would he bring a dead animal into his cabin? And when was he here?

I dropped down to feel for dampness on the floor among the dead leaves. It was not only damp but still wet, as were the leaves. Near the rug, there was a wet patch that could have been a boot print, and something had dripped at the outer edge of the bedpost. It was too dark for water, but it could have been mud. There was a thin trail of sand on the other side of the bed. I stood with my back to the door for as long as I could, trying to concentrate on what I was seeing: the bedspread with its distinctive squares, the blond wooden walls, the Remington case, the deer head, the partition for the space where he hung his clothes, and that ghastly rug. They were all horribly familiar, yet suddenly very strange, as if I had wandered in from somewhere else, another dimension maybe.

Focus.

I stuck the cork into the bottle, held it to my chest, and backed slowly out of the cabin. I jumped down the steps and ran stumbling over the rocks toward the lake. I think I held my breath until I was on the dock. Sat down hard where Mother's chair used to be and started to take those deep breaths the therapist had said she swore by. She had told me that she, herself, made use of them whenever she felt anxious, or out of her depths.

I drank some whiskey. Maybe I should roll back the time for perspective. I felt utterly disconnected from reality, light-headed, floating almost. The brightness of the sun hurt my eyes. Yet there was no longer that clear sky. Clouds hung like curtains on the horizon. There were tiny waves rolling toward the shore. I felt for the phone in my pocket, in case there had been a message from the marina. The screen lit up with a text but it was hard to see it in the sun. I swiveled to turn my back to the sun, refusing to look down into the water where I had seen that thing the first day. There was a message from James that must have appeared earlier, but I had been too terrified to look. Now, when I tried calling him, there was no signal. Of course, there was no signal. Maybe closer to the end of the dock where sometimes James could call his office . . . Slowly, I moved down to where the ladder was, where James and Father would stand in their bathing suits, facing away from the cottage, talking too quietly for me to hear.

There was still no signal but at least now I could read the message.

"Eva called. She says you must get off the island. Right now. She sounded worried. Said she had spoken with your mother. Please call me. If I don't hear from you, I will drive up there and bring you down myself."

Looking east, close to the shore, I saw the burnt orange sweater in the water again. It was undulating gently as the waves rolled over it and over the stones it had come to rest on. It was Father's cottage sweater, the one he often wore when it was chilly in the evenings. With its arms stretched out, it looked like it still had his torso inside, lying gently on the rocks, enjoying the last of the sun. Had I thought that before? Or had it changed since I last saw it? I thought I had seen it closer to the end of the dock, that first day, when I was too busy with the pump to care whether it was Father's sweater.

A flash of memory of his tottering backward, falling into the water, his arms flailing, on the side of the dock where that sweater floated. The look of shock on his face. Disbelief. His boots, loudly, angrily, banging into the dock. When was that?

Had he come to the island before me?

Had the police even asked whether he might have come here? If Father had decided to vanish, wouldn't this be the first place he would come?

The police wouldn't have searched for him here—if they had searched for him at all—because it was early March when we first went to them to report that he seemed to be missing. In March the ice was just breaking up.

I jumped off the dock onto the rocks, slipped, righted myself, and slide-walked to the sweater. Knitted wool, heavy when wet. I remembered washing his sweaters here and wringing the water out, as much as I could, then carrying them up to lay them on the deck to dry. We never got a washing machine at the lake. "Those things belong in the city," Father had said, but he did like his clothes clean, and when we were children, before we began to think for ourselves, I hadn't minded washing his clothes for him. This was the sweater he had worn the day he'd taught me how to use his favorite Remington. Long before he killed Scoop. And maybe William. William. For sure, he had killed William. Had I even asked him about William? Had I been afraid to ask because I thought I knew?

Hadn't he said that we would all be happier without William, that Gina would, finally, get the time to do whatever fool things she had wanted to do with her life?

One day the last summer I was at the cottage, William's last summer, Father had asked me about Gina. What was it she had wanted so much to do when she was free of that lumbering worry? I told him Gina had taken up pottery. She had signed up for classes at the Craft School, making cups and vases, and she had been learning how to use a kiln.

Father had laughed so hard, he spat in his glass. "And you?" he inquired.

"Me?"

"What are you doing? Still writing?"

"That, and looking after Mother," I lied.

"Not having children, after all?"

"After all?"

"Weren't you pregnant last summer?"

I shook my head, didn't trust my voice to say "no." I had no idea how he had known.

I had barely known it myself.

Then, too, I had been feeling dislocated, worried about how my life was unfolding and what I wanted from the rest of it. It took several mornings of light-headedness and vomiting to suspect that I might be pregnant. I had been drinking too much wine and way too much scotch. James, if he were around, would have told me that there was nothing unusual about my drinking, that I had come to think of a bottle or two of wine and scotch chasers as normal, that this was the way I had chosen to deal with my problems. Perhaps he would have repeated how lucky I was to still feel sick in the mornings (and sometimes all day, at least until I had my first glass of whatever was in the offing), because these were signs my body was still resisting the alcohol, my liver was fighting back, telling me I had to slow down. "Try drinking water, or ginger ale to calm yourself." James had prepaid the therapist's going rate for ten sessions.

If I was pregnant, he would share the blame. I hadn't had sex with anyone other than James for some time. His moving out of my apartment did not mean that we stopped having sex, what it meant was that I could pretend I was independent again. Nor had I stopped enjoying my comfort drinks.

Many times I remembered waking up in James's bed but not knowing how I got there. I remembered how fluffy his duvet was and how I had always liked the smell of his aftershave. Even when I had begun to find his presence in my life suffocating, when I no longer knew where he ended and I began, because the lines had become blurred by our

closeness, even then, I loved waking up with him. It was almost as comforting as alcohol.

The idea of being pregnant had been terrifying. I thought I was too
old to have babies. Much like my parents—or the people I thought of
then as my parents—I was too set in my ways to rear a child. Yet, there
had been times when listening to children's voices in the cottage had made
me feel happy. I did not think that listening to our voices had made our
parents happy. We made them irritable.

I had liked playing LEGOs with William. It had been challenging
but fun, and I remembered holding him close to my chest in the evenings,
while Gina slept, and feeling his butterfly breath on my face. No matter
how hard I tried, I had no memories of Mother or Father holding me.

Father, having asked about my being pregnant, turned and started
out the cottage door. "You don't have to be a damned fool," he said over
his shoulder, "you can get rid of the little bastard." He lumbered down to
the deck, still not looking at me as I trailed behind. "You're not a bloody
Catholic like some of the idiots around here."

"No," I said.

"If you were, you could give it away, it's what Dogans do. They hand
their little bastards to other people to raise. Unless it turns out to be defec-
tive, like Gina's."

I was barely breathing. I shouldn't have been surprised, as he had
never hidden his disdain for William after he was diagnosed, but the cold-
ness of his voice took me aback. I had never forgotten it.

"Gina inherited her mother's idiocy," he said. "She should have
known what she was carrying and got rid of it."

I turned away from him, ran past him on the dock, and dove into
the lake.

In the early fall, I had gone to my doctor, who had assured me that
I was no longer pregnant. Sometimes, she said, a pregnancy will end in
spontaneous termination. "Usually, it's because the fetus fails to develop

and dies in utero. But it's nothing for you to worry about. You can try for another baby," she assured me.

I hadn't even told James.

Now, LONG AFTER HE HAD been buried, I suddenly found myself weeping again for William and hating my father. I had tried not to weep at the funeral. I had been almost too angry to cry.

The way Father had returned to the cottage when we were all looking for William. He had driven the *Hunt* to the dock when we were all shouting William's name. He had seemed so calm. He had tied up the boat with only the stern rope. The dock line was missing. And he was calm, almost cheerful later, when William's body was brought in by the police. I thought no one else had noticed that the rope dangling from William's arm was exactly like our dock line, or if anyone noticed, they would not have made the connection. After all, all ropes look the same. Except that this rope had been broken and Father had tied the two frayed ends together to last until he had time to get a replacement.

I stood staring at the sweater, the waves bubbling under it as it undulated close to shore. I remembered it on him, how it had been a little tight these last couple of years. Maybe he ate more now that he no longer had to look at Mother at dinnertime. The orange shoulders rose and lowered themselves again, as if he were shrugging. The red on the chest had started to leak into the water. I thought I should pick it up and take it to the deck, but I couldn't. I bent over it, looking at the leaching stain, reached for it, but my hands refused to touch it. It was the strangest of feelings, part of me wanting to raise it and part of me not wanting to see it ever again.

Bending over the sweater, I was aware, again, of that rotting smell at the end of the dock and in his cabin and, looking up from this angle, I noticed something solid, dense, and dark wrapped in the tarp under his elevated deck. I approached it slowly, at a half-crouch. It was blue with dark brown patches, thick at one end, tangled in some weeds at the other. Closer, I saw that it had been rolled in the blue carpet from what used to be the kids' room, the one I had bought for William's fourth birthday, so he could sit there and play when he wanted to be alone. He had an imaginary friend who lived in the closet, and he liked to talk with him quietly, but only when he was sure there was no one else in the room. Once, when I quietly went into the room and William hadn't heard me, he looked at me, put his forefinger to his lips, and said, "Shush." I waited inside the door. We were both looking into the darkness of the closet. I had imagined I heard something softly stirring in there. Father's country-and-western music almost disappeared in the stillness. William gave me his customary somber off-side stare and motioned for me to leave.

Now the blue carpet was stained brown and it reeked of decay, the stench growing stronger as I approached. I yanked the end of the tarp closest to me. It was too heavy to lift, but the dreadful stench was suddenly so overwhelming I almost retched. I lifted a corner, exposing more of the carpet. Crouching, I pulled the carpet toward me, keeping whatever was underneath covered. A dead animal? But would he cover a dead animal? Coyotes, he had said, were easiest to kill when the lake froze over. Had he sat on his deck, holding his gun, waiting for them to come close enough to kill?

I sat on my haunches, feeling the aches in my legs and my arms, the pounding in my head where I had banged it that first day on the dock. The light filtered through the slats in the cabin deck, it was dancing on the blue carpet, as if it were moving, though I knew it was motionless, except for whatever was underneath. Giving in to the pressure of my fingers as I pulled, it moved, slowly. A green jacket. No. Green and brown in a splotchy pattern. Studs in the middle. Hunter's camouflage. Father's favorite jacket for killing things. "They won't see me coming." A thick arm flopped to one side, neck turned away. Gray hair. Matted. The face. Yes. I would have to look at the face. I pulled the tarp off and stood up, waiting for him to move. Dizzy from standing up too quickly, I reached for the side of his steps to steady myself. I heard my nails scrape the wood. The flash of recognition. The memory of his falling. The red spraying on his chest and on his face. That look of shock. Disbelief. He had tottered backward and fell heavily into the water. His boots smashed into the dock. He lay there with only his feet out of the water. I had looked closely because I thought he was still moving, but he wasn't. Except for his arms floating up and down with the waves, his hair drifting in the water.

Hadn't I noticed the drag marks on the path toward his cabin? They were surely there now, as was the blood. He had been so much heavier than I thought he would be. Dead weight as I pulled him out. I had held him by the ankles. His boots came off first, then the sweater rolled upward, over his head and off him into the lake. I had taken my time putting on his hunting jacket. Given everything that had ever happened here, that was the jacket he should be wearing. I had covered him with William's carpet and covered it all with the tarp.

I had left him there.

Staggering up the steps to the cottage I heard the crows' loud throaty caws, but they were no longer on that branch, they had all descended behind Father's cabin. They were hopping toward the body under the blue carpet and calling to one another, excited. A murder of crows.

Breathing in the almost clean air, I felt unusually calm and at peace, with even the seagull that was no doubt still lurking inside. I would leave the door open for it.

I strode—not in a hurry but determined to be in control—into my room, where that wretched smell had never permeated. Maybe the only safe place. Threw myself on the floor to see more clearly where I had left it. The Remington repeat rifle, the one he had kept in that special soft case, the one my no-longer-mother had tossed into the lake. I pulled it out and cleaned it with my blanket, rubbed the barrel and the trigger, polished the stock, exactly as he had shown me. "Always clean your gun, always put it away, never leave it lying around." I ran with it, still wrapped in the blanket, to the end of the dock and tossed it in. I made sure I held up the blanket so I could put it back on my bed before anyone came.

If James was right about my father's business, he could have been killed by one of his customers, someone whose money he had laundered. That person could have taken the gun, cleaned it, and dropped it into the water. My fingerprints wouldn't be on it.

No matter how many turkey vultures gathered at the top of the island, waiting for me, I would go back there and call the marina. Then I would call James. I would tell him I had found his ring and I was wearing it again. Someone would come and pick me up. Before they came, I would have one more sip of whiskey, throw the bottle into the lake, and read the last of *Sapiens*.

ACKNOWLEDGMENTS

I wrote this book during Covid lockdowns, when it seemed that the darkness would prevail. Several people helped to bring it to its current incarnation, in type and between covers. Many thanks to my daughters, Catherine and Julia, my sons-in-law, Graeme and Cam, and always, Julian. I owe a huge debt to my meticulous and sympathetic editor, Laurie Grassi, and my publisher, Kevin Hanson, who took a chance on this book. Thank you also to John Pearce, who has, in past years, been my editor and publisher and now, for many years, my agent.

ABOUT THE AUTHOR

ANNA PORTER is the award-winning author of ten books, both fiction and nonfiction, most recently *Deceptions* and *In Other Words: How I Fell in Love with Canada One Book at a Time.* She has written five mystery novels, including *The Appraisal,* which was shortlisted for the Staunch Book Prize, and *Mortal Sins. Kasztner's Train* won the 2007 Writers' Trust Prize for Nonfiction and *The Ghosts of Europe* won the Shaughnessy Cohen Prize for Political Writing. She cofounded Key Porter Books, an influential publishing house she ran for more than twenty years. In addition, she writes book reviews, opinion pieces, and stuff about Central Europe. She is an Officer of the Order of Canada and has received the Order of Ontario. Visit her at **AnnaPorter.ca** or connect with her on Twitter **@AnnaPorter_Anna.**